# IN T...
# OF OMIZANTRIM

## The War of Powers: Book Five

While her Sky City is in the hands (claws?) of treacherous lizards, Princess Moriana desperately tries to arouse the complacent inhabitants of High Medurim. Unfortunately, the passion aroused is not blood lust but just plain old lust.

That's bad for Moriana, but good for those two intrepid genies, Erimenes and Ziore. They are caught up in the heat of things as their molecules of mist go zinging around the confines of their jugs. But where there's a will there's a way, and eventually the two ethereal genies manage a very substantial meeting.

Well, at least one thing gets accomplished during this trip....

"Rough, bawdy, glowing with barbaric energy. It reminds me of *The Godfather* set in a world of fantasy."
—*Fred Saberhagen*

# THE WAR OF POWERS SERIES

## THE WAR OF POWERS: BOOK FIVE

# IN THE SHADOW OF OMIZANTRIM

### ROBERT E. VARDEMAN
### AND VICTOR MILÁN

PLAYBOY
PAPERBACKS

Published simultaneously in the United States and Canada by Playboy Paperbacks, New York, New York. Printed in the United States of America. Library of Congress Catalog Card Number: 81-82972. First edition.

Books are available at quantity discounts for promotional and industrial use. For further information, write to Premium Sales, Playboy Paperbacks, 1633 Broadway, New York, New York 10019.

ISBN: 0-872-16999-5

First printing February 1982.

For Joseph Wm. Reichert
A prince of a fellow.

—vwm—

*Por mi querida.*
*Hoy, mañana, siempre.*

—rev—

# A Chronology
## of the Sundered Realm

—20,000    The reptilian *Zr'gsz* settle the Southern Continent and begin construction of the City in the Sky.

—3,100    Istu sent by the Dark Ones to serve the *Zr'gsz* as a reward for their devotion.

—2,300    Human migration begins.

—2,100    Athalau founded by migrants from the Islands of the Sun.

—1,700    Explorers from the Northern Continent found High Medurim.

—1,000    Tension increases between the *Zr'gsz* and the human settlers.

—31    *Zr'gsz* begin active campaign to exterminate all humans.

—3    Martyrdom of the Five Holy Ones.

0    *The War of Powers*: Unable to wipe out the human invaders, the *Zr'gsz* begin to use the powers of Istu. Most of the Southern Continent is desolated. In Athalau, Felarod raises his Hundred and summons up the World-Spirit. Forces unleashed by the struggle sink continents, tip the world on its axis (bringing Athalau into the polar region), cause a star to fall from the heavens to create the Great Crater. The *Zr'gsz* and Istu are defeated; Istu is cast into a magical sleep and imprisoned in the Sky

7

City's foundations. Conflict costs the life of Felarod and ninety of his Hundred. Survivors exile themselves from Athalau in horror at the destruction they've brought about.

Human Era begins.

100    Trade between humans and *Zr'gsz* grows; increasing population of humans in the Sky City. Medurim begins its conquests.

979    Ensdak Aritku proclaimed first Emperor of High Medurim.

1171    Humans seize power in the Sky City. The *Zr'gsz* are expelled. Riomar shai-Gallri crowns herself queen.

2317    Series of wars between the Empire of Medurim and the City in the Sky.

2912–17    War between the Sky City and Athalau; Athalau victorious. Wars between the City and Athalau continue on and off over the next several centuries.

5143    Julanna Etuul wrests the Beryl Throne from Malva Kryn. She abolishes worship of the Dark Ones within the Sky City, concludes peace with the Empire.

5331    Invaders from the Northern Continent seize Medurim and the Sapphire Throne; barbarian accession signals fresh outbreak of civil wars.

5332    Newly-proclaimed Emperor Churdag declares war on the City in the Sky.

5340    Chafing under the oppression of the Barbarian Empire, the southern half of the Empire revolts. Athalau and the Sky City form an alliance.

5358    Tolviroth Acerte, the City of Bankers, is founded by merchants who fled the disorder in High Medurim.

5676    Collapse of the Barbarian Dynasty. The Sky City officiates over continent-wide peace.

5700    The Golden Age of the City in the Sky begins.

6900    General decline overtakes Southern Continent. The Sky City magic and influence wane. Agriculture breaks down in south and west. Glacier near Athalau. Tolviroth Acerte rises through trade with Jorea.

7513    Battle of River Marchant, between Quincunx Federation and High Medurim, ends Imperial domination everywhere but in the northwest corner of the continent. The Southern Continent becomes the Sundered Realm.

8614    Erimenes the Ethical born. Population of Athalau in decline.

8722    Erimenes dies at 108.

8736    Birth of Ziore.

8823    Death of Ziore.

9940    Final abandonment of Athalau to encroaching glacier.

10,091    Prince Rann Etuul born to Ekrimsin the Ill-Favored, sister to Queen Derora V.

10,093    Synalon and Moriana born to Derora. As younger twin, Moriana becomes heir apparent.

10,095    Fost Longstrider born in The Teeming, slum district of High Medurim.

10,103   Teom the Decadent ascends the Sapphire Throne. Fost's parents killed in rioting over reduction in dole to cover Imperial festivities.

10,120   Jar containing the spirit of Erimenes the Ethical discovered in brothel in The Sjedd.

Mount Omizantrim, "Throat of the Dark Ones," from whose lava the *Zr'gsz* mined the skystone for the Sky City foundations, has its worst eruption in millennia.

10,121   Fost Longstrider, now a courier of Tolviroth Acerte, is commissioned to deliver a parcel to the mage Kest-i-Mond.

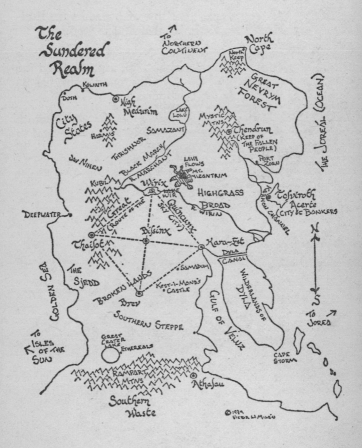

The Sundered Realm

To Northern Continent

North Cape

The Joreal (Ocean)

North Keep

Great Nevrym Forest

Kolinth

Dush

High Medurim

Lake Lolu

Mystic Mtns.

Chendrun (Keep of the Fallen People)

City States

Harmis

Samazant

Port Zorn

Thrushior

Jav Nihen

Black Marsh

R. Marchant

Lava Flows Ms. Mizantrim

Kubil

Wirix

Lake Wir

Highgrass Broad

Toshiroth Acerte (City of Bonkers)

Nhou Caesandel

Great Route of the

Qubnauru (Sky City)

R. Wirin

Deepwater

Thaisot

Bissinx

Kara-Est

N

Golden Sea

The Sjedd

Broken Lands

Byev

Samadur

Kest-i-Mond's Castle

Dyll Canal

Wildrlands of Dyll

S

To Jorea

Southern Steppe

Gulf of Veluz

To Isles of the Sun

Great Crater Lake

Ethereals

Cape Storm

Rampart Mtns

Athasau

© 1979 Victor W. Milán

Southern Waste

# CHAPTER ONE

For a woman plummeting a thousand feet to her death, Synalon Etuul was uncommonly relaxed. The rushing air caressed her naked body like a thousand subtle hands. Her black hair, charred and frizzled from her contest of magics with her sister Moriana, fluttered inches above her seared scalp.

Overhead floated the City in the Sky, a vast soundless raft of gray skystone. Around the mandiblelike double docks at the prow of the City swarmed hundreds of rafts of the same substance, from eight-foot flyers to hundred-foot barges, swarming with warriors both human and inhuman. A few of the eagles of the City's war force circled dispiritedly, herded by small two man flyers. For the first time in their long history, the warbirds of the Sky City knew defeat in the element over which they ruled as haughtily as kings: the sky.

The dethroned queen paid attention to neither the birds nor the rounded hills cloaked in green that spun around and around beneath her feet. All her concentration was devoted to a single mental summons. Her eyes closed and the thought formed, surged outward, questing, commanding. In a moment, she heard a distant piercing cry and knew that her call was heard.

Without warning, the arrow shape of a huge war eagle shot by her, wings folded to its glossy black sides, head thrust forward so that its yellow beak sliced the air like the prow of a ship. Synalon smiled and sent the bird encouraging thoughts.

Once beneath her, it unfolded its full thirty-foot wingspan with a thunderous crack. Synalon fell by it again.

Still, no concern touched the sorceress's aristocratic features.

The wings furled like sails. The black warbird fell until it flanked Synalon, then spread its wings carefully so that they dropped side by side.

"I'm ready, Nightwind," she called, no longer requiring the tiring mental communication. The bird let itself drift down until it was directly beneath her. She spread her legs and floated down until she sat astride the bird's back, her legs thrown over its churning shoulders. She let her head slip back and uttered a small cat cry at the pleasure of the bristly feathers brushing between her slender legs. Defeated, exiled, and without so much as a cloak to her name, Synalon still took pleasurable sensation where she found it, and savored it well. The better, perhaps for the novelty of the circumstances.

Slowly, the eagle increased its wingspan and the tempo of its wings' beating, until the full weight of the tall, lean woman was borne upon it. As it pulled into level flight, it curved and began winging along the City's track. Its mistress had prepared well for this eventuality, though her power in the City had been absolute, and her favor in the eyes of the Dark Ones had seemed to render her invulnerable. Its blood had seethed with the need to be out of the confines of the special aerie in the depths of the City, but Nightwind had waited patiently as instructed, for its mistress's mental call. Having rescued her according to plan, it strained powerful muscles to put as much distance as possible between the former queen and her former domain.

A cry of pleasure broke from Synalon's throat and was whipped away by the wind of Nightwind's passage. Stolidly, the bird flew on. Only once did it have to correct its flight as the woman suddenly shifted her weight back and forth. It knew its mistress's foibles well.

Flushed and breathless, Synalon cast a glance upward. The City was several miles distant. Her sister was undoubtedly on her way to having herself crowned Queen of the

City in the Sky. Synalon reached forward and stroked the straining bird's neck, feeling the taut muscles beneath her fingers.

"The silly slut," she said, "is probably wiping away a tear for her evil twin," she said to her eagle. Synalon grinned savagely. "Ah, yes, the evil but great-souled twin who took her own life rather than face the disgrace of being exiled among the groundlings or lifetime captivity." She laughed, long and loud.

Synalon had feared only one thing as she stepped to the windowsill in her throne room. The heat from the living firestorm of the salamanders summoned by the traitorous Uriath to slay both her and Moriana had abated slightly. But under no circumstance did she fear the fire elementals —or even the Destiny Stone Uriath had stolen and which had destroyed him. The major obstacle to overcome had been Moriana's lover Fost. He might suspect trickery and check to see if she had actually fallen to her death. He may have been a lowborn groundling but he was as cunning as if he had spent his life untangling the threads of intrigue in the Imperial court at High Medurim.

In other circumstances Moriana might have suspected some ploy on her sister's part. But she had been exhausted physically and spiritually by the last duel with Synalon for possession of the Sky City they both coveted. Besides, she had wanted to believe her sister capable of making such a noble choice as suicide over imprisonment or exile.

Wary of pursuit, Nightwind swiveled his head back and forth constantly studying the horizon and the sky to both sides. Looking back the way they'd come, he gave a sudden sharp cry.

Synalon came immediately alert. Her vision wasn't that of an eagle but it was far sharper than an ordinary human's. On a distant knoll almost swallowed by the shadow cast by the City in the noonday sun sat a small figure. Before the figure a great black cruciform object lay on the ground. Synalon's eyebrows arched in surprise. Her thin lips drew back in a smile. With pressure of her knee, she set Nightwind into a long banking curve and headed back.

The procession turned into the alley and stopped. Quiet lay like a blanket on the streets. From the center of the City came wild cries of celebration. Most of the population had massed in the great Circle of the Skywell to acclaim the new queen. Of the rest, some waged a final hopeless fight against the invaders in back streets and warehouses, or huddled behind shuttered windows fearful of the forces that stalked the City in the Sky that day. The backs of deserted buildings looked down blankly upon the knot of the faithful.

It was an unremarkable wall constructed of seamless gray stone shot through with veins of dull green, worn to a glossy smoothness by the passage of wind and countless ages. Like the older structures in the City, like the bulk of the City itself, it was a gigantic crystal grown in the ages before the coming of man to the Southern Continent. Rooms, passageways and doors had been hollowed out of it by the patient labor of clawed hands.

A hand like those of the original builders, dark green, finely scaled, possessed of thumb and three clawed fingers, held aloft a black diamond that smoked as though plucked from a furnace. The huge gem's facets glittered dully, not in the light of a sun masked by a high cloud layer but with an inner luminescence of its own. The worshippers fell silent. The hand pressed the stone against the wall. The jewel smoked furiously and a section of wall vanished soundlessly, leaving no trace.

The jewel bearer stepped through the oblong opening into a passage that had lain hidden for a hundred centuries and more. Heads bowed, twinned hearts pounding with religious rapture, the faithful followed him into the dark—into the Dark. No light penetrated the downward-winding tunnel. The noonday light outside seemed incapable of crossing the threshold of the secret passage. But the giant diamond carried by the leader provided enough dark illumination of its own to guide its bearer and his twelve followers.

Downward, ever downward they trudged. Darkness deepened, became tangible. No fear touched their hearts. The Dark was their element. They drew comfort and strength from it. The expectation of a great gift grew among the faithful.

They came to a door. It was twice as tall as a man, made of oak and bound with brass that showed no tarnish, no sign of the ages that had washed over this door like a flowing stream. All was illusion: the door was not wood and brass. It was wrought of a substance no mortal could work or even alter. The physical aspect given to a binding force of incredible power, it defied any other power in the world.

Any other but one. And the source of that power was only lately rediscovered.

The twelve threw themselves to their knees. The thirteenth raised the smoking jewel above his head and began a reptilian hissing, a triumphant chant.

In the bosom of the Dark a Demon slept, as it had for ten millennia. Hatred and despair washed over one another in an endless ebon swirl. But lately the Demon's dreams were shot through with bright threads of hope. Presences long unfelt had drawn near, uttering soft words, seductive words, promising that which the sleeping Demon desired above all things: freedom.

Or had that been another fragment of dream, the mind of the sleeper taunting itself with a hope it knew must remain unconsummated?

The nebulous awareness of the being existed without volition, could not summon events into focus or bring back recollections. It had no tests of truth or falsity. Still, the memories of newborn promise carried a sharpness, an appealing immediacy, that set them apart from the vagueness of dreaming. Like the memories of soft white flesh, and pain, and pleasure. . . .

Something tickled the Sleeper's mind. It stirred within its womb, within the stone that imprisoned its limbs as the old enchantment fettered its mind. For a long moment the Sleeper believed it was just another taunting shard of dream. Or did it hear once more the voices of those who had worshipped it in the days of glory, lost so long ago?

It sensed presences. As the words of the Song of Awakening came to it, a pulsation of power ran through the Sleeper's body and mind. The Demon's consciousness began to swim upward through the clouds that had lain so long on it. Many times in eons past it had attempted this crazy hegira. But now it felt the singing certainty that this time would be different.

"Well met, cousin," Synalon called cheerfully as she circled Nightwind in to a landing on the rounded hilltop. Prince Rann looked up from contemplating his warbird's corpse. The fallen eagle was a twin to Synalon's save that it bore a blazing scarlet crest. It lay spread out on the hillside before him, the butt of a *Zr'gsz* javelin protruding from beneath one wing.

"Rather absurd of you to say so, isn't it?" he asked, rubbing at the gingery stubble on his chin. He noticed her nakedness then, and looked away, blushing.

She laughed and jumped down from Nightwind's back. The eagle spread its wings above the corpse of its nest brother and uttered a single desolate cry.

"A pity about the bird," the princess said. "He was such a noble creature."

Still looking away from her, Rann nodded.

"I suppose it's reassuring," he finally said.

"How do you mean?"

"To know that I can feel remorse over the death of a friend."

Laughing easily, Synalon sat beside him. The warmth of her body washed over him. He began to fidget. He was a small, intense man who seemed put together of wire and spring steel. His eyes and swept-back hair were tawny, his

face displaying the same haughty, almost ascetically clas-
sic sculpting as Synalon's. The perfection of his features
was marred by a tiny network of white knife scars
stretched over the skin like a mask. The nearness and
nudity of his cousin was for him as exquisite a torture as
any he might devise for victims of his sadism.

"You're turning soft," she taunted him. Then, as mer-
curial as always, she switched from banter to flashing
anger. "Perhaps that's why you lost my City for me. The
security of my realm lay in your hands. You let it slip!"

He jumped to his feet, glad of the chance to get away
from the smell of her, the feel of her provocatively bare
thigh pressing against his purple-clad leg.

"You're a fine one to talk," he said quietly. He paced
away. His scabbard flapped empty at his hip. His scimitar
had plummeted to earth sheathed in the body of Darl
Rhadaman, Moriana's champion. "*You* fought the real
battle. What happened in the air was secondary. I grant
you, I failed to stop Moriana's entry into the City. But
ultimately, cousin dear, it was up to you to prove your
superiority in a test of wills and magic, face to face,
alone." He turned back to regard her sardonically. "And
evidently it was a battle you lost. Or else you wouldn't be
in such . . . dishabille."

She leaped to her feet.

"Don't lecture me, half man! How can a eunuch such as
you understand what I have lost this day?"

"What you have thrown away this day!" His face was
taut and pale under the lattice of scars. "With the favor of
the Dark Ones, you thought, no prize lay beyond your
grasp. And now look what you've won. Exile to a lonely
hilltop without so much as a cloak to cover your nakedness. A prize fit for a queen—of nothing!"

She smiled at him, savage and evil, raised her arms and
stretched so that her heavy breasts rode lazily up her rib-
cage. His tongue flicked lizardlike over his lips. He turned
away again.

"What will you do now, cousin?" Synalon asked silkily.

"Will you leave me on this hilltop fate has set me to rule?"

His head drew down between his shoulders.

"You know I cannot do that." For the first time in Synalon's long memory, the prince's voice was hoarse and choked with emotion. She laughed musically in delight.

"No, of course you can't abandon me. Because, while you hate me, you love me far more. And vastly more even than that, you desire me, O cousin Prince!"

Abruptly, Synalon flung forth her arm. Blue lightning coruscated from outstretched fingertips and struck Rann full in the back. He uttered a croaking cry and fell forward onto his knees, arms hugging his chest, bobbing and gasping in a paroxysm of agony.

"And because you fear me, my good and loyal Prince," said Synalon, sneering. "Because you fear me well."

Painfully Rann struggled to his feet.

"It would . . . seem that you're the one—oh!—who grows soft," he said, enunciating each word as if a dagger twisted in his bowels at every syllable. "Still you fail . . . to exact the final price of my failure."

"I'd prefer having you available to redeem yourself," she said in a matter-of-fact tone. "You are adroit, for all that your recent efforts have not exactly been crowned with success. And you're a tough bastard, Rann. A normal man would at this moment be lying before me unconscious or dead from the bolt I gave you."

Turning, Rann gradually forced himself to uncurl and stand upright before his cousin. He felt like he was stretched on the rack. He forced his lips to smile.

"A normal man, perhaps, but not a half man, eh?" He shook himself as though throwing off the last of the pain the lightning had left. "What now, cousin?"

Synalon paused, rubbed her palms together, as if rolling a pill between them.

"We travel to Bilsinx, or Kara-Est perhaps, and marshal our resources. That bitch Moriana found some way to increase her powers. So will I. And those damned lizard allies of hers—their magics seemed all of a defensive sort. They were potent, but even more so is my hatred. I will find the way to defeat them in spite of that damned smoking jewel of theirs, and then pull Moriana down to a lingering death in the sight of all the City she thought to wrest from me!"

Rann might have pointed out that Moriana had indeed wrested the City away from Synalon. He didn't. He was too preoccupied staring past the pale angle of Synalon's shoulder, past the charred fall of her short hair. She frowned at him. The roundness of his eyes, the elevation of his brows and the slight parting of his lips were equivalent to a shout of horror and disbelief from another man. She followed the stare.

Small objects detached themselves from the rim of the floating City and fell. First a few, then hundreds spilled from all sides of the Sky City like beach sand from a child's palm. The objects rotated as they fell. Synalon's wondering eyes made out the flail of limbs desperately seeking purchase on the air. Screams came to her ears like the cries of distant gulls.

# CHAPTER TWO

Fost Longstrider sat slumped in the bishop's stool someone had produced for him and wondered whether or not to get drunk.

All around a crowd cheered itself hoarse. Moriana stood proudly beneath the winged crown of the City in the Sky, her arms outflung as if to embrace her new subjects. For having just fought two desperate battles, one of arms and one of sorcery, and then having come close to flaming death from the stolen magics wielded by High Councillor Uriath, she looked remarkably fresh and radiantly beautiful.

Fost, on the other hand, was slipping from the frenzy of battle into the fog of after-action depression. He was charred all over from his own near incineration by one of Uriath's fire elementals, and was uncomfortably aware that the stench of burned flesh clinging to his sweat-lank black hair had come from Luranni. He shuddered at the memory of the woman whom he had bedded and who had interposed herself between the salamander and her lover. She had bought his life with hers. Where he wasn't black, he was bloody; where he wasn't scorched, he was scored by swordcuts. His helmet and shield were gone, his breeches blackened and torn beyond recognition and his hauberk reduced to a few rings of steel mail hung around his powerful torso. He still had his broadsword hanging at his hip in a well-smoked hornbull leather scabbard.

He looked more like the vanquished than a conquering hero.

In battle he'd always felt a vivid, singing awareness, had felt alive in a way he didn't at other times. Lately he had

22

started to go into a berserker's fury that grew madder as the battle grew more intense. Afterward, however, he felt depleted, soiled, and not at all proud of his prowess at wreaking destruction on his fellow man.

His only consolation was that the venerable ghost of Erimenes the Ethical wasn't crowing in his usual fashion over the glorious bloodletting he had witnessed that day. At the moment Erimenes argued with yet another ancient Athalar ghost, that of a nun named Ziore who had spent her earthly life denying herself all fleshly pleasure in accordance with the philosophy espoused by Erimenes himself in life—but which he had renounced after surviving the death of his body and awakening to what he had missed. Ziore blamed Erimenes for what she herself had forsaken, the more so since discovering he had recanted. After accompanying Moriana and Fost respectively, the two genies were now engaged in highly vocal, childish bickering.

Still, Fost thought, his lot wasn't so bad. The woman he loved stood by his side and received the adoration of her City. She had succeeded, as had he. Moriana had regained her precious Sky City; he had been reunited with his lover. An added bonus was that Synalon's madness would never unleash a second War of Powers on the world.

A fatuous smirk crossed his face when he realized he was a hero. Like in all the fairy tales of his youth, he was a hero and had won the privilege of living happily ever after.

He drained his goblet of wine and eyed the swell of Moriana's rump inside her tight breeches. Living happily ever after was a marvelous prospect, he decided. He just wished this state business would be finished soon so they could get down to doing the happy living in earnest.

With harsh shouts and proddings with spears, a mob of prisoners was herded into the circle to stand before their rightful queen. Some cowered on their knees pleading for forgiveness with clasped hands and desperate voices. Others stood aloof, disdaining to beg for their lives. Even they had a certain hunted look to their eyes. Fost guessed that their apparently prideful refusal to prostrate themselves and grovel for mercy sprang from a knowledge that it would do them no good. Moriana was an Etuul, from the same stock as Synalon and Rann.

Most of the troops guarding the prisoners wore the ragged garb and odd bits of armor of the Underground's street fighters, the brown and green of the Nevrym foresters or the bright colors and well-tended armor of Moriana's handful of allies from the City States. A few, though, wore the black and purple of the City's military, and here and there Fost caught a glimpse of the brassards of the elite Sky Guard worn alongside the blue and red ribbons of Moriana's sympathizers. The captives were an equally mixed lot: common bird riders and Sky Guardsman still haughty and erect despite the numbing shock of their first defeat; Bilsinxt auxiliaries in drab earth tones; gaudy Palace Guards; even a few scattered Monitors bereft of their leather helmets and looking about wildly like beasts being led to the slaughter. So hated were Synalon's Monitors that only those fortunate enough to find outlanders— Nevrym foresters, men from the Empire, even Hissers—to surrender to before the mob caught them had survived this long. Now they faced Moriana's justice. But unlike the other prisoners, to them it made little difference whether she chose to be harsh or lenient. The crowd had seen their faces. Their fates were immutable.

As the crowd backed away as if to set themselves apart from those who had dared oppose the return of the City's rightful queen, Fost wondered again where Moriana's reptilian allies were. He hadn't seen one yet. But he knew Moriana had won their cooperation by promising to give them certain religious relics they had been forced to leave behind when Riomar shai-Gallri and her sorceress adventurers wrested the City from them millennia before.

One of the religious artifacts was in view at this moment, and not as far away as Fost would have liked. Across the Skywell from where he and Moriana stood, squatted the Vicar of Istu, leering at the proceedings with a grotesque basalt face. The statue's form was manlike and exaggeratedly male. Its head bore horns. This was the most disconcerting feature of the great icon, because all of the world's horned creatures wore them decently on snout or forehead and pointing forward. The Vicar of Istu's sprouted unnaturally from the sides of its round head and curved upward.

A substantial pedestal had been carved from the foundation stone of the City, but the Vicar didn't occupy it. Fost felt cold all over remembering the sight of the statue coming alive and moving from that pedestal to threaten Moriana so long ago. He hoped that the Vridzish were nearly finished rounding up their precious religious treasures. The sooner they got that ghastly mannikin out of his sight the happier Fost Longstrider would be.

"Men of the Sky City!" Moriana's voice rang like a trumpet, stilling the murmurings and occasional catcalls cast in the prisoners' direction. "You stand before me because you have committed a most grievous deed: resisting by arms the return of your legal and rightful queen to claim her throne."

Instantly, a dozen men fell to their knees, sobbing and pleading and shaking clasped hands in the air.

"We did no wrong! Your Majesty, there has been some terrible mistake!"

A short, slightly built youth in black and purple pushed his way arrogantly through the crowd to stand before Moriana, his black hair thrown back, his blue eyes blazing defiance. The brassard of the Guard surrounded one wiry bicep.

"We fought in defense of our City and our crowned queen, so acclaimed by the Council of Advisors in accordance with ancient law. Your claim to the Throne of Winds may be just but you chose to come as an invading enemy. If resisting you was a crime, then my comrades and I must plead wholeheartedly guilty!"

A wild babble filled the air. The crowd growled like a

hungry beast, and a guard shouted, "On your knees before the queen, scum!" The captive Monitors and sallow men in the robes of Palace bureaucrats and mages swore that this madman did not speak for *them*. The other Sky Guard captives raised a shout in a different key.

"Well said, Cerestan! We fly and fall with you!"

Moriana raised her hand, commanding silence. The uproar died.

"You are Cerestan, young man?" she asked. Fost watched, judging the man to be a year younger than the new queen—which made him older than the courier.

"I am flight lieutenant of the Guard," Cerestan said proudly.

"Very well, Lt. Cerestan. You are brave. Since you have thrust yourself forward so boldly, then you shall hear my judgment upon you and upon your comrades, as well." More piteous outcries broke from the captives. Cerestan paled but set his jaw resolutely.

"You, and those who fought beside you in resisting my entry into the City in the Sky—and your fellows of the Guard particularly—hear now your doom. You are from this moment free men and women, to leave the City or remain in her service, with the thanks of monarch and people, providing only that you are willing to swear fealty to me, your new and rightful queen."

The crowd uttered a formless, astonished gasp. The prisoners looked stunned. Cerestan blinked rapidly and cocked his head as if uncertain he had heard correctly.

Moriana laughed at his confusion.

"Did you think I was insensible to your dilemma? Being the younger sister I was heir to the throne by City law, but the Council named Synalon rightful queen. Which was right? You chose what you thought was the moral course. You fought for your City as best you knew how, and you fought bravely."

She paused. A few cries of disbelief floated from the spectators, and she noticed that the men in Sky City uniforms who guarded the captives were beginning to acquire an angry look.

"I am most grateful now and forever to those who chose to side with me, and I shall do you all the honor it is in my power to do. But I will not punish loyalty to my beloved City, nor courageous striving on her behalf. So you who fought against me are no longer prisoners—not pardoned, for you have done nothing to be pardoned for.

"As for the rest of you, you Bilsinxt are likewise pardoned, but you are to be exiled at once from the City." Some of the Bilsinxt cried out in terror. The usual form of exile from the City was to be given a hearty push into the Skywell to fall the thousand feet to the ground. Moriana raised a placating hand. "I mean nothing drastic. You'll be allowed to collect your belongings and be given transport to the surface by balloon. Your city is still occupied, but I intend to withdraw the Sky City forces. With Synalon dead, no reason remains to maintain such a force."

Startled comment rippled through the listeners. Though everyone knew that Synalon was dead, it had not been confirmed in words before. Moriana waited until the commotion was over before going on.

"For the rest of you, for the functionaries who officiated over the reign of terror waged by Synalon and Rann against the people of the City, and the Monitors who were the instruments of that oppression, I remand you to prison, to be tried individually according to your acts, by a tribunal over which I personally will preside. Look to your conscience, gentlemen. On my own behalf I am not vindictive, but on behalf of my people I harbor no mercy!" She gestured imperiously, the graceful but definite handsweep of one born to rule. The wailing mages and officials were hauled to their feet and hurried off to prison, Moriana's men forming a cordon to protect them from the fists and feet of the crowd.

A noise tugged at the fringes of Fost's mind. The mindless oceanic sounds of the crowd blanketed all other sounds, but beneath the roar he felt more than heard a discord, unidentifiable and unsettling. He shook his head to clear it. The aftermath of the battle was getting the better of him. And he knew the precise way to combat it.

He held forth his goblet. A grinning serving youth refilled it with amber wine.

"Here, Chasko, refresh yourself," he shouted to the bearded man who stood beside him with Erimenes's satchel slung over one shoulder. His friend Prudyn, normally inseparable from him, stood some distance away holding an identical satchel loosely by the strap. The two had moved apart so that Erimenes and Ziore could no longer rant at each other.

Fost took Erimenes's satchel and slung the strap over his shoulder. Chasko accepted a fired clay vessel of liqueur and moved off to rejoin his comrade.

"You've made a sorry spectacle of yourself, old smoke," Fost told the spirit, knowing Erimenes could read the words from his mind if he didn't hear.

"It's all the fault of that brainless witch who claims to be an Athalar. She couldn't be one, or if she is then my city decayed greatly in the years following my death. Imagine the weak-mindedness and credulity to be so taken in by an obviously spurious doctrine as to waste one's whole life on it!"

"That's your own spurious doctrine you're talking about," Fost reminded him.

"If I've told you once, I've told you twelve thousand times," Erimenes said loftily, "I despise your barbaric imprecisions. Neither I nor that foolish cow Zir or Zor or Zoot or whatever she's called could possibly have made a spectacle of ourselves, since we're not visible. Why do you insist on changing the subject?"

"Majesty! Your Majesty!" Standing near Fost, Moriana looked up from a consultation with a group of officials who for reasons of conscience had allied with her.

A girl in her teens pushed her way through the throng almost to the queen's side. She wore breeches and a tattered tunic and a shortsword so thoroughly nicked as to appear sawtoothed. Her face was deathly pale beneath a coating of soot and grime, and one cheek was laid open to bleed freely and disregarded. Ribbons in Moriana's colors circled one arm.

"What is it?" asked Moriana, brow creasing in annoyance. She restrained the men who moved forward to disarm the girl, though the functionaries clucked with disapproval at her raggedness and impudence.

The girl took a deep breath. She swayed. Moriana caught her arm and supported her.

"The Hissers, Your Majesty," she got out, and then her knees buckled with the onslaught of a coughing fit. She finally controlled herself long enough to blurt out, "The Vridzish're attacking, Your Majesty! All over the whole damn City they're falling on top of us, armed and unarmed alike. It's t-treachery!" She fell forward so abruptly that Moriana scarcely prevented her from smashing face down on the pavement. It was only then that the queen saw the broken shaft of a black *Zr'gsz* arrow protruding from the girl's shoulder.

At the aft edge of the Circle, screams announced the arrival of the Hissers.

The stink of burning warehouses stung Fost's palate as his mind, fogged by drink and post-battle depression, struggled to come to grips with the girl's jagged-voiced warning. A flickering caught his attention, a quarter turn around the Circle of the Skywell. He looked that way in time to see a black flash and a fountain of scarlet. The Hissers swarmed into the Circle from the broad avenue that ran aft along the City's main axis. They freely wielded obsidian-edged swords.

He turned to Moriana. Her face was the color of a corpse's, and her lips moved without sound.

Then, "Ziore!" she cried. Without waiting for the genie

to answer, Moriana spun away to snap orders at the warriors who stood about staring in horror at this unexpected attack.

Gathering a knot of armed men and women about her, Moriana set off toward where the street mouth disgorged a stream of greenish *Zr'gsz* into the wide Circle. She and her troops made slow progress, bucking the current of humanity fleeing the wrath of its ancient enemies.

Fost felt a pang of surprise and betrayal that Moriana had called upon her Athalar spirit rather than upon him in her anguish. Then he decided that she was far more used to turning to Ziore in recent months than to him. The leaden lethargy that had gripped his limbs evaporated into a bright humming of adrenaline frenzy. He hitched Erimenes's satchel higher on his shoulder and drew his sword with a jerky motion.

A hand gripped his biceps. He whirled, swordarm preparing for the thrust. At his side a Sky Guardsman who bore Moriana's colors turned ashen but didn't flinch.

"Sir Longstrider," he said, not quite knowing how to address this obviously important groundling. "The captive soldiers—what shall we do with them?"

Fost glanced after Moriana, who was fighting her way through the panicking crowd like a fish swimming upstream, shouting for her men to come to her aid. It was hopeless trying to call to her over the wails of the multitude. Off toward the end of the City he saw thin trails of smoke twisting into the air.

He looked at the captive bird riders and Guardsmen, who stood where they had before, still unable to assimilate that they were free.

"Tread warily, my impetuous friend," advised Erimenes from his jug. "If you presume to give orders that Moriana finds objectionable, you may regret it later. The lady has shown a marked propensity to place the dictates of statecraft above those of the heart."

"Shut up, Erimenes," snapped Fost. Worry and anger grew. He felt the Guardsman's wondering eyes on him.

"The Hissers are unlikely to distinguish between us and them," he told the waiting soldier. "Arm them."

With Erimenes belaboring him as a fool, Fost dashed off in pursuit of his queen and lover.

Faint and distant, the sounds of conflict seeped through rock and penetrated the awareness of the thirteen who wove mighty magics in front of the ancient door. Khirshagk paused, the harsh incantation rattling to a stop in his throat.

"Our people strike prematurely, Instrumentality," one of his assistants reported.

He nodded. His long, handsome face was composed, serene. Despite the absolute darkness in the long-sealed and forgotten chamber, his twelve followers discerned every detail of his features, of the feathered ceremonial cloak he'd donned over his scratched green cuirass, and of the immense black diamond held smoking in one clawed hand. A black radiance pulsed from the depths of the stone, its tempo increasing second by second, like the beating of a heart touched with growing arousal.

"It matters little," he murmured. "The Children have waited many centuries for this moment. After such patience, the Dark Ones will forgive them their impetuosity. It will not alter the outcome." And so saying, Khirshagk, Instrumentality of the People, raised the black diamond that was the Heart of the People and resumed the chant to weaken the spells laid long ago by Felarod.

"Come, lads, we've got them on the run!" cried a bearded Northlander, brandishing his broadsword so that the rings of his mail shirt tinkled musically. Up the narrow street a clot of low caste *Zr'gsz* in loincloths broke and fled under a vicious rain of arrows from Nevrym foresters and grounded bird riders. Knowing something of the Nevrymin and their attitudes toward the Hissers, Fost had been concerned over which side they'd take in this fight. However, the Vridzish had made savagely clear their intention of slaying everything human in the City. The foresters allied with the Sky Citizens by default. Their longbows did much to roll back the advantage of surprise gained by the *Zr'gsz.*

Seeing Moriana's troops strike the attacking Hissers with spear, sword and a singing cloud of arrows, a group of defenders had veered down a sidestreet to meet a probe by the lizard men. Fost had gone along, and already felt useless. By his own estimation the very worst archer in the world, Fost wished to close and use his sword.

He trotted up the street between the clanking mailed City States man and a rangy Nevrym forester with one eye. They passed the bodies of several of the *Zr'gsz* quilled like porcupines by the human archers. An obsidian-tipped spear lay by one's outflung talon.

"Ha! What fuss to make over these decadent savages," Erimenes said scornfully. "If they craft weapons of stone they cannot be too formidable."

The one-eyed forester glanced at Fost. Having accompanied Moriana and Ziore in the assault on the City he was accustomed to disembodied voices emerging from satchels.

"You'd soon learn better had you a body, old one," he told the genie. "The volcano glass of the *Zr'gsz* holds—"

A small, light-skinned lizard man popped from the doorway of a shop a few steps ahead and brought his arm whipping forward. An obsidian axe whirled to embed itself with a crunch in the mailed chest of the bearded Northlander. The man coughed astonishment and blood. His legs gave way beneath him. The Nevrymin drew and loosed his arrow as the Hisser dodged back into the doorway.

"—holds an edge far sharper than the finest steel," he finished. He paused, only slowing the fluid rhythm of his run, and confirmed with a quick glance at the City Stater's unnatural posture and unwinking, glazed stare that he was beyond assistance. "Course, obsidian'll shatter against steel plate, or even good iron. But it can bust right on through mail."

Fost gulped. In his imagination, his own mail vest already rent by ill-use took on the consistency of wet paper. His grip tightened on his sword as he loped past the doorway from which the axe-wielding Hisser had emerged. The Nevrymin didn't spare a glance. The Vridzish lay huddled inside the pointed archway with his sharp chin slumped to the shaft of the arrow jutting from his sternum.

Fost's peripheral vision noticed the timeworn frieze graven around the shop's arched door. The architecture and ornamental stonework of the City in the Sky had disturbed him before, though he'd never been able to understand the reason. Now he knew the cause of that uneasiness. The City had originally been constructed by the *Zr'gsz*. The many additions later wrought by humans had imitated the original style. While these additions lacked the eldritch quality of the older structures, they still jarred the unaccustomed eye. But it was the ornamentation that bothered Fost the most. The figures in the bas relief were wrong in nameless ways, subtly distorted, yet apparently human. But they were not human; they were *Zr'gsz* or the products of *Zr'gsz* imagination.

The City turned alien and cold around him.

The two of them continued their curving course and spilled into an intersection. Fost yelped as a streak of yellow lightning crackled past his elbow and blasted the cornice of a building. Glowing gobs of stone spattered in all directions, drawing sharp yips of pain when they struck flesh.

"Fost!" cried Moriana. "I'm sorry. I didn't know it was you."

"Think nothing of it," he said sarcastically. Her deathbolt hadn't singed him, nor had the molten masonry hit him. But he now had a fused patch in the mail beneath his left arm to match the one a salamander had given him that morning. "I didn't know you could do that."

She showed her teeth in a grin of wolfish satisfaction.

"Neither did Synalon," she said. "I've learned a few things since we parted, my love."

A shout turned her attention back to the street, where more Zr'gsz had massed. Fost jumped to avoid the javelins and slung stones that glanced off the walls and clattered on the paving.

Several of their followers died from the missiles. The rest dodged back into doorways or around corners to avoid fire. Moriana stood her ground. She held a High-grass bow in her left hand, but made no effort to pull an arrow from the few remaining in the quiver slung across her back.

She raised her right hand. A short arrow whirred by and dug a furrow in her cheek.

"Damn you, treacherous serpents!" she screamed. "Die for your faithlessness!"

The hand came down. Blinding white light exploded from her fingers. Fost saw bright orange and blue after-images dancing before his eyes, but from the corners he glimpsed Zr'gsz bodies flung in all directions by the blast.

"A most impressive display, Queen," remarked Eri-menes. "However, I wonder if your prowess will suffice against the forces I perceive are about to be—"

"Silence, rogue!" squalled Ziore from her jug. "Moriana is the most powerful mage in all the world."

Weaving like a reed in a breeze from the energy spent on the deathbolt, Moriana turned a stunned look toward the leather bag carrying Ziore. Her expression showed she was unused to this facet of the genie's personality.

Moriana staggered. Fost caught her arm and supported her. Her fingers gripped his forearm and squeezed down weakly.

"You've grown more powerful," he said, "to be able to toss lightning around like that so soon after your duel with Synalon."

"I have." She swept hair from her forehead with a

quick thumb movement. "And my anger gives a greater store of power than I'd have otherwise."

"You should rest and marshal your power."

"No! If I stop now I'll collapse." She shook her head tiredly. "Even without my magics, we're winning. The human warriors of my army and Synalon's are too many for them."

She gestured up the street. As far as a distant curve, it was strewn with arrow-skewered *Zr'gsz* corpses. Near at hand several Underground fighters fished a limp green-scaled body from the sunken stone pond of a aeroaquifer. The magic fountain continued to produce water and music alike from thin air. The calm beauty of the sound drove back the warlike clamor from the surrounding streets.

"Now, where's that foul pact-breaking Khirshagk?" demanded Moriana. "I'll scatter his ashes over the Keep of the Fallen, and the Heart of the People be damned!"

The warriors raised a cheer. Fost started to ask what the Heart of the People was, but a giant hand slammed into his ribs and dumped him on his rump in the street. An instant later, a tidal wave of sound crashed into him and sent him sprawling.

He rolled, recovered, found himself tangled with Moriana. A strange, dead silence descended. Moriana's lips moved but no sound emerged. Fost wondered what had happened to her voice, to the sounds of battle and the soothing song of the aeroaquifer. Then he saw a Sky Guardsman sitting a few yards away. A trickle of blood ran from one ear.

Fost felt his own ears. His fingertips detected no wetness and a quick inspection of Moriana showed her ears weren't bleeding either. The concussion had deafened them but hadn't burst their eardrums.

The Guardsman had gone as rigid as a marble statue. His arm was extended, pointing along the street they'd just cleared of the Hissers. Fost and Moriana exchanged looks and turned their heads that way.

A rolling black cloud rose above the dizzying spires and rooftops of the Sky City, burning a hole in the sky as it climbed. Blackness shone from it like light from the sun. They had to look away, the bright afterimages dancing in their eyes.

Moriana's cry pierced the armor of Fost's numbed ears. He looked back to see a great shape hovering just above the steep roof of the armory directly below the rapidly receding cloud. It was manlike in shape, though many times larger than the largest of men. And the horns that grew from either side of its blunt head were anything but manlike. It was the very image of the Vicar of Istu.

*No, you idiot,* Erimenes's voice rang in his head. *It's the original.*

The Demon of the Dark Ones shot upward and was gone.

# CHAPTER THREE

The spells were sung, the aspects properly aligned.

The mystical forces Felarod had forged to contain Istu had been hammered thin like gold beaten on an anvil. Yet still they held the ancient and mighty Demon caged in his stone prison. It would still take unearthly power to break the barrier.

"And now that which we have awaited so long," cried Khirshagk, *"shall come to pass!"* For a long minute, he held the blackly blazing Heart high above his head. The others turned up their faces in rapture. His own twin hearts close to bursting, the Instrumentality brought his arm down and flung the diamond against Felarod's magic.

The giant gem exploded. The ancient door was volatized by a ball of jet flame, as was the living stone for yards in all directions. Khirshagk and his twelve followers had only a split second to scream out their ecstasy before being engulfed and destroyed. Khirshagk and the others had known what fate awaited them and embraced death with the fanaticism of true martyrs. Not just their own lives but ten thousand years of their People's history had built toward this instant.

Khirshagk fulfilled his role as Instrumentality. His hand released the Demon Istu and began the Second War of Powers.

*Free!*

The Demon's being crackled with unfamiliar energy. Its first reaction had been the reaction of its id: sheer terror. But its awesome mind awakened to the knowledge that centuries-old chains were no more.

*Free!*

With the fullness of that knowledge, awful and magnificent, Istu soared upward following the path the dark fireball had slashed through the foundation of the Sky City. Nothing dimmed his exaltation. Not even the sunlight, the contact with that hated aberration Light. He shouted defiance at the sun and soared upward to once again touch the Void, the disruption of order that was Dark.

*Free!*

In a single beat of the massed hearts of the tiny paleskinned ones who infested the City of his children, Istu surged above the atmosphere, filling his being with the essence of the Void and Dark. The sun ball blazed at him, furious and impotent, and the stars looked down with malice. His laugh rang among them, echoing to eternity. In Dark and Void had the Universe begun, and to them it would return. Once again would the Dark Ones rule over placid oblivion, and their child and servant Istu would become One with them, One with Nothingness.

*Free!*

Great joy surged at being liberated from the walls of stone and magic that had pinioned His mind and body for so long. Greater still would be the joy of revenge.

*Free!*

The Demon of the Dark Ones turned his attention downward.

Stunned, Fost, Moriana and the rest scarcely had time to pick themselves up from the flagstones before Istu descended again like a flaming black meteor. With a strange, high keening the Demon flashed over their heads to touch down out of sight among the towers of the portside quarter of the Sky City.

"Moriana?" asked Ziore from her jug. "What happened? I feel the most peculiar presence . . ."

*"Don't!"* screamed the woman. "Keep your mind away from it. Don't try to read its thoughts or emotions. Don't even *try!*"

"But . . . oh." Ziore read the knowledge of what had just occurred from Moriana's mind. She knew better than to disregard such advice. If Moriana told her to keep her perceptions clear of the Demon, she must obey. The sorceress-queen had more intimate experience of Istu than did any living entity. Ziore read exactly how intimate that knowledge was and sent ripples of mental horror radiating outward.

Fost wiped tears from his light-blinded eyes. First Moriana's firebolt, then the eruption from the center of the City and now the Demon's return had all etched their patterns on his retinas.

"It's real, isn't it?" he asked, appalled at the power of the thing he'd witnessed. "A demon. A real demon."

"The most powerful of all," announced Erimenes, managing to sound melodramatic despite the enormity of the moment.

Fost didn't feel his knees give way. He was simply standing one second and sitting the next.

"Istu. He's real." He had seen the Demon manifest itself before, had seen the Vicar touched with unholy life, seen the hellglare of the Demon's soul burning yellow through the slits of the statue's eyes. But the Demon, the *Demon,* Istu, child and servant of the Lords of Infinite Night, had never been real to him. The Vicar had been evil and horrifying, but no more than a golem to be outsmarted with a simple cunning twist from an agile mind. Fost had defeated it and rescued Moriana. A mortal had vanquished an animated statue.

But that force animating the Vicar had been the tiniest splinter of an immensely potent and incomprehensibly ancient mind. Before, Fost had faced only Istu's id, childlike and primal, a mass of drives and desires. He had witnessed awesome power—and this was only the smallest fraction of the true force of the Demon.

And this!

Above the highest spires of the portside district Istu reared up from the street, appearing to be a man-shaped hole cut into the overcast sky. His eyes blazed like windows to the surface of the sun. From them darted beams of impenetrable blackness. The tower of the Palace of Winds exploded. Moriana cried out as if her nerves were twined with the tower as it was dashed into a million fragments.

Gazing numbly into the sky, Fost watched a block the size of a hornbull turn end over end and crash through the starboard wing of the Lyceum. Head-sized fragments rained into the intersection about them, knocking smaller chunks from the edifices. One boulderlike fragment struck the magic-powered aeroaquifer, forever stilling its voice and stemming its waters.

The Demon laughed.

His laugh pierced souls, rimed hopes and aspirations with quickfrost like that which Fost saw glazing the shards blasted from the Palace. Warriors whose bravery had gone without questioning a dozen times that day fell to their knees sobbing in dread.

"He's real," Fost repeated over and over to himself. No one else listened to his dazed litany. "It's all real. Gods, Dark Ones, the War of Powers and all."

"Yes, you bemused jack-fool!" Erimenes snapped acerbically. "Don't you understand? This day has truly seen the opening of a *Second* War of Powers!"

Fost's response was to drop his face into his hands and moan. It did add up. One didn't need to be a bespectacled clerk in a Tolvirot counting house to arrive at the sum.

He felt someone tugging at his shoulder. He shook his head with a peevish motion. All he wanted now was to crawl into his mother's lap—what did she look like? What was her name?—and cry himself to sleep. And maybe if he were very lucky, he'd awaken and find this all a nightmare sent by Majyra Dream Mistress to bedevil him.

An openfisted blow slammed into the side of his head and sent him sprawling. His panic had been stripped from him like a wrapper, to uncover sudden fury.

Moriana stood over him. Her expression was one of

stark contempt. She thought him a cowardly groundling seeking the comfort of despair. He snarled and started up.

When he gained his feet he saw the hauteur was gone from her face. Her eyes met his and he understood.

"Let's go," she said simply.

They raced back toward the center of the City and the broad promenade of the Circle. The Sky Citizens who had not been there to acclaim the new monarch now gravitated there naturally after escaping the Hissers and their demon ally. Moriana rapped orders, brisk and businesslike in the face of calamity, marshalling her armed forces for resistance.

A warning cry sounded. A platoon of *Zr'gsz* broke from a nearby avenue. An arrow storm cut them down. A triumphant shout rose from the crowd.

"They don't know what they've got to contend with yet," said Erimenes. "But they will soon. All too soon," muttered the spirit. Fost didn't bother listening. He stood frozen, his gaze riveted to the spectacle unfolding in the Sky City.

Far down the avenue the Demon appeared, striding on two legs like a man. Edifices of grown or graven stone slumped into ruin as his swinging arms casually brushed them. The Vridzish were massed about him, insignificant insects beside the stories-tall entity.

Arrows winnowed the ranks of the People. Dauntlessly, they came on, trotting to match the bandy-legged strut of Istu. Unbidden, the Sky Citizens rushed to the attack, black and purple-clad troopers and Underground fighters together, brandishing swords and spears.

Istu stopped. The horned, misshapen head bent down to inspect these presumptuous pale worms. The burning eyes narrowed, reminding Fost of shutters closing on a magical vessel containing a fire elemental. But the glare of a salamander was mere heat and mindless malice. Istu's eyes burned without heat, but the hatred of old, soul-destroying evil that shone forth made Fost shrivel inside.

Istu blew forth a black breath. The miasma billowed downward, impenetrably dark. Some of the advancing Sky Citizens quailed and fled. Others stood their ground. The same fate took all. Like a living fogbank, the black breath rolled over them. As it did, each of the soldiers exploded into a pink cloud of bodily fluids and shards of skin, leaving the skeletons to clatter hollowly to the street. The bones, still joined by sinew, gleamed pale and white.

The black breath cloud enveloped all those who had been so bold as to rush upon the Demon of the Dark Ones. The noise of the explosions reminded Fost of unpierced fruit popping in the oven, a sharp sound with wet undertones. His stomach gave a queasy heave. Onward came the cloud. The crowd realized it would soon overtake them. In terror some of them turned and flung themselves into the Skywell rather than have the Demon's breath claim them.

Moriana stepped forward from the line of troops she'd ordered across the avenue. Istu stood impassively, waiting to see what this golden-haired mortal made of its deadly exhalation. Silence seeped up from the very stones of the Sky City as Moriana raised her hands. A golden radiance sprang from her, resolved itself into a spear of light that leaped forward to pierce the cloud of darkness. The cloud exploded as had its victims. A few tatters of blackness danced on the wind, then vanished.

An avalanche of sound rumbled deep in Istu's throat.

"It recognizes Moriana," suggested Erimenes.

Fost's throat constricted. For the queen's sake he hoped the Demon didn't realize this wasn't its first encounter with the tall, slim, defiant woman.

Moriana flung out her arms. Her fingers reached, grasped, drew back toward her breast. The facade of a tall structure on Istu's left toppled forward onto the Demon.

Istu roared and staggered. His horned head was above the level of the buildings and mere stone couldn't harm him. But the torrent of masonry affected him like a sudden gout of water would affect a human. He was driven back even as the falling stone crushed the *Zr'gsz* clumped around his feet.

"She's learned a great deal, that girl," Erimenes remarked approvingly.

The black beams lashed from Istu's eyes. Moriana was prepared. Her hand was already in motion, drawing a curtain of shimmering flame across the air in front of her. The black radiance struck the flame shield; both disappeared.

Breath pumped rapidly in and out of Fost's powerful chest. He felt helpless in the face of such magic. He clutched his sword, wishing for action and knowing this battle far outclassed his abilities.

"Can she defeat him?" he whispered. "Has she gained power greater than Felarod's?"

Somewhere in the fracas, the lid of Erimenes's jug had come loose. In a whirlwind of blue fog and sparkling light motes, the genie appeared at Fost's elbow. As his long narrow head took form, it was shaking, a look of paternal disappointment on his ascetic features.

"I hardly think so. Nor would you, if you truly thought on it. Consider, my foolish young friend. How alert are you after waking from a long, long sleep? Especially one deepened by wine or drugs. I suspect the after-effects of Felarod's compulsion have a similar effect on the Demon. Yes, they are definitely analogous to those of more mundane soporifics used extensively in the . . ."

"I get the drift," said Fost, waving a hand to stem the tide of Erimenes's pedagogy.

Istu had shouldered through the rubble. He strode purposefully up the street, and Fost wondered if it was only his imagination that perceived a fiercer light in those yellow eyes.

With a crack like thunder, a vast circular pit yawned before the Demon. Istu dropped instantly from sight in a welter of debris. Buildings to either side, their fronts undermined, slid into the hole. From the rush of air through the Skywell at his back, Fost knew the hole went all the way through the stone slab on which the City rested.

Almost at once a black hand appeared, three fingered and taloned like a Hisser's. Once more Moriana had cast magic of incredible power at the Demon—and had only succeeded in delaying his progress along the avenue. With icy shock, Fost realized the Demon was playing with his mortal opponent. He could simply have flung himself to the Circle of the Skywell with the speed of rushing wind had he so desired.

"Perhaps Istu treats this duel as a warming up exercise," said Erimenes, reading the courier's thoughts.

A look of alarm gripped Erimenes's features, and he shouted, "Oh, no, you can't take that upon yourself!" The genie had mind read Fost's intentions.

Unheeding, Fost looked around, then went to the young loyalist officer Cerestan, who stood with bow and arrow in his hands and glared with impotent fury at the Demon.

"We need balloons and birds," Fost shouted as the lieutenant's head whipped around. "We have to evacuate the City. *Now!*" he added as the young Sky Guard started to protest.

Still Cerestan objected, "We cannot abandon our City!"

"This goes beyond the fate of your damned City! Any human who stays here will be dead within the hour. Don't you see? A new War of Powers is upon us. We need live humans to fight back, not dead fools who threw away their lives in useless heroics."

Fost watched as understanding sank into Cerestan's mind. He nodded, lank black hair falling across his forehead. He turned to obey, then halted with a jerk like a dog reaching the end of its tether. He faced Fost.

"The queen! What of her?"

Fost read the look in those fervent blue eyes and inwardly groaned. He may have battled against Moriana but Cerestan was smitten with her all the same.

"I'll take care of her," he said, emphasizing the first word more than was necessary.

Cerestan wheeled and raced off, calling to uniformed men and women as he passed. Some wearing Moriana's ribbons hesitated, but only for an instant. What side each had fought on before didn't matter now. They were all the same in the yellow eyes of Istu. And Cerestan was an officer of the Sky Guard, which meant that his orders were worth heeding. Rann promoted no fools to command his elite.

Fost worked his way through the crowd, yelling to warriors and unarmed civilians alike to evacuate. Erimenes floated by his side, pleading with him to stop this folly and see to the security of his own hide. For Erimenes to encourage the courier to flee the scene of imminent violence was tantamount in likelihood to the spirit again adopting his old philosophy of abstinence. Fost realized the situation was grave if Erimenes was willing to forego bloodshed in favor of what he had termed cowardice on many prior occasions.

"Get out, it's hopeless, get out!" was all the genie said. But he repeated it continually, his voice rising to shriller and shriller pitches.

To Fost's astonishment, Cerestan led a tentacle of the frightened crowd aft from the Circle along one of the lesser streets—seemingly into the face of the Hissers. Even though his wits were dulled by fear and fatigue, Fost figured out the ploy. Istu himself was playing cat and mouse games on the main avenue with Moriana and most of the *Zr'gsz* were with him. The Hissers Cerestan and the rest ran into could be quickly dispatched. Then the Sky citizens would get to work inflating the huge cargo sausages in the aft hangars. Since Istu fought forward through the City, they'd be safer there than those who retreated to the City's prow, at least until Istu and his reptilian allies consolidated their hold on the Sky City.

Then no human would be safe.

"—have you impaled for impertinence, if she doesn't feed you to Istu," babbled Erimenes as Fost broke from the ranks of soldiers and raced for Moriana. "Great Ultimate, you know how fanatical she is about her City!"

Moriana had blocked the avenue with a shimmering, rippling curtain of light burning scarlet and blue and gold and white. Buzzings and fat black sparks burst forth as Istu touched it. The Demon fell back with a bellow of pain. Fost saw all this as he sprinted after Moriana.

With a sound like water sizzling on heated iron, a black hand reached through the shimmering curtain. With another anguished, angry roar, Istu hurled himself through the auroral wall. It caused pain but no damage. Pain was enough to infuriate him; he reached a clawed hand for Moriana.

"Duck!" screeched Erimenes. The courier had only a split second to evaluate the situation. Moriana stood poised, her face strangely calm, a blue nimbus of energy scintillant around her form. Her arms slowly rose, as if imploring the gods for aid. Fost dived headlong, not wanting to be caught in whatever defensive magic Moriana was about to unleash.

He felt a tingling close about his middle like a noose. He hung suspended in midair, the pressure around his waist threatening to crush him. Fost gasped, then reached out and gripped a protruding cobblestone with his fingertips. Straining every muscle in his body, he pulled. Like a seed squeezed between thumb and forefinger, he squirted out of the magical grip holding him. He tucked his shoulder and rolled on the hard street.

"What're you doing here?" Moriana's voice sounded odd, flat. Fost sat up and saw that they were encapsulated by a dome of dull silver. "The force shield will keep him out for a few minutes." She shook her head tiredly. "I learned this magic years ago but have never been strong enough to use it before."

Fost thought about frail mothers who lifted impossibly heavy blocks to free their trapped infants. In those moments of adrenaline fury, they became more than human. The urgency of battle against this cosmic being had elevated Moriana's powers in the same fashion.

"The City is being evacuated," he told her. "I came for you."

*"Evacuated!"* she screamed. Her face twisted in rage. "On whose craven order?"

"I told you, friend Fost, nothing good would come from that rash action of yours, but you didn't—"

"My order," Fost said, cutting off Erimenes.

Moriana raised a slender hand. Fost stood firm, though he knew magics capable of fending off Istu for the barest fragment of a second would blast him into a scorched cinder.

*"You!* By what authority?"

"As your acknowledged consort. But mostly common sense." He cast a quick glimpse upward at the pewter-colored wall of force. It held. The Demon seemed unsure how to deal with it, but Fost didn't doubt that Istu would eventually penetrate the curtain.

"The City's lost. All that remains is for her people to save themselves. And you, too. You most of all."

"I'm holding Istu!"

"You hold him—barely. He hasn't fully recovered from his enforced ten-thousand-year nap."

"But I grow stronger with every instant. I feel it!" Her eyes burned like balefires. She had won her City at horrendous cost. The thought of losing it almost in the same instant of seizing it drove forth her sanity like a beast.

"Are you Felarod?" he shouted at her. The dome began to bulge inward like a tent roof filling with rainwater. Istu had decided to push his way through using brute strength. "Do you control the power of the World Spirit? Can you overcome a demon born among the stars?"

"He's right, Moriana." The calm voice seemed to come from nowhere. Fost finally realized it emerged from the satchel so much like his own that Moriana carried over her shoulder.

The queen's shoulders slumped. The sight squeezed tears into Fost's eyes. He knew again how much he loved her, and her loss was a shared wound.

"Come," she said, almost imperceptibly. Serpentlike her hand darted out to catch Fost's wrist. She dragged him toward the wall of the dome. He hung back, recalling what it had felt like going through the barrier as it formed.

The silvery hemisphere burst like a soap bubble. Istu's iron-black claw plunged deep into the pavement where they'd stood only seconds before.

The Circle was almost deserted when they reached it. At the fringes of the great plaza Zr'gsz began filtering in from the side streets. Moriana stooped to gather a full quiver of arrows and kept running, pausing now and then to cast some enchantment at the Demon following them. Fost didn't even look back to see what spells she hurled at Istu. It was too painfully apparent they were little more than annoying inconveniences to Istu.

Forward of the Circle, they ran into a crowd. Off to their left an elongated cargo balloon surged into the sky. Screaming people dangled from its gondola as the sausage rose from the streets to be dragged clear of the City by a laboring eagle. Bird riders helped refugees mount eagles. Each could carry only a single passenger, and Fost saw more than one scimitar fall and come up red as hysterical men and women tried to fling themselves onto already overburdened warbirds.

Moriana's step faltered.

"My poor people!" she cried. "Only a handful will escape!"

Fost knew beyond doubt she was about to decide that she had to remain until all the Sky Citizens possible had been saved. He prodded her with his broadsword.

"Go on, damn you! We need your magic if we're to have a prayer of winning this!"

Her eyes were green daggers, but she picked up the pace again. Something whined past Fost's cheek. He slapped at it, thinking it an insect. His palm came away red.

He glanced back. The Vridzish had taken the Circle and were slaughtering refugees intent only on fleeing forward to the prow decks. The lizard warriors moved with in-human swiftness, their weapons all but invisible as they struck yielding flesh. Behind them, Istu stood in the Circle of the Skywell, horned head thrown back, raping the sky with his basso profundo laughter.

A pressure on Fost's arm brought him up short. They were at the waist-high wall ringing the City.

"Now what?" he asked.

Moriana's answer was to sling her bow over her shoulder, jerk out her longsword and parry the blow of a mace with one smooth motion. The snarling lizard man riposted with incredible speed. Moriana scarcely weaved out of the arc of the flanged mace before Fost lopped off the gray-green arm and plunged his blade through the Hisser's chest.

Other lizard men ran toward them.

"Can you hold them?" shouted Moriana.

"No!"

Ignoring his response, Moriana turned and leaped as lithely as a cat to the top of the rimwall. She stepped forward into space. Fost cried out in loss. Her despair had driven her to suicide!

"It's you who's about to suicide, dolt! Turn around. Fight!" At Erimenes's urging, Fost moved to slap away a spear jabbing for his midsection. The spear pulled back only to shoot forward again and take him in the belly. He doubled over, gagging. The Hisser's throat swelled in tri-umph.

Grabbing the haft of the spear, Fost stabbed out with his sword. The Hisser gave a croak of surprise as the blade pierced his throat sac.

Fost rose, ripping his sword free and wrestling the spear from the lizard man's death grip. The Vridzish hadn't struck with enough force to drive the obsidian-pointed spear through Fost's mail, though links had parted under the force of the blow.

Luck had been with him, this time.

A high caste *Zr'gsz* stood before him, breastplate gleaming green. The finely scaled skin of face and hands were so dark as to be almost black. The Vridzish flicked a two-handed mace at Fost. Instinct made Fost turn and block with the spear, which was almost knocked from his grasp. He cut at the Hisser's head. The mace knocked his sword aside, lashed out again. It struck chips from the wall as Fost dodged to one side.

Recovering his balance, he launched a whining multiple attack, one-two-three cuts in rapid succession. The mace met and countered each. He only saved himself from the crushing head by falling forward. The wooden shaft that had saved his life once now slammed into his left shoulder. He gasped in pain as his clavicle snapped.

He hacked at the Vridzish noble's side. His blade met the metal breastplate and was robbed of its force. He heaved, bringing his sword up along the inhuman's armored side to slice into the unprotected armpit. The Hisser dropped the mace between his body and Fost's and shoved the courier back.

Wary of the head with its five ugly flanges, Fost was caught off-guard when the Vridzish shifted his grip and whipped the butt of the weapon into Fost's face. Fost heard the crunch of his nose breaking. Lightning ricocheted inside his skull and nausea turned his flesh to water. He reeled, blinking to clear his eyes, saw the gleaming metal head rise up, up, up, poising to smash in his brains. . . .

Shot from pointblank range, the broadheaded arrow stuck the Hisser in the neck with such force it nearly severed the neck. Fost saw the lizard man's look of final surprise as the head lolled to one side. Then the *Zr'gsz* fell flopping and kicking while black blood fountained from its neck to spray the lower caste Hissers behind.

They shrieked mad sibilants and lunged forward with weapons raised.

"Jump, you fool! It's your only chance!" Impossibly, the voice was Moriana's.

His skull pounding, his sight blurred, his left arm swinging at his side like so much dead meat, Fost couldn't hold back the reptilian Hissers for even a heartbeat. Knowing he was going to his death and loath to fall to these villains from a child's fable, he spun and dived over the rimwall into open air.

The ground loomed up at him from a thousand feet below.

# CHAPTER FOUR

Fost Longstrider fell only four feet.

He had both arms crossed in front of his face. They took most of the force of his landing on the slate gray stone platform. His broken nose smacked hard against his forearm, sending a white-hot lance of pain into his brain. The wire-wound grip of his broadsword twisted in his hand, giving him a nasty cut on his left forearm. Even worse than the other abuses to his body, the force of his fall caused the stone platform to sink beneath his weight, leaving his stomach inches above his spine.

He felt the platform stir, rise. Fost lay dazed, watching the fireworks in his head and wondering whether or not he was glad he hadn't plunged the other 996 feet to the ground. The stone slab rocked gently like a boat bobbing at a dock. The nausea he felt from his broken nose was made all the worse by the motion. He guessed what had happened and where he was, but he kept his eyes clamped tightly shut. At this stage he didn't want to *know*.

"Is he all right?" he heard a worried feminine voice ask. Since it wasn't Moriana, it had to be Ziore. Her voice came out sounding elderly but strong and resonant and distinctly different from the screeching sounds she'd made at Erimenes.

A thump and a scrabble of claws came only a foot away from his head. The raft rocked under the impact of the added body. He heard the swish of a weapon cleaving air, the thunk of Moriana's longsword intercepting the axe-cut aimed at the back of his head.

The reek of *Zr'gsz* stung acridly in his nostrils. Anger filled him and drove back nausea and pain. If the reptilian

52

bastards weren't going to let him lie in peace, he'd make them sorry for it.

He seized the lizard man's ankles. The skin rippled smooth and dry, its texture differing only slightly from human skin. Before the reptilian Hisser reacted, Fost yanked hard on the ankles and flipped the creature into space between the blunt nose of the slab and the City wall.

He still wanted little more than to lie down and die, but the berserk fury he'd come to know in moments of battle settled on him like a cloak. He rose up and scythed three Zr'gsz from where they stood poised to leap from the rimwall.

"Bravo!" cried Erimenes, as the three sundered bodies plunged from view to the ground so far below.

Moriana thrust by him with a spear, not at a Vridzish swarming up onto the wall to attack but at the gray stone of the Sky City itself, pushing the skyraft clear. With a speed he didn't know himself capable of, Fost parried the stab of an obsidian-headed spear, then severed with a rapid backslash the claw that gripped it. Surprised, the Zr'gsz spearman lost his balance and fell into the rapidly widening gap between skyraft and City.

With the raft slowly drifting from the City, Moriana flung the spear at the Hissers, striking one in the shoulder. Panting with the fury of his own bloodlust, freshly roused and scarcely satisfied, Fost chanced a glance at the young queen.

"Faith-breakers!" she screamed. "I'll pay your folk back as I pay you now!"

Like sheet lightning, a wave of red flame burst from her body. The dozen Zr'gsz crowding onto the rimwall screamed, not screams of agony but the screaming of superheated air blasting from their lungs as the flame consumed them. So frightful was the energy blazing from Moriana that when the fire died it left a huge glowing yellow spot etched on the very stone. The few Zr'gsz left alive in the vicinity of the rimwall broke and fled toward the Circle of the Well of Winds and the comforting presence of the Demon.

Fost opened his mouth. Before he could speak Moriana's sea green eyes dimmed and closed. She fell heavily. Only reflexes honed to unnatural keenness by the berserker fit enabled him to catch her before she pitched headlong over the nose of the raft.

Squatting, he lowered her to the stone. Strength drained from him like water from a tub with its plug pulled. His legs refused to lift him upright. Instead of trying to stand, he sat beside her, staring back at the City as it slowly receded.

His first thought was of pursuit. Hundreds of rafts nosed against the forward edge of the City as the one they now rode had been, bobbing gently on passing air currents. Had the *Zr'gsz* wanted to, they could have sent flyers to run down the fugitives in a matter of minutes like hawks bringing down a fleeing dove. Somewhere in the dizzy whirl of that day, Moriana had mentioned to Fost that she didn't know how to operate the Hissers' skyraft. He certainly didn't have the foggiest idea how to maneuver it or to speed it up.

If the *Zr'gsz* wanted them, they were easy pickings.

But the Vridzish obviously didn't care about the fugitives. The pale green faces of lower caste Hissers watched the raft blankly from the ramparts of the City. Here and there the darker features of a noble turned their way to scrutinize them briefly, only to turn away again. Fost sensed that they knew well that the potent human sorceress whose friendship they'd betrayed, whose vengeful might had actually given the mighty, eons-old Demon of the Dark Ones pause, escaped them on the tiny raft. And they did not care. Their indifference chilled him more than pursuit.

Nowhere did the *Zr'gsz* show any sign of pursuing the humans as they fled from the City in the Sky. Fost saw shrieking women and children hounded like beasts through the streets, saw the shapes of the Vridzish hunch over the bodies of fallen human warriors, some of which still writhed with life, tearing at the bloody feast with their sharp, inhuman teeth. Only those humans they brought down did they bother with; their main purpose seemed to be to rid the City of the pale, soft-skinned creatures who had stolen that realm from them so long ago.

Like men hunting vermin.

Fost's flesh crawled at the thought.

And the vermin were fleeing the City. The sky above the lofty spires and buttressed wall of the Sky City seethed with eagles winging away in search of refuge, burdened with human cargo. Balloons broke from the confines of the City and floated downwind, humans dropping from their gondolas like ill-shaped raindrops. Too numb to feel horror, Fost wondered distractedly how much of the City's populace had escaped. There had been so little time, though Cerestan and the rest seemed to have wrought miracles in saving those they could. A large number of the sausage kites and round passenger balloons drifted in the City's wake.

But there were too few balloons, too few eagles to hope that any significant number had been rescued. As Fost watched, scores of giant warbirds beat back to the City gathering frantic humans onto their backs or into their strong claws to make a second, or third or fourth trip to the ground. The sheer number of refugees mocked their efforts. Those not fleet enough to outrace the hissing, croaking Vridzish died horribly. Those who outdistanced their pursuers, only to reach the rimwall with no means of transport to the ground, cast a single look over their shoulders at the horror being wrought on their City—and jumped.

In the middle of the Sky City Istu made sport.

He was kicking the haughty Palace of Winds to pieces and flinging giant building blocks for miles in all directions. Great pillars of smoke rose from a dozen locations within the City. A minaret of some noble merchant's mansion collapsed in the street, undermined by unseen claws.

Streams of trotting low caste *Zr'gsz* made their way to the rimwall and back into the tangled streets bearing varied bundles: rolls of cloth from warehouses, tables and chairs, cabinets and crates. Some bundles had human shape and some of these still kicked with frantic life. All to no avail —over the edge they went, along with the oddments and artifacts of human existence in the Sky City.

"See what they do, my young friend," intoned Erimenes. During the battle he had retreated into his jug, leery of getting caught in the nimbus of some stray battle-magic. Now he appeared in the air at Fost's side once again. "They seek to expunge all trace of the hated interlopers from the City in the Sky. I suspect that even those structures they originally built themselves, but which have been extensively modified by men, shall be razed." He shook his head. "It is an awful hate that can bide for eight millennia."

Fost had no ready retort. His head felt like a ball of lead and his eyelids like leaden shutters. His own exertions overwhelmed him. He had fought two desperate battles, faced dangers mortal and mystic a dozen times, and seen the realization of the fear that had been nurturing since Jennas of the Ust-alayakits had begun hinting to him months ago that a new War of Powers could be in the offing. It was enough action, danger and horror to last a hundred lifetimes. He had no idea how Moriana felt after her ordeal. He was only glad she was unable to see the singleminded ferocity with which her former allies cleansed the City, even to the point of casting her people over the side like so much rubbish.

He heard a vast, many-throated squawk and a cracking of wings like sails snapping to a stiff breeze. His last sight before unconsciousness was of Synalon's ravens billowing upward from the rookeries like a huge evil black cloud.

"Good morning, friend Fost," a cheery voice said. The words were muffled by layers of fog and pain. "You know, you actually look quite dashing with your nose mashed

down like that. It makes you seem positively rugged. And
since it has never lain altogether true, it's no detraction
from your personal beauty, such as it is. An improvement
on the whole, I'd say."

"Shut up!" bellowed Fost, heaving himself to a sitting
position. His roar set his head ringing like a bell. He
groaned and fell back, clutching at his temples.

"Tut, tut, my dear boy." He heard the philosopher's
infuriating tones as if they came from far away. "You
really do need to curb that impetuous nature of yours."

"Shut up, you querulous old fool," Ziore's voice
snapped. Through the tear glaze covering his eyes, Fost
became aware of an unfamiliar outline bending over him.
He blinked to clear his vision. He saw an elderly woman
clad in a long, flowing robe similar to the one Erimenes
"wore." Her aged features were smooth, serene, beautiful.
Erimenes was blue; this apparition was pink, with long
unbound hair so pale as to be almost white. Tiny reddish
sparks danced within her substance.

Fost felt peace and comfort suffuse his body. His face,
which had felt as if a heated torture mask had been
clamped to it, began to relax from agonized contortion.
He still felt agony in his head and aching weariness in
every limb, but somehow the sensations no longer trou-
bled him.

"Moriana woke briefly and let me out. She's sleeping
again. I hope she sleeps a long time, the poor girl. She's
suffered many hurts. Only a few of them are of the body."

Fost moved his head tentatively, gingerly shaking it as if
unsure whether or not pieces might break off or fall out.
When nothing untoward happened, he straightened and
spoke.

"Water," he said in a voice sounding like it came from
another's throat.

A look of concern passed over the slender, aged face.

"I cannot help you. But I perceive you have your magic
water flask with you."

In objective terms, it probably would have taken more

out of Fost to climb hand over hand from the ground to the Sky City on a rope than to open the satchel in which he carried Erimenes's jug and bring forth the silver-chased black flask. But certainly the chore seemed onerous. With fingers that felt as agile as the City's great sausage-shaped cargo balloons, he unstoppered the flask and held it to his lips.

The tepid water was as sweet as nectar rolling through his cottony mouth and down his parched throat. When he had found the body of Kest-i-Mond the mage murdered in the sorceror's own study a few thousand years ago—was it only last fall?—it had seemed at first that his only reward for braving the Sky City soldiers to deliver Erimenes's spirit to the enchanter was to be the flask and a silver-covered bowl of similar make. A paltry reward, the flask produced a perpetual flow of lukewarm water and the bowl gave an inexhaustible supply of tasteless thin gray gruel. However, this wasn't the first time Fost had cause to be thankful for those items.

He wiped his lips and tossed back his head, which was a mistake.

When the sledgehammer pounding in his brain had given way to a tackhammer tapping insistently at his temples and forehead and the bridge of his nose, he dared a look around. The raft was an oblong eight feet wide and twelve long. The gleaming black sphere at the stern controlled the raft's movement—under the guiding hand of a Zr'gsz.

Around him the day was overcast. A rumpled ceiling of cloud hung above his head. The clouds thinned to admit rays of watery sunlight of a sour lemon shade more unpleasant than plain shadow. Aft he saw a massive purple bulwark he eventually identified as the Thail Mountains dividing the continent. Oriented, Fost scanned all around, swivelling his head slowly to keep it from falling off his neck. North he saw the green of forests, bordered by the broad brown flood plain of the River Marchant. Beyond that the play of light and shadow on fallow lands and those planted in spring wheat turned the Black March into a giant's board game.

Off to starboard lay an irregular metallic splotch with a dark mound in the middle. Its color was that of an Imperial klenor-piece whose silver wash had worn away to reveal base metal. Fost recognized Lake Wir, with Wirix unapproachable at the center. The lake was ringed with an irregular dark line that the courier didn't think was vegetation. After a moment, his eyes moved involuntarily to Moriana, who lay huddled at his side, her shoulders rising and falling to the tidal motion of her breathing. She had mentioned leaving a force of Hissers camped on the shores of Lake Wir. Now they had become a besieging army, and a sizable one at that.

Fost wondered where they'd come from in such huge numbers.

"Moriana often pondered that question," said Ziore, causing him to jump. "When we visited Thendrun, the place appeared deserted. More of the Vridzish were involved in the attack on the Sky City than the princess thought were exiled." Her face grew thoughtful. "I suppose I should call her queen now."

"Princess is probably as accurate as any other term," sneered Erimenes, "since she has no domain to rule." He wagged his head censoriously. "Her ambitions cost her dearly. Though I daresay others will pay far more before this mess is done."

"How can you say that!" flared Ziore. Her form became darker and redder, the light flecks within her substance blazing like tiny suns. "This has been terrible for her! She knows well what she's caused. Indeed, she blames herself far too much since all she did was what she believed to be right."

"She couldn't possibly blame herself too much. Should she accept an adequate share of guilt for the evils she's wrought, she'd cast herself over the edge."

Ziore's form turned almost white in rage.

"You dare . . ."

"Shut up!" Fost bellowed. Ignoring the aftershocks in his head, he scowled at the two genies and went on in a low, deadly voice. "I have endured as much of your squabbling as I intend to. Another word of argument from either of you and I'll cast both your jugs over the edge of the raft."

Both shades opened their mouths at the same time. Fost's eyes became slits of a gray ice. Both mouths promptly closed.

"That's better." He lowered himself back on his elbows and continued his cursory survey. Black clouds obscured the country to the south, belaboring the Highgrass Broad and the Quincunx territory around Bilsinx with lightning and heavy rain. "Where's the City?" he asked.

"Due south of us," said Erimenes after a moment of sulking, his eyebrows lowered and his thin mouth pouted to let Fost know how miffed he was at such cavalier treatment. "It's hidden by the clouds."

Fost nodded, very deliberately, as if he had an egg balanced on his head and didn't want it to roll off.

"They can't see us. And I can't see *them,* which makes me just as glad."

He put a hand up and gingerly explored his face. The contours weren't altogether familiar.

"How long was I out?"

"You've slept since yesterday," Ziore answered. She didn't seem as angry over Fost's outburst as was Erimenes. She was a forgiving soul, save where Erimenes the Ethical was concerned. "We do seem to be slowly outdistancing it."

"Not that it matters now that they can't see us." Being able to contradict his antagonist brought a pleased smile to Erimenes's lips. "We floated in plain sight of the City until night came, and they showed no sign of molesting us."

Fost lifted the flask for another drink. He still felt no hunger; the thought of food made his stomach surge and roll like a boat in a moderate sea.

"Are we just floating at random, then?"

Erimenes shook his head.

"Where are we going?"

The genie inclined his head. Fost followed his gaze and found himself staring at the smoke-wreathed fang of Mt. Omizantrim. His stomach dropped away beneath him.

When he awoke, the first thing Fost saw was black Omizantrim looming over them like a hammer poised to fall, its head dense smoke shot through with lightnings. The steady rumble of the angry mountain beat against his ears. Brimstone clutched at his throat and wrinkled his nose. Even his skin gritted unclean with a sheen of ash and volcanic dust.

The second thing he saw was Moriana, sitting with her knees drawn up and her arms encircling them. Her face was haggard and pale. She turned toward the fury of the volcano as if with longing.

"Moriana," he said softly. She neither spoke nor stirred. Cautiously, he raised himself. His head didn't start vibrating like a gong. He reached out and took her arm.

She turned to face him. Her eyes were like coals and only vaguely the green he remembered so fondly.

"Erimenes is right." Her voice fell heavy and black like a burnt ember. "I should fling myself over the side."

After an ugly glance at the philosopher who stood by the port edge looking idly at the thunderhead piled above them, Fost said, "Nonsense. You should know better than to listen to him."

She pulled away and looked back toward the mountain.

"I've brought disaster on the world. I wanted to save my City. Instead, I destroyed it. And I murdered you, the man I loved. Oh, you live, thanks to my error in taking the wrong amulet. But the deed was done, is done, and cannot be revoked."

She dropped her face into her hands. Her hair hung in lank strings, its normal glorious gold dimmed to mousy brown.

"Was it power I truly sought all the time I quested and connived and killed to regain my throne? Am I no better than Synalon?" Her body jerked with sobbing, convulsive despair.

Ziore's pink, smoky body fluttered in a slight breeze crossing the raft. She looked in appeal to Fost.

"I've tried to gentle her from this dark mood," the genie said. "But she will not be consoled. She loves you. Can you do something for her?"

A quick stab of Fost's eyes spiked the contribution Erimenes was about to make. Dragging himself forward on his arms like a cripple, he took Moriana's shoulders and turned her around.

A bright spark of rebellion blazed and died in her eyes. Knowing by that sign he was right, Fost spoke roughly and to the point.

"Whatever your motives, the deed is done," he said. "The Fallen Ones are in control of the City again and Istu is loose, and I doubt the Dark Ones will fail to press their first real advantage in ten millennia." Her face tightened as he spoke. That was good, too. It was more encouraging than the slackness of depression it replaced.

"You're the most powerful magician in the Sundered Realm, probably in the world," he went on. "Back in the City you were potent enough to hold Istu off while some of your people escaped."

Her eyes dropped. A single tear spattered onto the gray stone.

"Only my fury at the *Zr'gsz* for their betrayal—and at myself for *mine*—gave me that power. I doubt it will come again."

"I don't say you'll ever have the power to *stop* the Demon of the Dark Ones. But you can do more against him than anyone else alive. We need whatever power you've got if we're to have a chance."

"We?"

He paused.

"Uh, humanity." It sounded bald and grandiose. But it was the truth.

Realization nerved him to say what must be said.

"You brought this about, Highness, Majesty, whatever I should call you. By the Five Holy Ones, you should stay alive and try to undo the disaster you've wrought!"

He released her. She slumped, her slender shoulders hunched and shaking in reaction.

"Die, if you want," he said harshly. "That's the coward's way out."

Her slap bowled him over onto his back and set loose an avalanche in his head. For an instant, fireflies danced in front of his face. They faded to orange and yellow points and the accompanying pain slowly subsided to a dull aching.

"No one calls me coward!" she screamed. "Take it back, you groundling worm!"

Despite the agony in his skull, Fost grinned when he pulled himself erect. He got his feet under him and braced his arms on either side of his knees, the roughness of the stone assuringly firm.

"Is that all I must do, Princess dear?" he said. "Welcome back to the living."

She was in his arms, her tears hot on his cheek.

# CHAPTER FIVE

"It's apparent these rafts return automatically to their place of origin on being abandoned." Erimenes was in his best pedantic form, not one whit deterred by the unorthodox setting for his lecture. "I assume the function is intentional, though it may of course be serendipitous. Further, I reason that abandoned skyrafts follow lines of magnetic force back to Omizantrim, which accounts for our circuitous route from the City to . . ."

Thunder drowned him out. Fost ducked reflexively, spilling a spoonful of gruel into his lap.

"I think the mountain's building up to a major eruption," Moriana announced.

She had resumed her previous station in the bow of the raft, gazing at Omizantrim as the volcano grew ever nearer. Fost gulped a last mouthful of the tasteless gray slop, covered the bowl with its silver lid and replaced it in his satchel, then slowly crawled forward to sit beside her. Cautiously, he stationed himself several inches farther back from the rim.

No one—no human, at least—had ever accused Mt. Omizantrim of being beautiful. It looked threatening and grim from far away, which was the only way Fost had seen it before. Close up, it was a tall cinder cone, dark gray, its flanks slashed with black striations and scarred with fumaroles. The open-wound pits in the mountain exuded thick clouds of dark blue and maroon gas, then lit them from below with a lurid glare. The very crest of the mountain was obscured in a billow of slate-gray smoke spilling away into the northwest. A gaudy necklace of lightnings surrounded the heights, both from the smoke and dust cloud and from the storm clouds above. Sulfur stung eyes, nose and throat; dust clogged them.

Omizantrim was far from beautiful. But Fost failed to discern the reason why Moriana thought it was going to erupt. As far as Fost could tell, the mountain looked little different than it had when it hiccuped to noisome life on the eve of the Battle of Chanobit Creek.

Fost couldn't figure it out. He asked her. Moriana shrugged, still studying the mountain with wrinkled brow.

"The displays seem more violent than at any time when we were camped there. And do you smell the ozone, the prickling in the very air? You should see yourself. It's making the hair stand up at the back of your neck."

"It wouldn't take dormant lightning in the air to cause that, let me tell you," said Fost. "But couldn't it be due to our height alone?"

Moriana glanced down. The gray and black landscape writhed below like a tortured animal. Patches of vegetation clung tenaciously to the jagged, blade-sharp lava, deep green in some places, dusty and faded like old dry moss in others. One-horned and domestic deer moved below, not browsing but running in full flight across the broken land away from the great mountain.

"It's just a feeling," she confessed. "See? The animals feel it, too. They're more sensitive to such things than humans. They know the moods of the volcano from long exposure."

"Our height isn't great enough to make much difference," Erimenes cut in. "We've stayed about a thousand feet up since leaving the City. That puts the mountaintop eight or nine thousand feet above us. Even that noxious looking cloud is easily thousands of feet above our heads."

Fost felt the skin on his back try to creep into a bunch at the nape of his neck. An instant later, a brilliant yellow flash burned itself into his retinas. The light was so intense he wasn't even aware of the wall of sound that struck him. But several minutes later as he blinked away the last of the purple afterglow, his hearing had only just returned.

"Weather magic," Erimenes said in his usual peevish tone. "Can't you keep the lightning off us, at least?"

Ziore stared at the blue shade, her expression remarkably reminiscent of the clouds overhead. Mindful of Fost's injunction against further squabbling, she stayed silent.

"Perhaps I could," Moriana said. "But the battles I fought in the Sky City drained me so."

She broke off to look at Fost with peculiar intentness. A wan smile played about her mouth.

"No, since you told some harsh truths to snap me out of my self-pitying fog, you've lapsed back into being too perfect a gentleman to point out the obvious. Yes, I have to start using my powers again sometime, and the longer I wait the more painful it'll be."

She stood and stretched, oblivious to the emptiness yawning an inch in front of her toes. Fost shuddered. It was easy to forget what an insane disregard for heights the Skyborn had.

"Now's as good a time as any," she said firmly. "I've slept for two days and have a stomach full of that delicious provender of yours." Her sarcasm elicited an uneasy smile from Fost. Though they had both devoured the gruel from the magic bowl so avidly it seemed its supply must be exhausted in spite of the self-replenishment spell, neither was ravenous enough to mistake the stuff for anything but clammy glop.

Moriana folded her long legs beneath her and closed her eyes in concentration. Fost saw her lips flutter, heard the ghost of an incantation above the grumbling of mountain and clouds.

"She needed a brazier and special herbs to make weather magic at Chanobit," Ziore said in an awed whisper. "She's learned so much since then."

Erimenes grumbled, but all ignored him. Seeing that Moriana required total concentration, Fost took an oiled rag from his satchel and drew his sword. He examined it, clucking over its condition. Its blade was dimmed, streaked with blood and grime, and dirt had caked in places. Though the blade itself was fine North Keep steel, its edge was nicked and pitted from heavy use. Fost rummaged in his sack and brought out a whetstone, then began to rub the sword down with the rag.

As he cleaned the weapon, he kept one eye on the mountain. It grew until he scarcely saw where the cone disappeared into the wreath of greasy smoke. The heat of its many mouths washed over him like the uneven breathing of some immense creature. Throat of the Dark Ones, Omizantrim meant. Fost wondered if that was Their sulfurous breath that blew so hot on his face.

Just when he began to worry that the craft would drive head-on into the mountain, Omizantrim swung across the bow and began to slip by to port.

"We're circling," said Erimenes unnecessarily. "Probably going to the very skystone drift where the raft was mined."

Lightning barraged the mountain's stony flanks, but none came near.

"Your magic's working," he told her. She replied with a distracted smile. In fact, he didn't have the slightest idea whether it worked or not, but he wanted to encourage her.

"We're losing altitude." Reluctantly, Fost glanced down and saw that Erimenes spoke the truth. The crags and folds of the mountain's skirts grew closer as he watched and the landscape took on more detail. Cave-sized openings were soon revealed to be great bubbles that had burst. Drifts of white ash and a gray stone touched with a curious sheen appeared in sharp relief that he guessed was skystone itself. Small animals scurried among the stunted stems of bushes, tails streaming behind as they fled the coming wrath of the mountain.

They passed a cluster of huts. Blocks of the incredibly durable lava had been hewn laboriously by hand and fitted to form walls capped by big slabs of basalt. The buildings, while grim, were suited to withstanding the mountain's caprice. But not even the stout construction of the watchers could withstand the cosmic disease of change. The massive roofs had been levered from their places, the walls that held them pulled down into jumbles of black stone. Ash had fallen since the destruction, piling like blown snow against the few walls and doorposts that remained standing, filling in the outlines of the ruined huts so that they resembled a collection of haphazard children's sandboxes. Splintered pieces of wood thrust above the dust in some of the buildings, and Fost saw a few drably colored scraps of cloth waving in the breeze.

"They didn't loot," he said to himself. "Only destroyed."

Moriana's face had turned the color of the ash strewn below.

"Wise Ones," she whispered, "have they slain the Watchers?" The thought of this new guilt showed on her face like a fresh swordcut.

"This isn't the main camp. It's only an outpost. The Vridzish were gathering the Watchers out of the smaller camps when we were here before. The Watchers are no doubt held captive at their village, as they were before." Ziore's expression belied her hopeful tone.

"Who do you think works the skystone mines?" came Erimenes's question.

Lightning cracked dangerously close. Fost jumped, almost losing his whetstone and small oil flask over the edge of the raft. The conversation took a turn that was not only distressing to Moriana but distracting as well.

"Where are the Hissers, anyway?" he asked.

"Look beyond you," said Erimenes.

Despite the heat, Fost's throat had become a column of ice leading from the glacier in his stomach. The spirit wasn't lying. A two-man flyer had just rounded a stony buttress behind them, and three more appeared followed by a much larger barge teeming with green-skinned figures. Fost swallowed hard, thinking that the *Zr'gsz* flew much sloppier formation than Rann's bird riders. Per-

versely, he wished Rann could be here now to pit his
genius against the lizards.

Moriana looked up as he touched her arm.

"Forget about the lightning. We've got worse things to
worry about."

She glanced back at the pursuing raft. The craft bucked
now in updrafts from malevolently glowing mouths gaping
below. She picked up her bow and began replacing the
string, which had been ruined by a shower sometime while
she and Fost slept.

Repacking his cleaning gear, Fost watched the enemy
rafts gain on them. Under control of *Zr'gsz* pilots, the
craft moved much faster than the human's drifting raft. A
three-man flyer edged out in front of the others, and a
Hisser stood amidships whirling a sling. He loosed. Nervously, Fost watched the stone arch up and then down,
apparently headed straight for the bridge of his nose. He
watched in hypnotic fascination that didn't lose its grip
until the missile dropped harmlessly in the raft's wake.

An angry bee whined past his right ear. The slinger
stiffened as two more arrows sped past Fost, aimed with
uncanny precision. The slinger pitched over the side of the
small raft when the pilot slumped across the skewered
corpse of the third *Zr'gsz*, an eagle-feathered arrow jutting
from his eye.

Upon this attack, the loose formation of the skyrafts
broke apart. They climbed rapidly out of range. Moriana
shot two more arrows and killed the pilot of a second
small raft which skidded sideways, spilling its occupant
out over a lake of lava that glowed perceptibly brighter
orange when the Vridzish struck.

"Damn them," Moriana said. "They're sharp. They've
put their rafts between themselves and me."

"They'll have to show themselves to shoot at us," observed Fost. As he said the words, a head and shoulders
appeared at the side of one raft. A javelin rocketed toward
them. The dart went wide; so did Moriana's return shot.

The woman cursed reptilian reflexes and nocked another arrow. She drew the shaft to her ear and waited. Another Hisser leaned out to aim a short bow at the humans. Her arrow took him in the throat. The bow dropped from clawed hands, and the body dangled a moment before its fellows released its ankles.

"Your reflexes match theirs," Fost said admiringly.

The look she gave him was not what he expected. He felt chilled by the flat, almost hostile expression. He was starting to speak when the mountain blew up.

The shockwave bowled him over. Moriana's witch sense gave her a split second's warning of the blast, and the same reflexes he'd just complimented saved his life. Bracing herself, Moriana caught hold of Fost's swordbelt just as he pitched over the brink. She dragged him back, aided by his groping fingers tearing on the gray stone of the raft. Erimenes shrilled terror as his satchel momentarily hung above nothingness.

"Thanks," shouted Fost over the roar of the eruption.

Moriana bobbed acknowledgement to the thanks she read on his lips. She couldn't hear anything. The mountain was roaring in the voice of a million angry hornbulls. Fost stared in wonder that transcended fear as an orange prominence reached heavenward from the crater. The blast had blown the dust free of the mountaintop, and the heat of the geysering lava dispelled the clouds above like an enchantment gone insane. The top of the flame stream wavered, tipped, arced toward the far side of the volcano in a fountain of molten rock.

Something exploded nearby with a sound loud enough to hear even through shockwave-deadened ears. A fragment grazed his cheek. He blinked at ash and cowered inside his mail shirt.

*A bomb,* he heard Ziore say inside his mind. *A partially cooled lava shell surrounding hot gases. It must have struck the mountainside nearby.*

He cursed. Apparently all Athalar waxed pedantic at

the damnedest times. Fost glanced back at their pursuers in time to see something streak down and smash the big raft amidships. The stone platform came apart in midair. Fost saw superheated gases strip the living flesh from the Hissers' bones as the blast scattered them away among the debris of their vessel.

*That sort of thing happened a lot when I had the Destiny Stone.* It was Moriana's voice now inside his head. He guessed Ziore acted as a repeater for the woman, since oral communication was out of the question in the din of eruption.

A spire of black stone flashed by on their left, its pitted face almost near enough to touch. Fost's head snapped back to see where they were heading.

*I'll bet things like this did, too,* he thought at Ziore. *Look where the damned thing's setting us down!*

Moriana looked where he pointed. A patrol of Vridzish stood gesticulating at a torrent that flowed through a cut in the same glossy gray stone Fost had seen before. A few hammers and prybars lay scattered about, and a knot of unarmed *Zr'gsz* huddled near the soldiers, staring at what resembled a cascade of extremely muddy water—or watery mud. Fost knew from the mad dance of superheated air above the stream it had to be lava. Water would hiss instantly to vapor. The Vridzish stood on the side of the lava stream. The raft was making for a point just beyond them—in the midst of a river of melted rock!

The ground raced by beneath. Fost sheathed his sword and clutched the edge of the stone slab, leaning out to judge the distance to the ground. The agonizingly slow progress of the raft had become a mad careening—or so it seemed. Fost hoped this was only illusion. If they were moving too fast when they jumped from the raft, they'd tumble end over end across the cooled lava on the slope. It would be like rolling across a field of razorblades.

"We'll have to jump!" he screamed at Moriana. She nodded assent. Ziore's satchel was already slung over her shoulder. The pink genie hovered by her side, looking concerned. Erimenes had disappeared back into his own jar. Fost heard his whimpering even above the god's bellow of the exploding volcano.

A hundred feet short of the patrol and the lava flow, they jumped. Fost landed with a jolt that seemed to drive his ankles up to his knees and went on over to slash his arms and face on the jagged lava rock. Some good fortune spared his much-abused nose. Wiping at the blood pouring into his eyes from a nasty forehead cut, he looked up in time to see Moriana hit, tuck and roll with perfect form. She continued rolling on down the slope and came to her feet with barely a scratch. He cursed her Sky City training. He'd jumped from a few second-story windows in his time, to spare himself unpleasant scenes with unreasonable husbands bearing swords, but he'd never had occasion to jump from a second-story window that moved.

His plaints inaudible in the uproar, he accepted a hand up from Moriana.

"You heedless barbarian, how could you endanger me with such utter recklessness!" Erimenes screeched. "My jug could have been smashed to flinders!"

The abandoned raft brushed the feathered headdress of a *Zr'gsz* officer. The Hisser looked up and gaped in astonishment as the raft drove on to plunge into the rushing lava stream. One of the lizard men clutched his face and fell kicking as molten stone splashed him.

The others turned their heads to see pale distorted shapes scrambling across the lava field. No vocal commands were needed. The officer waved his two-handed mace and the patrol raced in pursuit.

"Here they come!" Neither Fost nor Moriana needed Erimenes's warning to know the patrol slowly closed the distance between them. Choking and coughing on the dust clogging the air, the pair ran as fast as they could over the treacherous, broken ground. After what seemed an eternity of struggling in the sulfurous atmosphere, Fost turned to see how near the *Zr'gsz* were. The Hissers had lost interest—or perhaps their lives, since they were nowhere to be seen.

The mountain shuddered under Fost's feet. And the black stone was fever hot, burning him despite his thick bootsoles. With every third step it seemed a loose rock turned under him, twisting his ankle and adding a gash on unsuspecting calf or thigh.

"You incomparable dolt! Watch where you're going!" screamed Erimenes from the relative safety of his satchel.

Tricky as the ground was underfoot, Fost refused to look down. The spectacle of the volcano in full throat riveted his attention. A column of maroon smoke shot through with sheets of fire blasted upward from the crater. A ceiling of black cloud hung over the mountain. A hellwind raged within. Fost glimpsed the glow of incandescent gases swirling in the guts of the cloud.

It was as if battle raged between sky and earth. The Throat of the Dark Ones vomited lava and smoke and boulders and searingly poisonous vapors. The sky retaliated with incessant whip strokes of blue-white lightning. Rain lashed down all around, but no longer fell on the mountain itself. The monstrous upswelling of heat from the Throat cast it back upward again as steam.

A barbed spear struck a humped rock in Fost's path. Erimenes howled incoherently as a hammerblow landed on Fost's left shoulder.

The man bent and spun with the force of the blow. Instinct made him draw steel as he turned, and the training he'd bought from renegade fighting masters in High Medurim made him turn the draw into a savage backhanded cut at the black shape looming on the fringes of his vision. A black-clawed hand released its grip on a mace to make a frantic, futile effort to stuff back in the greasy, green ropes of guts spilling from the lizard man's opened stomach. The intestines tangled the Hisser's feet as it fell.

Fost kept spinning until he faced the way he had before the attack. He lit out running after Moriana. With his left arm numbed by the slung stone, he was at a worse disadvantage than usual against the inhuman reflexes of the Vridzish.

"Stand and fight!" Erimenes yelled at him.

"You're crazy," he howled back. "That's what you always say!"

"No, you idiot! *They're almost on top of you!*"

Fost flung himself to one side without even looking. A vicious spear thrust missed him by scant inches. He tumbled onto his rump among the jagged rocks. A screaming Hisser lunged at him. He brought up both feet and kicked the creature in the belly. It fell away. He scrambled to his feet, hacked as he rose. The blade bit flesh. He didn't wait to see where. He just ran.

Perhaps the furor of the eruption was subsiding or perhaps it was his imagination that he heard the lizard men on his heels hissing triumph and baying like a pack of hunting hounds closing for the kill. There was no doubting they were almost on him. Over a long run his superior endurance would have told, but in this short, desperate sprint over jagged ground they were fleeter than he.

Fost dashed up a long slope of relatively smooth lava and found himself flying across a crack that yawned abruptly under his feet. On the far side of the crevice, he turned and lashed with his sword, taking a Hisser in the torso as it leaped after him. The lizard man fell back into the six-foot gap.

The crack ran up and down the slope as far as he could see in both directions. It was a natural place to make his stand.

"Run!" he shouted at Moriana as he set his feet and took his sword in both hands to prepare for battle.

Moriana's voice rang in his brain: *No! Don't be a fool. You haven't a chance!*

He took this mental communication as an indication that Ziore still relayed their messages.

"It's the only chance," he shouted, not sure how to form the thoughts for Ziore to translate. He immediately regretted even opening his mouth. His throat was raw from breathing dust. "You're the one who matters. Now run." He saw Moriana start to protest. He shouted her down. "Do you think I like being a hero?"

He had no chance then to see if she obeyed. A second *Zr'gsz* scrambled up the lava ramp and launched itself at him, only to meet the same fate as its comrade. The tall, feathered helmet of the officer appeared, bobbing purposefully toward Fost.

Movement made him glance upslope. A stream of thin, fast moving lava slopped over a lip of rock and splashed down onto a ledge a hundred yards above. Fost swallowed, though it felt as if a metallic rasp worked on his throat.

The lava rushed straight for him.

"Moriana, don't go! Save me from this lunkhead's folly!" For the first time in Fost's recollection, Erimenes pleaded to be taken from a promising fight. He obviously didn't like the notion of spending the rest of eternity entombed in a lava flow. The courier had little time to savor the spirit's abject fear because the big, dark-scaled officer was closing fast.

Had he been smart, the Vridzish would have waited for his men to come up and had them finish Fost with darts and slung stones. But either he lusted for personal revenge or was simply headstrong. He gripped his mace in both hands and swung at Fost.

Fost knew how fortunate he was that the officer had immediately attacked, but his heart dropped just the same. He recalled his last duel with a mace-wielding Vridzish noble.

Even the mace's long haft had a hard time reaching

across the crack. Fost avoided the first swing simply by leaning back. He couldn't retreat from the brink, however, without allowing the lizard man to jump across. With the Vridzish's advantage in reach, Fost doubted his own ability to win should the lizard man succeed in crossing the gap.

The *Zr'gsz* swung again, leaning dangerously far out. Fost staggered as the volcanic glass head of the mace brushed across his belly. He cut recklessly at the Vridzish. The lizard man jerked away. The rest of the patrol had come up to join their leader. Only a half dozen could stand with the officer on the narrow lava ramp. The others milled behind, one of the javelin men hopping impatiently from foot to foot hoping for a clear cast.

Savagely, man and *Zr'gsz* duelled over the abyss. Fost held out longer than he thought possible and even managed to chop a feather from his opponent's green metal helmet. But the lizard man was quicker and stronger and could commit himself further due to taloned feet gripping the rock. They traded blows, wood cracking on steel with impacts that jarred Fost's arm. Then the inevitable happened. Fost extended his blade too far; the Vridzish swung with awful force and knocked the broadsword to the side, almost tearing it from Fost's grip.

Time flowed like the molten rock as the heavy mace swung back at Fost's unprotected body. He didn't have time to even duck. He took a breath and braced himself for the impact, the stabbing of shattered ribs through lungs and heart, oblivion.

A lava tide washed over the officer and swept him and his death-giving mace away like a twig in a millrace. Fost heard awful croaking cries as the molten stone engulfed the other Vridzish. He stumbled back, tears welling in his eyes from the awful heat.

He saw Moriana rise from the shelter of a boulder. She smiled.

"Did you bring down the lava?" he asked.

"No. The mountain did that." The smile widened. "But I diverted it where I wanted it to go."

She took his hand and led him off across the badlands. The lava river gurgled at their backs.

# CHAPTER SIX

Morning found the volcano quiet, at least in comparison to the prior day's cacophony. But its tip still smoked like a North Keep forge. The greasy smoke trailed off toward Lake Lolu in the north, but it was unadorned black smoke without lightning or glowing clouds or hurtling bombs. A constant peevish grumbling rolled from the depths of the mountain, as if it suffered indigestion. Erimenes, who claimed knowledge of volcanoes, said that the rumblings would subside over the next few days until the mountain lay quiet again. Unless, of course, it decided to once again erupt. Neither Fost nor Moriana found the tidings particularly cheering.

They had reconnoitered cautiously, Moriana alert with her bow, Fost ready to snatch out his sword at the first hint of danger. As expected, Erimenes derided him for not going forth with naked blade in hand like a proper hero. Fost decided it would be unheroic for a rock to turn under his foot and cause him to fall on his sword, as was likely to happen in such treacherous landscape.

They had worked their way well south of the smouldering mountain, both in the hopes that any fresh lava flows wouldn't extend so far and to come on the Watchers' village from above rather than from below. Otherwise, they'd have had to pass near the ledge where the Ullapag had kept watch over the skystone mines and the steaming fumarole into which Felarod had cast the Heart of the People. Moriana had a total horror of the place. Since yesterday they had exchanged snippets of their respective stories when they stopped to rest or eat, and Fost had learned enough of what had happened at that spot to understand why Moriana dreaded it so.

The sun had barely struggled above the humped flows to the east when they came upon the first new stream of lava. The guessed it to be the one which had swallowed the Hissers the day before. The surface had already hardened into a crust that showed rusty black in places through its coating over the ubiquitous gray ash. It looked solid enough.

Fost and Moriana exchanged looks, then Fost said, "There's only one way to make sure it's really hard enough to support us." He took a deep breath, then boldly stepped out, only to find the thin crust cracking beneath him at the same instant the stench of burning leather rose. He jackrabbited back to solid ground, scalding his feet thoroughly in the process.

"Look at him dance. Have you ever seen such a fine tarantella, even in the courts of High Medurim?" Erimenes howled in laughter which infuriated Fost even more.

"Fost," said Moriana over the genie's ridicule, "we must get across. The *Zr'gsz* will be after us. And I . . . I am uneasy in this place."

He agreed with her. He sat beside the solidified but still hot river of rock and thought. Eventually, he hit on the plan of lashing bits of loose lava to their feet and walking across using them as insulation.

"Yes," she cried, "it'll work. It has to! If the pieces of lava we use are wide enough, it will be like snowshoeing. The larger the stone, the better our weight will be distributed."

"And we won't break the crust," Fost finished. "Do you think the insulation from the rock will be enough?"

"Certainly," said Erimenes in his best professorial tones. "The thermal gradient in such a portion of the stone will be sufficient to prevent a repetition of your hotfoot." The genie began snickering again.

With her archer's skills, Moriana deftly wove strong cord from the tough bunchgrass that grew among the dog-thorn bushes. Then the two tied the chunks to their boots using projections to anchor the cords so they wouldn't come in contact with the hot crust more than necessary. Before they set off, Moriana insisted that each cut two stout staves of ofilos wood to use for balance. Reluctantly, Fost agreed. They spent an hour hunting for relatively straight limbs. Fost's allergy to the ofilos caused his hands to break out in a rash but this discomfort was offset by his enhanced ability to balance. With the ofilos poles to prop him, he made it to the other side with a minimum of flailing, cursing and hearstopping attempts to go facefirst onto the hot stone crust.

In less than an hour they came to another flow, the one into which their raft had dived. Fost was amazed at the distance between the two flows. Either they had diverged considerably in their course down the mountainside or the fleeing pair had made record time crossing the saw-toothed terrain.

"The same trick should work," stated Fost, gently prodding the tip of his ofilos pole into the semi-solid rock beneath the hardened surface. He pulled out the shaft when it began smoking. He beat out a tiny blaze, then began tying new lava rock to his boots.

Halfway across, the lashings on Fost's right foot burned through. He stood with one leg upraised like a nesting stork. His mind raced, trying to decide what to do next. Fate decided the issue for him. The other set of cords burned through, leaving him stranded twenty yards from cool, safe ground.

"Fost!" yelled Moriana. She had safely reached the far side of the frozen stream.

"Dark Ones take Fost," shrieked Erimenes. "Save *me!* I'll be marooned in this rock for all eternity. And gods, it is hot!"

"Of course it's hot," cried Fost. "It's molten stone. I thought you knew all about vulcanism."

"Don't drop my jug," pleaded the genie. "I don't want to roast for a thousand years!"

The crust began bending inward beneath Fost's feet despite the weight-distributing lava rock. In seconds he would be ankle deep in the fiery river, in minutes only his charred skeleton would remain. He forced himself not to panic. That meant instant death.

"Moriana!" he shouted. "Use some magic to get me out of here!"

"I can't, Fost. I . . . I'm too drained." Even as she spoke, she worked at weaving new cords. Fost watched uncertainly. He didn't think much of tying new lashings to his chunks of rock; the balancing act that would require seemed beyond his ability. He settled by perceptible degrees into the lava. He could only trust her.

Instead of bringing the new cords out to him, though, she sat down and tied them to her own feet, reinforcing the charred lashings that had already carried her across the flow. Then she trudged out to him.

"Climb on," she ordered, bending down and bracing herself on the balancing poles.

"You're joking."

"No, she's not," screeched Erimenes. "Believe her. Fost, damn you, do as she says! Don't let us die out here!"

"Hurry, Fost," said Moriana. "For once, Erimenes is right. Unless you like it out here, climb on!"

Despite the dryness in his throat, Fost swallowed. Casting aside his own poles, he gingerly climbed onto the woman's back. She sank alarmingly beneath him, then rose again, seeming to support his weight with ease. Though her own stone shoes made deep depressions in the elastic crust, they didn't break through. After a few heart-pounding minutes, they gained solid ground.

"She's quite a woman," Erimenes said now in a natural tone.

Fost agreed.

\* \* \*

Crows crossed the disk of the setting sun, black cruciform motes on an angry eye, any eye whose upper lid was a layer of dark, heavy cloud and whose lower was the tortured lunar landscape of the lava drifts south of Omizantrim. A bloodshot, angry eye.

Had Fost believed in portents he would have been catatonic with fright.

It had been a night and a day since the hazardous landing on the slopes of the exploding mountain. After Moriana's sorcery had changed the course of the lava stream to kill the *Zr'gsz* patrol, they had headed south away from the erupting cone and had laid up for the night in a wild land of knife-edged ridges and razor-cut draws. Their only company was the mournful howling of the hot wind down the slope of Omizantrim and the stunted vegetation that somehow thrived. The gnarled ofilos possessed a beauty of sorts. Early summer was their blooming season and the trees exploded with yellow-rimmed fragrant white blossoms that defied the gray dust all around. Such delicate beauty against the backdrop of stark desolation reaffirmed their faith in life itself.

After running, Fost decided it was time to be more aggressive. They had picked up spoor from the reptilian Hissers all day and had avoided it. Now he crawled on his belly over what felt like broken glass, but the discomfort proved worthwhile. Fifty feet away he spied a *Zr'gsz* sentry. He waited, watched. The lizard man's partner approached and the two exchanged words, then resumed walking their posts.

Fost cursed the ofilos and its beguiling blossoms. He was violently allergic to the frail five-petalled flowers. His nose streamed the way Omizantrim had leaked lava the day before; his eyes watered and his nose felt as if it had been broken again. Worst of all, he didn't know how long he could contain the sneeze caused by the pollen.

If a sneeze escaped. . . .

"It is only a histamine reaction," came Erimenes's soft

explanation. "The body attempts to reject the formation of . . ."

Fost stiffened. Why in the name of hell had he brought Erimenes along with him on this furtive mission? The same spirit who, when Sky City troops pursued Fost, had repeatedly called out to attract their attention to Fost's hiding spot and provoke a rousing fight?

"Ust," he moaned. He stifled a powerful sneeze and felt the pressure almost explode his eardrums.

"Bless you," Erimenes said softly. "And you need have no fear that I'll betray you, friend Fost." The shade was bottled up in his jar, but Fost felt the weary, wounded headshake. "To think you put so little trust in me."

He huddled, trying to make himself appear part of a dogthorn bush. Its two-inch spikes stung like fire ants as they pierced his flesh. The only consolation for the man was in the bush's cycle; it didn't bloom until fall.

Cautiously, he raised his head. The Vridzish sentries went on down the arroyo and disappeared around the southwest corner of a compound wall. He cursed to himself. The wall was impressive, built to more than man-height with blocks of dressed lava looted from demolished buildings and topped with dried branches of dogthorn in much the same way a rich man of High Medurim might top his wall with broken glass. But there was a difference. The wealthy Medurimite did it to keep out intruders; this barrier kept the occupants inside. As Fost spied, he came to the conclusion this was the prison for the Watchers.

Moriana had been astonished and horrified to see what had sprung up on the former site of the Watchers' village. What had cut deepest of all was the realization that in spite of her orders that the captives be well treated, her erstwhile allies had enslaved the Watchers the instant she left. The *Zr'gsz* must have worked dozens to death to build this compound so quickly.

The discovery had almost thrown her into another spell of depression. Ziore had said or done something to pull her out of it. Fost didn't know what since their communication hadn't been oral. Even lying on his belly being perforated by thorns, he felt jealousy at the intimacy Moriana and Ziore shared, an intimacy no amount of love would ever make it possible for him to share.

The guards came around again and this time Fost successfully timed their patrol, counting monotonous seconds with a childhood chant: *one fat courtesan . . . two fat courtesans . . . three fat courtesans. . . .*

When he reached three hundred and four the pair passed by his hiding place again. Five minutes.

He mentally directed the information at Erimenes and hoped the spirit passed it on. It had taken an hour's arguing, cajoling and threatening to get the two genies to form a communications link between Fost and Moriana. They weren't far apart—Moriana lay a hundred yards downslope hidden in a cave—but the mental noise from the captive Watchers inside the black thorn-topped wall made it impossible for Ziore to make out Fost's thoughts at that distance. Though his arrogance tended to obscure his real talents, Erimenes was an Athalar sage of sufficient mental power to survive his body's death. The two shades communicated by thought with perfect clarity. Fost guessed that they passed most of the long, hot afternoon in psychic squabbling, which was fine with him. He couldn't hear it.

Erimenes beamed Moriana's acknowledgement. The sun had sunk so that only a dazzling sliver remained in view. As Fost watched, it sank beneath the skirts of Omizantrim.

From the south came shouts and the tramp-tramp-tramp of trudging feet. Craning his neck and getting his left ear pierced by a thorn, Fost saw some of what was happening. A file of people, men, women and children, in drab clothing rendered drabber still by sun and dust and toil, dragged themselves up to the wooden gates of the compound. The Vridzish guards hurried them along with strokes of lizard hide whips and switches made from thornbush limbs, chivvying them in wheezy pidgin man-speech. The lizard men were eager to get their captives penned up before the cool evening rendered them torpid. The Vridzish could function after dark, but their reflexes slowed.

When the last straggling child was whipped through the gates, they thumped closed and Fost heard a bar rumbling into place across the outside. New guards replaced the old; a mental signal from Moriana confirmed that the setup was the same as before, two on the gate, two patrolling the perimeter.

Night settled in to stay. Crickets tuned up off in the scrub, their chirping joined by the warbling of night lizards distending purple throat sacs to sing plaintively. The ofilos closed their lovely, treacherous blooms and some night blooming succulents released sticky sweet perfumes. Though Fost found their odor cloying, he wasn't allergic to them.

Some of the buildings in the Watchers' main camp had been left standing by the new occupiers, and Moriana reported that most of the soldiers who had escorted the prisoners went into them for the night. There were fewer of the lizard men than she'd expected. From the patrol activity of the day before—and today, as well, when they had dodged skyrafts floating around the mountain—Moriana reckoned there must be several times as many camped around Omizantrim as were bivouacked in the Watchers' village. Probably the rest were posted around the flows to keep out intruders, and concentrated around the mines themselves.

Fost was glad of that. It'd be no easy task to sneak even a few of the Watcher captives out from under the noses of two hundred sleeping Hissers.

Knowing something of *Zr'gsz* military routine, Moriana waited until midway through the new watch, giving the evening cool sufficient time to weigh down the limbs of the patrolling Hissers and render them drowsy. Then she beamed her readiness to Fost.

He listened until the lizard men's sandalled feet crunched through the dust and gravel of the arroyo running along the western wall of the compound. When they passed, he started counting again. He counted two-twenty-five. The Hissers would be midway along the northern wall unless something had disrupted their routine. He'd heard no disturbance and Moriana informed him that the lizard men needed to relieve themselves less frequently than humans.

*Now!* he thought.

From her bubble cave, Moriana put a compulsion on the two armed guards at the gate. When she'd outlined that part of her plan, Fost expressed his surprise. He thought the mental compulsion worked only on her fellow Sky Citizens, who were steeped in the magics of their City and thus susceptible to them.

"The magics of the City," she'd replied, "are closely allied to those of the *Zr'gsz*." The peculiar light in her green eyes had discouraged further questioning, not that he cared. Fost knew as little of magic as he did of hydraulic engineering. Now he hoped fervently she was right.

He wished she could have compelled the lizard folk on the gate to slay their fellow guards. But she lacked the ability to impose so drastic an act as the murder of a comrade. She could turn them into living statues for as long as it took Fost to eliminate the patrolling pair and get to the gate, but that was all.

His heart thumped in his throat as the two appeared around the corner, two lumps of black against fainter darkness. He heard the crisp sounds of their steps, fancied he heard their breathing over the animal sounds of the prisoners on the far side of the wall. On the count of one-fifty he eased his sword from its scabbard. He shifted his hand to make certain of his grip on the wire-wound handle. Fear danced in his veins and pounded in his temples. He knew all too well the horrible speed with which the *Zr'gsz* reacted. He had to pit his merely human reflexes against two of them.

Part of him expected Erimenes to sing out a challenge at any moment. But the genie stayed silent as the footfalls drew nearer. Gleams of reflected starlight danced by in time to the footsteps. Fost sucked in a huge breath and sprang.

He landed with feet widespread and sword swinging, held two-handed in a madman's grip. He struck left and right with hysterical speed and power, crazed with fear that the lizard men's preternatural reflexes would cut him down before he could act. But even *Zr'gsz* reflexes take time to react; these Hissers were slowed by the soporific caresses of the chill night. When the pale creature materialized between them with his star-gleaming blade blazing a deadly trail through the darkness, they had no time to react.

The sword thunked home in the neck of the second sentry by the time Fost's nerves recorded the impact with the first. The leading Hisser fell, his head lolling from the half-severed neck that spewed dark blood onto the volcanic sand. The second's head simply sprang from its shoulders, launched by a powerful jet of blood.

Fost was so astonished that he just stood there staring for several heartbeats, his sword seeming to pulse like a living thing in his hands. Stinking black blood dried quickly on clothes and hair and skin.

"I'm alive," he whispered. "I'm *alive!*"

"Shrewdly struck," observed Erimenes. It was true. Fost had read about mighty warriors, generally great-thewed barbarians from the equatorial forests of the Northern Continent, who decapitated foes with a single swordstroke. Once he'd started learning swordcraft he'd dismissed the tales as mythic. A horizontal headcut was too chancy to be useful—a shoulder or upraised arm was too likely to get in the way. And it was *hard* to cut through a human neck, even with a well-honed steel blade.

In his panic, Fost had been unable to do anything but lash out horizontally and hope the sentries kept their arms by their sides. They had, and he'd chopped one of their damned heads off.

Maybe he *was* a hero.

"Don't get carried away," Erimenes advised him sourly, picking up the thought from his brain.

Grinning, Fost jogged down the arroyo. He felt a laugh rising in his throat and pushed it back down sternly. He hadn't honestly expected to survive the ambush. Reaction to finding them dead while he still lived made him giddy.

He reached the end of the wall where the arroyo wall was only a few feet high, scrambled up and peered around cautiously. The buildings beyond were black and silent like so many crypts; the garrison had finished its meal and gone to bed, wrapped in heavy cloaks against the cold. Two more sentries stood as rigid as statues exactly where Moriana had predicted.

But the *Zr'gsz* could stand motionless far longer than a human. Were these under Moriana's compulsion or just standing their usual watch? Fost knew only one way to be certain.

He dropped from the wall and slowly walked around the corner. Nothing. The sentries might have been carved from basalt. He repressed a lunatic urge to whistle as he glanced around. Far away a pink glow stained the eastern horizon. The lesser moon was poised to fling itself into the nighttime sky. Fost picked up his pace.

Affecting a boldness he didn't feel, he walked directly between the sentries to the gate. Neither Hisser stirred. He reached for the wooden beam securing the gate.

"Kill them, idiot," hissed Erimenes.

Fost paused to consider. Neither sentry showed any more life than the blocks of lava in the wall, but there wasn't any guarantee Moriana could hold them much longer. Fost had considerable cause to fear and loathe the lizard men, but he didn't like killing helpless beings.

But he saw no alternative—and time passed. He made two swift jabs with his dagger and turned back to moving the massive wooden bar.

The creak it made coming free of the brackets could be heard all the way to Port Zorn. But as soon as Fost had freed Moriana of her need to hold the sentries under compulsion, she'd shifted her attention to the buildings where the Hissers slept. She relayed via Ziore and Erimenes that no movement occurred at his slip. With a grunt of satisfaction, Fost heaved the bar away and opened the gate.

If the *Zr'gsz* hadn't heard him removing the bar, the captives had. A knot of men and women in ragged smocks clustered about the gate. Their reaction surprised him. A gasp of fear raced through the small group. Then it passed and he saw furtive expressions of hope dawn on their haggard faces.

Their gauntness appalled him. Obviously, the *Zr'gsz* fed their slaves only enough to enable them to drag their bodies down to the skystone mines every morning and toil the day away. That their slaves' numbers diminished every sundown made no difference to the reptiles.

A man pushed his way through the crowd. Not a tall man, he walked erect despite the air of deprivation, exhaustion and despair that swirled about him like a cloak. He'd once been a stocky man, Fost judged from the folds of loose skin on the scarecrow frame. But his eyes blazed clean, firm.

"I am Ludo, Chief Warden of the Watchers of Omizantrim. Who are you and what is the meaning of this?"

"I'm Fost. This means you and your folks are escaping. But they have to *move*."

"The Hissers—"

"Are taken care of. We can have a nice chat later. But get your people moving and do it now unless you love such lush accommodations." He waved his hand at the rude makeshift huts, little more than slumping piles of rock or tents made from tattered clothing.

Ludo took a deep breath and came to his decision.

The Watchers moved silently and efficiently, even the children. While Fost hovered by the gate watching the barracks nervously for sign of movement, they filed out through the gates and dispersed into the night. Leery of the apparent ease of their rescue, Fost advised them to scatter so that pursuers would have the hardest time possible rounding them up. In a few minutes all but a few lean men and women Fost took for the leaders had slipped out the gates and blended into the darkness.

"I can't believe it's gone this easily," Fost said.

"It won't be," came Ludo's calm voice. "They'll have their hounds on us as soon as they realize something's amiss. I only hope enough of us get free to wage effective war against the evil ones."

Moriana hadn't mentioned hounds, but she couldn't know everything about the *Zr'gsz*.

"My partner's hiding that way in a bubble cave," Fost said, pointing toward Moriana's command post.

"We know of it," said Ludo.

"I'll meet you there." The Watchers made for Moriana's cave. Fost admired their skill. They didn't beeline for the cave and risk being spotted on the open ground. Instead they bent over and scuttled to the jumble of rocks and bushes on the far bank of the arroyo and worked their way down from there, all but invisible in the light of the pink moon.

Before he followed them, Fost had work to do. Hurrying, he shut the gate and dropped the bar back into place. Then he picked up the guards one by one and propped them back in place, their spears serving to support their slack bodies. One he couldn't get into more than a slumping squat, but he thought it would fool anyone casually glancing down from the buildings. A close inspection would give the whole game away. But the deception might buy precious minutes, and time was more precious than gold.

Grabbing his scabbard so it wouldn't flap against his legs, Fost followed the Watchers into darkness.

"You!" Ludo's face turned to a mask of blood-dark fury in the light from twin moons. "You witch! Traitor to all mankind! What are you doing here?"

Moriana faced his anger squarely, hands on hips and head held high as she replied, "I'm setting you free."

"And who caused our imprisonment?" the Chief Warden hissed. Fost respected the man's self-control. Despite the consuming rage, he kept his voice low. Fost and Moriana and the band of fugitives had travelled a good ways from the prison compound across terrain that gripped at them with knife-edged fingers before stopping and revealing to the Watchers the identity of their second benefactor.

"You speak only the truth, Ludo," said Moriana. "But I didn't know the Hissers would do this to you. Indeed, I had instructed that you only be detained so that you didn't impede the . . . the Vridzish mining operations."

Ludo spat into the sand between her feet.

Her lips pulled back in a snarl, then relaxed. She was better able to accept impertinence from this lowborn groundling than any other of her kindred, but it was by no means easy. Still, she had to empathize with the man.

"I was wrong." A note of desperation pushed its way into her voice. "I thought allying myself with the Fallen Ones was the only way to prevent my sister from seizing control of the Realm for the Dark Ones." Her eyes dropped from his. "Now it seems I and not my sister was the tool of the Lords of Endless Night. But I did not know!"

Fost's gaze made a nervous circuit of their surroundings. He saw nothing but the blank black walls of the draw and the hunchbacked shapes of trees along the banks. The pink moon had ridden past the zenith and the blue one just began its mount of the eastern sky. This took too long. And Moriana revealed too much before the hostile Watchers.

"It doesn't matter." No scion of the Sky City could have bettered Ludo's haughty disdain. "You served the interests of mankind's enemies. You are a traitor; your life is forfeit. Were it not for the dilemma posed by the fact that we now owe you our freedom, we'd take your life."

Fost cleared his throat and loosened his sword in its scabbard. Moriana laid a hand on his forearm.

"Yes, kill the witch!" a woman's voice hissed from the darkness, sounding almost like one of the Hissers.

"Idiots." Glowing softly, Erimenes hung in the air by Fost's right shoulder. "The past is gone. You must deal with what pertains now—and the simple fact is that only Moriana's sorcery gives humanity any chance of defeating the Fallen Ones."

Ludo looked at the spirit, his face still bleak with anger.

"The princess knows she did wrong," continued the genie. "She said as much, and if you don't know the effort that took, you know little of the Skyborn. Now she's set you free. The Vridzish are militarily naive. The ease with which we released you proves that. Instead of wasting the night with recriminations you should be laying out a guerrilla campaign to deny the Hissers access to their skystone."

The Watchers murmured among themselves. Finally a man whose chin was fringed with a silvery beard spoke.

"This is true, Ludo. Killing the princess won't bring back the Ullapag or pen the damned lizards in Thendrun once more. If she'll help us we can't say no. Or so it seems to me."

Scowling with fierce brows that were still as black as the surrounding lava, Ludo turned on his followers.

"The witch has brought ruin on us all, on all of humanity," he exclaimed. "Justice must be done!"

"We failed in our charge," a woman's voice cried. "That's what's rankling you, isn't it, Warden? Moriana helped the Hissers overcome us—but we were charged to guard the mines and we failed. Don't we share the guilt?"

Ludo's broad shoulders slumped. He turned back to Fost and Moriana, as if his limbs had transmuted to lead. Fost almost hated to hear the acquiescence of this proud, strong man.

"Charuu is right," he said slowly. "So be it. On behalf of the Watchers of Omizantrim, I hereby . . ."

He broke off to stare past Fost's shoulder. Fost felt a soft breeze tug at his sleeve, heard a quick, soft moan. Ludo jerked. He raised his hands to his chest, spread them against the dark stain spreading across his smock from the arrow embedded in his chest.

Fost spun, sword ready. Brilliant light blinded him.

"Don't do anything foolish, my friend," came the command. A soft chuckle accentuated the order.

And it was a voice as human as his own.

# CHAPTER SEVEN

"And what of my sister?" Synalon leaned forward, her eyes narrowing into slits. "What became of my sister?"

She hissed the words like an angry serpent. The young Sky Guard lieutenant flinched but held his ground.

"Your Majesty, I did not see—"

"I am not my Majesty until I know whether or not my sister lives!" she snapped. The young officer's gaze slid around nervously, looking for something other than the blazing pits of his queen's eyes. The walls of the makeshift tent around them were made of the collapsed skin of a silk hot air balloon. Giant ruby red, blind, legless spiders who ate the Sky City's organic refuse produced the light, virtually unbreakable threads. Saplings cut from a nearby stand of tai had been lashed together to provide a dome framework. The covering silk was rolled some feet off the ground to provide shade without cutting off the sultry breeze.

Prince Rann, despite the rents and stains disfiguring his black and purple uniform, managed to look as neat and collected as if he'd just turned out for a morning inspection. He appeared to be uninterested in the byplay between officer and queen; this made Lt. Cerestan even more uneasy. He forced himself to look directly at Synalon. She leaned forward even farther, waiting for his answer with the predatory intensity of a falcon watching its prey.

"You must have seen it!" persisted Synalon. Her words snapped like a banner in a brisk wind.

He flushed. Cerestan felt even more uncomfortable for what he had to report.

"Y-Your Highness, I was commanded to organize the evacuation of the City."

Synalon's eyebrows shot up. Her right breast popped out of the robe she wore loosely wrapped about her lush body.

"What? My sister ordered the City in the Sky *abandoned?*" Sparks popped and ozone edged the air. "That weak-kneed, cowardly slut! How *could* she!" She brought her hands up to angrily tear her garment. It resisted her wiry strength. Fat blue sparks travelled the length of her frizzled strands of hair and exploded in the air.

Cerestan made himself watch the princess's head shed sparks as a duck's wing sheds water. It kept his eyes off the naked breast which bobbed about in tempo with her efforts to rip her robe. The skin was the translucent white of snow the upper crust of which has melted in sunlight and then frozen again to a fine glossing. The nipple was a dainty blossom pink. . .

"She thought it necessary to save as many of our people as possible." He forced himself to hold his head high. But it put a severe strain on his nerve to face Synalon this way, a fact that only peripherally had to do with her spiritual and temporal power. "She herself battled the Demon Istu and bought time for as many to escape as possible."

Rann had been watching the officer sidelong, his tawny eyes distant. Now they fastened on Cerestan.

"You did well. You saved several thousand of our subjects."

Hardened as he was, Cerestan shuddered. Several thousand people—perhaps a quarter of the City's population. And the rest . . .

He looked out under the rolled tent wall. In all directions vultures crowded the sky and dotted the landscape in grave clumps, strutting stiff-legged with hooded heads drawn between their shoulders, bending down to partake of the unprecedented feast. The voracious birds extended in a line hundreds of yards across and a mile long, following the route of the Sky City. Though the hills were bright with fragrant wildflowers, the smell riding the wind was a ghastly charnel stink.

"So?" Synalon slumped back on her stool. "Well, she defeated me and that made her the most potent wizard alive." She propped her chin on one hand. Sparks stopped dripping like raindrops from her hair. "How did she fare?"

"I couldn't see—not more than quick glimpses—Your, uh, Highness. But she must have survived because she kept the Demon at bay for a long time."

Synalon slapped her knee. Her other breast bounced into view. Cerestan swallowed hard.

"That's my sister! I knew she could achieve real power if only she'd quit dabbling with her pathetic healing spells."

Glancing toward Rann in his growing discomfiture, Cerestan noticed that the prince, too, was looking pointedly away from his cousin. The scarred cheeks showed pink like sunburn, though no bird rider of Rann's experience could possibly sunburn. For a fleeting instant, Cerestan almost shared a human bond with his commander.

"Very well." Synalon settled back on the stool as if it were a throne. "Now tell me," she said, purring the words, "tell me, good Cerestan, which of your brother and sister officers did you happen to observe wearing the armband of my sister's faction?"

Cerestan squared his shoulders and took a deep breath. Conflicting loyalties pulled in opposite directions like dogs worrying a corpse, but one loyalty overrode all.

"I saw none, Highness." Then realizing how bald the lie sounded, he quickly added, "None so well I'd recognize them, at least."

A blue glow started to play around the roots of Synalon's hair. Cerestan prepared himself for death. She would either fry him with a lightning bolt or summon other soldiers to exact a painful penalty for his defiance. He cast a quick look out over the plain covered with feasting vultures. With luck, that was the least of all possible fates awaiting him at Synalon's hand.

"I'm sure you didn't, Lieutenant," Rann murmured. Cerestan stared at him, trying not to show his surprise at having such an unlikely ally. "In the press of prisoners you probably got no clear look at your captors. And later during the evacuation you had no chance to see which of your comrades might be wearing Moriana's colors. Isn't that so?"

The prince ended in a tone well-known to his men, one that clearly stated anyone contradicting him would shortly wish he had died in his sleep the night before.

"Y-yes, milord."

Rann nodded. Frowning, Synalon glanced from Cerestan to her cousin. It seemed to her that the young lieutenant should have recognized some of the traitors at least. By the Dark Ones, yes! But Rann was expert in internal security and he must have reasons for this action. She pouted slightly in frustration. It was bad enough that her own loss of the City was compounded by her fumble-witted sister losing the damned place the very same day. She had counted on at least a dozen agonizing executions of rebels this very night to take away the sting of her disappointments.

"Very well. You've done the Guard proud, Cerestan. Dismissed." Rann turned and bent his head toward Synalon. Cerestan stood as if his feet had put down roots. It couldn't be this simple.

Rann's head swiveled.

"I said, *dismissed*. Are you waiting for your mother's beak, Lieutenant?" It was a bird rider taunt referring to a weak fledgling that must be physically shoved from the nest. Cerestan saluted and fled.

Once more Rann bowed his head to speak to Synalon. A slim, raised finger cut him off.

"Cousin dear, what was that young man's name again?"

"Cerestan, Your Highness. Flight Lieutenant of the Guard. A good man."

She smiled wickedly.

"I judged as much." He was a well-proportioned youth, tall for a Sky Citizen, wide-shouldered, with black hair and blue eyes and a look of innocence hidden behind the veneer of veteran hardness that marked so many of Rann's officers. And Synalon hadn't missed the bulge between his legs and the way he oh-so-carefully looked anywhere but at his monarch's naked breasts. "But tonight, I think, I shall find out for myself what kind of man he is. We should always strive to know the more promising underlings. Well, Rann, isn't that so?"

Rann licked his lips and his cheeks flamed scarlet.

"Yes, Your Highness."

Blinking into the sudden glare, Fost was momentarily transported back to his childhood. Night was the favorite time for street urchins of High Medurim to play their games. Usually there was some reward. Always there was penalty for losing. Adding spice to the game was the possibility of being caught by the watch for violating curfew. What happened next depended entirely on the whim of the arresting officer. A low caste, impoverished out-Guild youth pulled in after sunset could be let off with a lecture, whipped . . . or enslaved.

It was all in the luck of the game.

The yellow beam shining directly into his eyes came from a bull's-eye lantern exactly like those the Medurim city guard used. Fost felt the familiar, clammy thrill: *caught!*

An almost pleasant voice brought him back to reality.

"Ho, my friend, don't do anything foolish now. It would be a shame for you to end up like that dolt on the ground."

He tore his gaze from the lantern's shine. Ludo lay on his back, kicking spastically at the black sand, his motions becoming more and more feeble. Moriana knelt by his side, but the man was clearly beyond the reach of her healing magics.

Dark shapes detached themselves from the misshapen trees along the bank. The men appearing held flexed bows on the huddled people in the arroyo.

"Why was it necessary to shoot the Warden, Fairspeaker?" a voice from the darkness asked.

" 'Twas necessary so that these rabble shouldn't attempt futile resistance, great Sternbow," replied the first disembodied voice in tones both oily smooth and suasive. "It brought their helplessness home to them. So now it proves unnecessary to slaughter them. Such forebearance does us all credit."

The lantern was uncovered and flooded the draw with sallow light. Tall men jumped down from the banks with swords drawn and herded the recaptured Watchers together. They wore tunics and trousers that reflected black and gray in the torchlight. In sunlight they would have been forest green and brown.

Beside the lantern at the head of the draw stood a tall, stately forester, his arms folded across his chest, his sword sheathed. His blond hair and beard were sprinkled with gray. His brow creased and the frown-lines deepened as he studied Fost.

"Longstrider," he stated quietly.

The courier folded his own arms across his breast.

"Sternbow."

"What? You fail to recognize me? I'd thought your memory more tenacious, good Fost." The unctuous voice belonged to the lantern-bearer who stood at Sternbow's side. He was young and slender, with a chestnut fringe of beard adorning his jaw and brown eyes that laughed at some private jest.

"I know you, Fairspeaker," Fost said quietly.

Slowly and ponderously, Moriana rose from the side of the fallen Warden.

"He's dead," she said. "What's the meaning of this senseless murder?"

A look of pain crossed Sternbow's angular face.

"No murder," Fairspeaker put in quickly, "to shoot a fleeing felon."

"Felon?" Moriana's eyes blazed. "How can you call him that? He was a victim held as a slave by the *Zr'gsz*."

One of the Watchers moved to touch her arm.

"Save your breath, Lady. These are the very hounds of the Hissers set to hunt us down even as Ludo foretold."

"But they're *men*," she said, stunned. The Watcher's chuckle was as dry and bitter as an old root left in the searing desert sun.

"On behalf of our ally the Instrumentality of the People I hereby place you under arrest for aiding and abetting the flight of prisoners of war," Sternbow said formally.

"Am I not your ally, as well?" demanded Moriana.

"The wise Sternbow takes cognizance of the fact that you have been an ally of the foresters," said Fairspeaker. "Yet he is also well aware that relations between Thendrun and the Tree go back to a time long before the name of the Princess Moriana was ever heard in the Great Nevrym."

"Don't you understand? The Hissers turned on me— turned on us. They helped me capture the City, then they wrested it from me. They mean to drive all humans from the Realm. They've freed the Demon Istu to help them do it!"

Shaking his head, smiling sorrowfully over human duplicity, Fairspeaker looked to Sternbow.

"Honored sir, is it not clear that she has had some falling out with our friends the People and means to turn us against them with these fanciful tales?"

Sternbow's already thin lips disappeared in a pensive line. Moriana's pulse raced. She had touched him with doubt. She could tell.

"Father." A stocky young man, face wreathed in golden ringlets, pushed his way into the draw to stand beside Sternbow. "She's telling the truth, can't you see? I've told you repeatedly we can't trust those lizards."

Fairspeaker laid a hand on Sternbow's shoulder, squeezed reassuringly.

"A sad burden it must be to you," he said softly, "that your son Snowbuck has not learned the meaning of faith among friends."

Sternbow shook himself free of the hand.

"We waste time here," he grated. "Brookrunner, Stagsnarer, disarm the princess and Longstrider." Fost and Moriana stood in stony silence as the Nevrymin relieved them of their weapons.

More torches were lit. The Nevrymin, a score of bow and swordsmen, ranged themselves around their captives and began to drive them back down Omizantrim's rocky slope. Above them the mountain rumbled to itself, and a brimstone smell stung their nostrils.

"Do those boorish forest dwellers all have doubled names?" Erimenes demanded from his jug. "Frogbaiter. Leafeater. Shitkicker." He produced a decidedly unphilosophical snort. "Absurd."

"They seem to know you, Fost," Ziore said hesitantly.

"Indeed they do." In spite of their predicament, a lopsided grin appeared on the courier's face. "In fact, they gave me the name Longstrider."

With neither gentleness nor excessive force, the foresters guided them around a seething fumarole.

"Ah, well, of course, there is a certain bucolic charm to the custom of bestowing two-part descriptive names," said Erimenes loudly, his wavering form peering down into the fumarole. "In fact, I once composed a monograph on . . ."

A loose rock turned under Fost's foot. Moriana caught his arm, steadying him.

"How did that come to pass?" she asked, cutting off the philosopher's nervous word flow.

"Lawless men plotted together to assassinate our king," said a forester walking nearby. "The outwood courier learned of the scheme and went to warn Grimpeace. Though he couldn't match the woodscraft of the rebels, he was able to outpace them and reach our king in time." He spoke without looking at the captives and he continued to hold his bow relaxed but ready. "In reward for the feat, the King in Nevrym bestowed upon him the forester's name Longstrider."

"It is indeed a pity that one who so nobly served the interests of our king should now place himself in opposition to noble Grimpeace." Fairspeaker had materialized out of the night. The forester clamped his bearded jaw tight and kept trudging through the lava flows.

The former village of the Watchers was awash in torchlight. Armed *Zr'gsz*, torpid with the chill, milled about the compound without apparent aim. An officer in feather helmet emerged from what had been the Watchers' assembly hall and held a vigorous discussion with Sternbow. The Hisser spoke in sibilant, garbled human speech augmented by violent gestures. Fost and the others were too far away to make out what was being said, but as far as the courier could tell the reptile was determined the escapees and those who had helped them should be put to death immediately. His only point of uncertainty was whether they should be speared where they stood or flung into the lava pits, thereby saving wear on obsidian spear tips. Fost did think Fairspeaker added his voice to Sternbow's in arguing they be speared. He found it cold comfort, somehow.

At last, Fairspeaker lowered his voice and, shaking his head with the lugubrious regret of an inquisitor ordering his assistants to crank the rack a few more turns, said something that caused the Vridzish officer to turn moss green and immediately begin issuing orders with even more histrionic gestures.

Sternbow strode to where the captives stood. He had to make his way through a mob of lower caste *Zr'gsz* surrounding the prisoners in unmoving, silent ranks. Somehow their silence, their apparent lack of emotion, seemed more threatening than a display of hostility. Fost saw little approval on the Nevrym leader's face as he pushed aside the scaled bodies.

"The Vridzish officer was adamant that you pay full price for your crimes." Though he stopped a foot behind Sternbow, Fairspeaker quickly thrust his presence to the fore. Sternbow showed no sign of irritation at being pre-empted. "But Sternbow, whom all know as a merciful and just man, prevailed upon him to let you live." Fairspeaker shrugged slightly. "For a time, at least. The People are much outraged by your treacherous defection, Princess."

"*My* defection?" She held her anger back with visible effort.

Sternbow locked his gaze on Fost's.

"You were a loyal friend to the Forest," he said. "I hope this breach can be healed."

"So do I."

The compound gates swung open. The Hissers made quick, menacing jabs with their spears. The prisoners were marched into the lava rock walled pen.

"Wait!" cried Erimenes as the gates started to swing shut.

Fairspeaker appeared in the gap between the gates.

"Why should we wait, friend spirit? I judge you are another bottle-bound shade, such as the one known to accompany the Princess Moriana."

"Yes. I mean no! I'm not like that vacuous creature at all. I'm much, much wiser. And I know many things that might interest you. Things your masters would give a great deal to learn."

An eyebrow arched.

"My masters, eh?" Fairspeaker pursed his lips, nodding to himself as he meditated. Then he bobbed his chin. Well, there's no harm in listening to you if you wish to speak."

He gestured. A pair of Hissers approached Fost with the curious sporadic movement of their kind, their spears at the ready. Fost plunged a hand into his satchel. The Vridzish stopped, pointing the spearheads at his heart. He ripped Erimenes's jug from the pouch and flung the red clay vessel onto the hard-packed earth at their feet.

Unfortunately, it bounced.

"Really, Fost, such petulance ill-becomes you," Erimenes sniffed. "I could never abide such a poor loser. Come then, Fairspeaker, let us converse."

"Let us, indeed." The young man accepted the jug from a clawed hand.

"I must confess the smell in that sty was quite revolting," Erimenes said as Fairspeaker walked out cradling the jug in one arm. "Say, you're a strapping young fellow. Are there any lively wenches in the vici—"

The gates slammed shut.

# CHAPTER EIGHT

The air in the prison compound lay like a thing dead, hot and still and decaying. Upslope toward the rear slit, latrines festered like wounds under buzzing clouds of flies. The tents and huts Fost had seen the night before were gone, torn down and trampled by the enraged Hissers. Crude makeshifts though they had been, they were sorely missed.

Fost had awakened with a pounding in his head and the sun pouring like hot wax on his eyelids. He lay near the gate, where exhaustion had claimed him when the curdled gray of false dawn started to seep into the eastern sky. Moriana sat nearby, her hair tied back from her face, her head bent in earnest conversation with Ziore. She and the spirit seemed to take turns reassuring each other.

Fost pulled himself upright. For a moment, he expected the longwinded complaint that was his usual morning greeting from Erimenes. Then he remembered. He spoke a heartfelt curse and dug his magic water flask from the satchel.

Moriana and Ziore noticed he was awake and greeted him in subdued voices. He handed the flask to Moriana and looked around the compound. The lava pen was almost empty. Two score Watchers stood in sullen knots. He spat to clear his throat.

"Most of the Watchers got away, I see," he finally said.

"But for how long?" Moriana answered, reluctantly pulling the flask from her parched lips. She pointed skyward. It was busy up there. No clouds were visible, and if Omizantrim breathed this morning its exhalation streamed away northward and out of their sight. But the skyrafts of the *Zr'gsz* teemed in the air like flies around the latrines.

"You'd know that better than I," Fost pointed out.

"I think they've got a chance," she said slowly. "If they have sense to lie up in the bubble caves during the day, the *Zr'gsz* will never find them."

With his usual touch of the inappropriate, Fost marvelled at the ease with which she pronounced the Vridzish's name for themselves. It wasn't intended for human tongue, yet she grated out the hissing and gutturals as if she'd hatched from an egg in the emerald depths of Thendrun. Fost took out his bowl and traded it to Moriana for the water flask.

As they ate, they talked about their adventures since parting in Athalau, the city in the glacier, the fabulous lost city of sorcerers and savants in which Ziore and the treacherous Erimenes had been born centuries before.

Fost's account was straightforward. He looked away from the hardness that came into Moriana's eyes when he spoke of having been discovered outside the glacier by Jennas, the hetwoman of the Bear Clan. Moriana had known that even before their precipitous separation in Athalau he and Jennas were more than mere friends. Fost recounted his journey north to find Moriana and tell her that the magic bauble she possessed wasn't the one she thought. Jennas had travelled with him, partly out of love, but mostly because her bear god Ust had revealed to her that a new War of Powers loomed, and that she must discover what that implied for her folk. Fost had nervously discounted Jennas's claims of visions and divine revelation. The farther they travelled, the less he was inclined to do so. They found powers afoot in the Realm beyond simple shades and sprites and hedge demons.

Most of the rest Moriana knew, including how he had gotten in touch with the Underground opposing Synalon in the Sky City.

He watched the skyrafts drift overhead as he spoke,

since this part of his journey held painful memories of Luranni and how the woman had given her life to save him from her traitorous father's fire sprite.

Fost fell silent. Moriana's slender fingers made patterns in the gray ash in front of her, then erased them. After a while she related her travails to Fost.

Moriana glossed over her stay in Thendrun, and not simply because thought of the place raised gooseflesh all over her body. Despite herself, she gave awed account of the Keep of the Fallen Ones, of the fortress hewn from giant emerald crystals grown eons ago in the heart of the Mystic Mountains by *Zr'gsz* magic. She talked about the witchfire that lived in the walls, and the emptiness of the castle that had made her think she treated with a dying and helpless race—she talked about everything but what actually went on within those walls of green crystal.

Fost studied her intently, sensing evasion, but did not speak of it. Instead they discussed the question of the numbers of *Zr'gsz* Moriana had seen since departing Thendrun. It had worried her all along and now was of vital importance. How many foes did mankind face? Fost could offer no insight. Their fellow captives might have but they remained aloof, refusing even to talk with Moriana, whom they blamed for their present troubles—and with good reason. Though their jailers hadn't brought the breakfast allotment of brackish water and rancid slop, all refused to acknowledge Fost's offer to share his inexhaustible stores of food and water.

As the morning wore on, it became apparent that the slaves weren't to be driven forth to work in the mines. The Hisser garrison had its work cut out hunting other fugitives across the inhospitable flanks of Omizantrim. Fost and Moriana moved into the shade of the eastern wall and continued to talk.

Without Erimenes on hand to incite her, Ziore turned out to be a warm and soothing presence, full of concern for her mortal friends. She made Fost feel as if she had

known him her whole long life and cared for him dearly.
He was even flattered when she told him he was fully the
man Moriana had described in such loving terms.

In the course of Moriana's narrative, Fost had picked
up the spirit's history and something of her attributes.
Now he asked, "But I thought you had the power to influence men's emotions. Couldn't you influence Sternbow to
let us go?"

"I tried," said Ziore, looking stricken. "Such was his
natural inclination, too. Yet Fairspeaker's influence
proved greater than mine."

"Is he a mage?"

"No. He holds Sternbow in bonds of love and fear and
duty. I don't fully understand their relationship."

"Perhaps I do. Fairspeaker is Sternbow's youngest sister's son. She died of fever not long after Fairspeaker's
birth. Her husband fell in battle not long after. Custom
provides that Sternbow should take Fairspeaker into his
own house and raise him as a foster son. But Sternbow's
wife wouldn't hear of it, claiming the boy was born under
an evil sign.

"Fairspeaker was raised by a succession of foster parents. Even when he was young, he earned quite a reputa-
tion for his skill with sword, spear and bow. And far more
for his prowess with words." Fost shook his head. "It's
strange, too. His talent is akin to magic, if not identical
with it. What he says sounds empty and often ridiculous—
as long as he is saying it to someone else. When he turns
his attention on you, it's damned hard not to agree with
everything he says. It's as if other folk are puppets, and he
knows just the strings to pull."

"An appeal that went beyond charisma," sighed Moriana. "Darl Rhadaman possessed a similar talent."

"It may be that I was wrong about Fairspeaker's not
being a mage," Ziore said musingly. "This ability you
speak of may be a talent of the mind, like Athalar magic,
though it is of a kind unfamiliar to me."

"Or perhaps too familiar," said Moriana. "It strikes me as similar to your talent for emotional manipulation, Ziore, but not as well controlled."

The genie looked first rebellious, then sheepish.

"You may be right," she admitted.

"In any event, he had grown to manhood when Sternbow's wife died. Fairspeaker returned from a campaign in which he had distinguished himself in battle against bandits from the Lolu country. He demanded the patronage Sternbow had withheld so long. Guilt wouldn't permit the older man to refuse."

He drew idle designs in the dust at his feet. The growing heat made him sweat. Fost wondered what it had been like for the Watchers in the skystone mines. Hell, no doubt. And the man he spoke of contributed heavily to a renewal of that living torture.

"When I was in Nevrym," he continued, "Fairspeaker was already something of a force to be reckoned with. He was little different from the way he is now. No one quite trusts him, unless you happen to be the subject of his immediate attention. Yet when he's around no man quite trusts his comrades, either. No one can tell who is under Fairspeaker's influence. And no one knows who Fairspeaker backs." Fost rubbed his chin. A wiry black stubble rasped under his hand. He'd lost his razor in the City, and the dagger he shaved with now had been confiscated by the foresters. "He keeps his own balance and keeps all others off theirs. He is dangerous," he finished.

"But why is he helping the *Zr'gsz?*" demanded Moriana. "He must know they're enemies of all humanity."

Fost shrugged.

"I don't know. One thing no one's ever accused Fairspeaker of lacking is a keen perception of where his own best interests lie."

A creak and a thump announced that the bolt on the gate was being withdrawn. Fost was on his feet instantly, Moriana beside him poised to take advantage of the slightest opportunity to escape. Deep down he knew escape was but a forlorn hope. The inhuman speed of the *Zr'gsz* and the keen eyes and ready bows of their human allies were too formidable a combination for them to overcome unarmed. Even if Moriana summoned up a fearful battle spell from inside her, all that would accomplish would be to take some Hissers and foresters down to Hell Call with them. That might be the only sensible thng to do, but despair hadn't progressed that far. Yet.

"My ears burn, gentle friends," said Fairspeaker, stepping through the gate with a brace of *Zr'gsz* spearmen at his heels. A leather pouch with a suspiciously familiar bulge swung familiarly at his hip. "Could it be you did me the honor of discussing me?"

Fost favored him with a long, dour look and folded himself back down to the ground.

"We've more pleasant topics to discuss, Fairspeaker. The state of the latrine, for example."

Fairspeaker threw back his head and roared with laughter, as if this were the choicest joke he'd ever heard.

"Ah, good Longstrider, you were ever the droll rogue. You are sorely missed in the Great Nevrym. The dullards and dotards who infest the Tree haven't among them the wit to fill a thimble."

Fost found himself listening intently, even thinking Fairspeaker wasn't such a bad fellow. After all, he did appreciate Fost's finer qualities.

Fairspeaker looked from the courier to Moriana who stood with legs braced and arms folded beneath her breasts, glaring defiantly at him. He met her eyes, shrugged at the message he read in them and turned his attention back to Fost.

"You'd be a valuable ally for the Dark Ones," he said. "Why throw away your life for this Sky scum?"

Why, indeed? It was all so lucid Fost wondered why he hadn't thought of it before.

"Are all Nevrymin allies of the Dark?" demanded Moriana.

"No, Lady," he said, laughing at her. "But soon they will be. As soon as those of us with the vision to see what's best for the Forest have assumed the mantle of power and cleared away a certain amount of the deadwood."

Moriana's answering laugh was as jarring as steel on stone.

"I, too, thought the Hissers my allies," she said, "and I gather my sister thought the same of the Lords of Infinite Night. You can see how wisely we chose those to trust."

A shadow crossed his pale face, then was gone, as fleeting as a bat crossing the disk of the lesser moon.

"I have my assurances from parties of great power—or Power, if you get my emphasis. Synalon was weighed and found wanting; you merely sought to exploit the People for your own base ends and found your wickedness turned against you. I, and those of like mind, deal with the Dark from a position of strength and good faith. We will be honored well when the final victory is achieved."

His brown eyes found Fost's gray ones. Fairspeaker smiled and Fost felt himself stirring to the gaze.

"Well, Longstrider? May I have your hand upon it . . . comrade?"

As if of its own accord, Fost's scarred right hand rose to touch Fairspeaker's slimmer, softer one.

*Idiot!* A voice cracked from the back of his skull. *He's playing you like a lute!*

He struck the proferred hand away.

"Go drown yourself in a bucket of shit!" he snarled, deliberately using the crudity to dispel the last of Fairspeaker's verbal spell.

Fairspeaker only laughed, and waved the fingers of his raised right hand languidly in the air as if to cool them.

"Well, that's your decision. All I can say is that I am deeply regretful." He turned to Moriana. "Perhaps you have a clearer perception of your own best interest, Princess. I can tell you that a high official of the People arrives on the morrow from Thendrun to interrogate you. You can save yourself much anguish—by which I mean earn yourself a quick and painless death—if you simply tell me now of your plans."

"Plans?" Moriana's laugh turned bitter. "I have none. Except to escape this stinking pen."

"Don't lie, Princess." The liquid eyes showed hurt. Fairspeaker patted Erimenes's new pouch. "Your former accomplice has revealed to me many of the salient features of your scheme to turn the skystone mines to your own purposes. But the servants of the Dark need details. For example, which traitor revealed to you the workings of the skyraft controls? We know you flew here on a craft stolen from the Sky City. I tell you this so you'll understand that we know enough to tell if you try lying to us."

Only instinct prevented Fost from dropping his jaw in amazement. It took iron self-control to keep from turning to see if Moriana was as dumbstruck. Where in the wide Realm had Fairspeaker gotten such an extravagant notion?

"Confess all, Fost." Erimenes's voice lacked nothing of the unctuous tones Fairspeaker carried off so well. "You've not been a bad companion, though you are uncouth and rather less valorous than I might have wished. I'd hate to see you suffer needlessly on account of your murdering wolf bitch."

Fost turned an ugly grin on Fairspeaker.

"I might even reconsider your offer to join you, my friend," he said in a deadly quiet voice, "if you could promise me one reward. Return Erimenes to a living, feeling body so that I could give him the fill of sensation he so craves. My vaporous friend, I think I've picked up some useful pointers from your old friend, the late, lamented Prince Rann." Fairspeaker guffawed.

"You'd jest on the gibbet, friend Fost."

"Who's jesting?"

"Mark my words, Fost! You'll regret this."

Fairspeaker looked at the sky. A few fat, fleecy clouds

gamboled in the southern sky. He let his gaze drift mean-ingfully at the traffic of skycraft streaming in from the northeast.

"You'll have until tomorrow morning to think over your refusal." Fairspeaker's eyes filled with concern. "You must understand, my friends, that once Lord Nchssk ar-rives, affairs will pass from my hands and I will be unable to win you any mercy."

They ignored him. He shrugged elaborately and walked out. The *Zr'gsz* guards waited until he had left the com-pound before backing out. The gates boomed shut and the lock fell with a sound like a headsman's axe.

Fost and Moriana exchanged looks. The tale Erimenes had fed the Nevrymin was a combination of truth and utter fabrication. Had the genie thought to insinuate him-self into the good graces of the Dark Ones by inventing an imaginary menace, banking on the near certainty that the more fervently Moriana and Fost denied the existence of such a danger the more fervently the questioners would disbelieve them?

Or had the ages-old spirit simply gone insane?

Fost slept through the heat of the afternoon. With a sentence of death looming over him as tangibly as the bulk of Omizantrim, it might have seemed strange he could sleep at all. But sleep shielded him from having to think of his fate.

He woke to find Moriana bending over a younger Watcher woman seated on a flat rock. Moriana worked on the woman's arm, which was twisted unnaturally. The woman's face was drained of color and feeling; it showed no pain.

Moriana finally stood, wiped sweat from her forehead and regarded the job of splinting and bandaging.

"It'd be best if you wore that sling for several weeks, Beiil. Right now the thing to do is sleep." The woman nodded dully and rose, walking to the nearest group of

Watchers who were busily not watching what the princess had done. One spoke to the woman in hushed tones and looked disbelievingly at her quiet answer.

"Damn the Hissers," Moriana swore fervently. "And thrice damn the Nevrymin for aiding them now that they've shown their true shade! That girl's arm was broken in the capture of the village. They locked her in a store-room with others wounded and dying. The others were too weak to help her; she bound her own arm, but set the bone wrong. By the time the Hissers let her out to join the others, it was too late to reset. I had to break it over again."

"She was certainly quiet."

Moriana mopped at her forehead with the hem of her tunic. Fost looked at the bare skin of her trim midriff with a pang of longing. It had been so long for them, and now they'd never have the chance to complete their reunion.

"Ziore helped. She suppressed sensation in the girl's mind while I worked. She even left a residual block that will keep the pain from becoming too severe."

"I keep being surprised at the way your powers have grown," Fost said. "Tell me. You'd rather heal with magic, wouldn't you?"

Her eyes answered for her.

When the sun dipped low enough in the sky to become entangled with the black tentacles of the Omizantrim flows, Fost broke out his bowl and flask. He and Moriana ate a little, then offered the vessels once more to the Watchers. Wan and shaky, Beiil rose from her pallet and came over. Fost helped her and Fost fed her with her own spoon. When she finished, most of the other Watchers lined up wordlessly to partake of the food and drink.

As the other prisoners ate, Fost lay back with his head in his hands watching the sky set in layers of color, slate-gray and blue and orange. His mind wandered. First, he thought about Moriana's account of her trip to Thendrun. There was something missing from her story. He didn't perceive the lack as he would, say, the hollow left by a missing tooth. Rather, it was like detecting wine watered by a dishonest innkeeper. Moriana had diluted the truth. Why?

He'd never find out. In a short time it would no longer matter. But it hurt him to think she'd keep anything from him.

His thoughts drifted to Erimenes. He had travelled so long in the company of the garrulous and horny spirit that he'd come to like him. Certainly there were scores—hundreds!—of times when he had felt like abandoning the sage. Yet he had come to regard Erimenes as something of a comrade in arms despite the genie's superciliousness and insatiable appetite for vicarious stimulation.

And Erimenes had repaid that loyalty with treachery. Fost had no one to blame but himself for his credulity. Erimenes had shown his true essence before, when as a messenger, Fost had been charged with delivering the genie in the jug to its original owner. It had seemed to Fost that the genie was gradually changing over the many months, though, was actively trying to aid Fost rather than goad him into impossible and potentially entertaining situations.

Aye, *seemed*.

The Watchers finished eating and drinking and, still wordless, returned the utensils to Fost. He sat unspeaking with his arms around Moriana while the light went out of the world. Then they lay down side by side and slept.

They awoke to light.

Instinctively, Fost groped for his sword. He found a handful of soft flesh. Moriana automatically brushed his hand from her breast and sat up beside him.

They blinked into the yellow eye of a hooded lantern. Fost's blood chilled. Had the *Zr'gsz* inquisitor arrived ahead of schedule? The light winked out. Fost's eyes adjusted to the darkness again, and he made out a stocky form in a narrow gap between the gates.

"Sir Longstrider? Princess Moriana?"

"What do you want?" Moriana asked cautiously.

"Save the hackneyed dialog for later," a familiar, testy voice snapped. "Right now, time is of the essence."

"Go play your vicious tricks elsewhere, you treacherous bottled fart," said Fost hotly.

"Yes! You're a disgrace to noble Athalau!" exclaimed Ziore.

"Gentles . . ." the husky young man said, raising his hands in a placating gesture.

"The just must suffer," Erimenes said. "May the Three and Twenty Wise Ones of Agift witness what dullards I am saddled with as friends!"

"You've small right to call upon the Wise," hissed Moriana.

"Gentles, now . . ."

"Must I bear such abuse heaped upon my noble head? After all I've done? Oh, it is a bitter lot dealing with such as you."

*"Silence!"* The command snapped like a whip. Fost peered most closely at the youth. Whoever he was, he had the habit of command. "Gentles, you may not know me, for you only saw me briefly. I am Snowbuck, Sternbow's son. I've come to rescue you."

"Then why are you signing your death warrant by carrying that jar around with you?" Fost got to his feet.

Erimenes called upon the gods to witness his sorry fate.

"But gentles," Snowbuck said, "it was the good Erimenes who talked these men into helping free you. I couldn't convince them by myself."

A tall shadow appeared at his side.

"It may do us little credit but it's no light thing to cross that devil Fairspeaker." Fost recognized the voice of the bowman who had told his naming story to Moriana the night before. "But when Erimenes told us what had happened in the Sky City, we could no longer doubt that the People are enemies of all our kind."

"As if it wasn't before all our faces long ago!" Snowbuck said passionately.

"Ah, Snowbuck, you've won now. Don't chop a tree that's fallen."

The rebuff was offered in a friendly tone and Snowbuck took it gracefully.

"You have the right, Firesbane." He gestured and men spilled into the compound. "Help these others out." He didn't have to tell them to be quick and quiet; they were Nevrym foresters.

As the Nevrymin began to usher out the Watchers into the night for the second time in two days, Snowbuck pulled Erimenes's fat clay jar from its pouch and handed it almost reverently to Fost. Fost accepted it with both hands. For a second, he considered drop-kicking it over the wall, then thought better of it. That would have been too noisy. He stuffed it back into the satchel.

"At least, you're not totally lost to feelings of gratitude," Erimenes said waspishly.

"Erimenes, what are you up to?" Fost demanded. He stood in front of the gate so that the escaping Watchers had to part and pass to both sides of him like a stream around a jutting rock.

"A scheme worthy of my high intelligence," the spirit replied smugly. "It was almost a pity to waste such ingenuity on so paltry a project as saving you from certain death. But it offends my sense of esthetics to contemplate a beauty such as Moriana's passing from this world."

"I'm flattered," the princess said, "but what was all that bizarre claptrap about our plotting to field our own fleet of skyrafts?"

"I had to tell that rogue Fairspeaker something that would convince him I was truly on their side—and, incidentally, would keep him from bowing to the insistence of the *Zr'gsz* commandant and allowing you to be killed."

" 'Allowing' us—what power has he?" Fost demanded.

"The Hissers realize it is Fairspeaker who keeps their Nevrymin allies allied. And he does have the favor of the Dark Ones. He wasn't lying about that."

In the starlight it seemed that patches of color had come to Snowbuck's broad cheeks.

"You owe Erimenes a debt, Sir Longstrider, and you, too, Princess," he said. "And . . . and I, as well. For he's made it possible for me to save my father's honor!"

His voice almost cracked the armor of his whispering. He collected himself and clapped the two on the arms.

"We must hurry."

"Lead the way," said Fost.

# CHAPTER NINE

Sure-footed in the dark, Snowbuck led Fost and Moriana up the arroyo that ran along the western wall of the
prison compound. He then threaded his way eastward
over the brushy slope of Omizantrim between the fumarole where the Ullapag had kept its vigil and the village
itself. The mountain was moody tonight. Its mutterings
crescendoed from time to time to a roaring like blood in
the ears. Purple lightning played around the summit. Explosions crashed in the crater playing lurid light on the
underside of the wide cloud that issued from the mountain's guts.

Fost sensed movement on both sides. He didn't waste
energy casting about to see who or what was nearby. He
trusted Snowbuck's sense better than his own. It would
have been foolish to fall down a hole simply to keep track
of unseen friends.

Like Moriana, he ran with sword in hand. Nevrymin
had returned their weapons as they emerged from the
compound. As dark as the night was, the princess had
decided not to string her bow and wore it slung over her
back next to a fresh quiver of arrows.

They passed through narrow draws, struggled up slopes
where the lava threatened to crumble underfoot at any
instant and fling them facedown on the sharp rock, and
once hopped across a recent flow that burned the soles of
their feet. Luckily, the crust didn't give way beneath them
the way the half-hardened lava had when they first made
their way to the Watchers' village.

At one point, Fost almost went headlong into the yawn-

119

ing pit of a skystone quarry. He drew a sharp rebuke from Erimenes for his clumsiness. The major drifts and mines lay downslope, which meant the *Zr'gsz* garrisons and patrols of Nevrymin still loyal to the lizard folk would be concentrated in that direction.

As he scrambled from the pit something flew up into his face. He struck at it, thinking it a bat or nocturnal insect. To his amazement it flashed by and continued soundlessly upward, losing itself in blackness.

He heard Snowbuck chuckle softly.

"Skystone," the youth explained, then pushed on, using the dark brush that grew upslope to pull himself along.

"How in hell's name does the stuff ever get deposited?" Fost grumbled.

"I believe," answered Erimenes, "that it is a component of the magma extruded through the crater to become lava. As it flows down the mountain it rises to the top of the flow. Yet it adheres to the heavier stuff of common lava, which holds it down until it cools."

"Is that true?"

"How should I know?"

The moons poked up into the eastern sky. Both were past full. The light made it easier for any pursuers to see them but also made the going quicker. As they put what Fost's experience told him were miles between them and the Watchers' former village, the courier began to believe they might actually escape.

Then a figure detached itself from a tall, dead tree at the top of a razorback of lava and stood looking down into their surprised faces.

"So," said Sternbow, "my own son." He shook his head. "I hardly believe it."

Snowbuck scrambled the rest of the way up the slope to stand beside his father. More figures rose out of the wasteland, drawn bows in hand. Fost groaned. He was already thoroughly sick of this routine.

"I must speak with you, Father," Snowbuck said. "As man to man."

Sternbow looked around. Fost wondered where his faithful shadow was. Sternbow's words told him.

"Fairspeaker became separated from the party as we made our way to wait for you," he mumbled. "He should hear this."

"No!" Snowbuck's voice rang loud and clear above the volcano's growl. "He should *not* hear! Or are you no longer capable of listening for yourself, Father?"

Sternbow raised his hand to strike his son. Snowbuck held his ground. The tall forester chieftain let his hand fall to his side and seemed to shrink an inch.

"It may be that I cannot." His words were barely audible. "But it is high time I learned once more. Speak."

"Father, the . . ." he began but was interrupted by a cry from behind.

"Snowbuck!"

At the sound of Fairspeaker's voice, Snowbuck spun, hand dropping to sword hilt. He was half around when an arrow struck him in the left temple. Snowbuck jerked, then dropped to one knee.

"F-father," he said. His eyes rolled up into his head and he fell, lifeless.

Sternbow uttered a ringing cry of rage and grief and desolation. For a moment, the mountain fell silent as if to mark the enormity of his loss. He raised his eyes to Fairspeaker on a hill fifty feet away, a bow held loosely in his hand.

"I came just in time, great Sternbow." The young man sounded out of breath. "Another instant and the faithless young pup would've . . ."

Sternbow tore forth his broadsword and flung it at Fairspeaker.

Paralyzed with disbelief, Fairspeaker stood and watched as the blade spun toward him. The whine of split air was loud in the awful silence.

At the last possible instant, Fairspeaker flung himself to the side. He was too late to save himself completely. The sword tip raked his cheek, opening it to the bone. He screamed shrilly and fell from view. As he did, a line of flame crackled from Moriana's fingertips. A bush burst into orange flame where he had stood.

Across the black nightland Nevrymin faced one another across drawn swords and levelled spears. A few Watchers stood with hands high, dazed by the course of events. One by one each turned until all faced Sternbow.

The tall man knelt on the unyielding stone, cradling his son's head in his lap. A thin trickle of blood, black in the moonlight, ran from the wound and stained his breeches. Slowly, he raised his head. He had aged ten years in one tragic minute.

"After him!" he cried. "Hunt down the traitor Fair-speaker!"

With a roar, the Nevrymin turned from confronting one another and raced off into the night. That was an order most of them had longed to hear for some time.

Sternbow rose to face Fost and Moriana.

"Apologies will not suffice for what I've done, so I will not offer them," he said. He composed himself visibly. "You are free to go. I wish I could call you friends, but I will not presume. O Snowbuck, you saw far more clearly than I!" His head slumped to his chest and tears flowed down his bearded cheeks, bright silver rivulets in the moonlight.

"What of you?" asked Moriana, reaching out to touch the man's quaking shoulder.

He raised his head with effort.

"Fairspeaker was—is—not alone in feeling that our interests and those of the Hissers lie along the same path. But I think the men of my band will be with me. We'll organize the surviving Watchers, wage hit-and-run war against the mines. It's a kind of war my men understand. The Watchers should learn quickly enough."

He looked down at his son's body. Snowbuck lay partially on his side with one arm crossed over his breast and the fingers of his right hand still grasping the hilt of his half-drawn sword.

"Now I will hunt the murderer of my only son. Or one of them—the real guilt rests on these shoulders!"

There was nothing more to say. Fost and Moriana started away. They hadn't picked a dozen cautious steps across the razorback when Sternbow's voice halted them. He walked to them, moving effortlessly over the uneven ground.

"I have something to give you, and something to ask."

"Very well," said Moriana.

"First, I beg you travel to the Tree and tell the King in Nevrym what has befallen Snowbuck. The Forest Maiden alone knows what schemes the People and their sympathizers have set in motion against Grimpeace, for he is known as a foe of the Dark Ones. That was why he agreed to ally with you, Princess, because you offered the best chance of thwarting your sister's aim to return the Realm to the Night Lords. Friendship with the People was not the way of Grimpeace, though I allowed Fairspeaker to convince me otherwise, to my eternal grief."

"It shall be done, Lord Sternbow," Moriana promised. "But I fear we will be a long time reaching the Tree afoot."

Sternbow almost smiled.

"Perhaps not. Don't forget the famed Longstrider accompanies you." His eyes turned somber once more. "But what I have to give you may solve that difficulty." He reached to the broad leather belt circling his waist and removed a heavy bag of sewn doe hide. "Uncut gems. My share of the pay from the Hissers. They should buy you adequate mounts."

Moriana's eyes widened. By the pouch's heft, the stone would buy adequate mounts for a squadron of cavalry.

"But we can't take it all!"

"You must." He slashed his hand through air in a peremptory gesture. "I couldn't touch those stones again, no matter how precious they are. Accept them or I shall drop them into Omizantrim's mouth."

"You are gracious, milord."

He bowed tautly.

"Farewell, milady, Longstrider. We shall not meet again."

A few days north of the frozen flows sprouting like tentacles from the ancient mountain, they came upon a breeding kennel. The land here in the Marchant Highlands ran to slow rises and wide dales like a gentle ocean swell made solid. The land was green and gravid and exploding with summer. They passed bawling herds of horncattle, lowing sheep and goats and flocks of tame striped antelope that fled at the strangers' approach. The country folk were close-mouthed and grim. The shadow of Omizantrim lay long across their land. And many was the morning in which the beauty of a clear blue sky was marred by silent black flights of raft, flying south in formations like migratory birds. At first, Fost and Moriana took cover whenever *Zr'gsz* skyrafts appeared overhead. They soon gave it up as unnecessary. None they had seen showed the slightest interest in what went on below. They did keep alert for any sign of rafts from Omizantrim, or any that searched rather than simply travelled from one place to another.

"What's your pleasure?" The kennel master was a long, lean sort with a face consisting mostly of wrinkles. Faded carroty hair had been trimmed to an alarming scalplock cresting his sunburned pate. A small white clay pipe hung from one lip as if glued there, emitting occasional wisps of blue smoke.

He didn't seem overly suspicious of the trailworn and heavily armed strangers who had trudged up the side road from the highway. But to read any expression on the face was beyond Fost's ability.

"We seek mounts," said Moriana.

The man stiffened. Her travels outside the City, often as a hunted fugitive, had rendered her broadminded in her dealings with both commoners and groundlings; the man she loved was both. But sometimes she slipped into the royal hauteur to which she had been raised. Fost saw it had an adverse effect this time. The face remained unreadable, but the man's posture spoke eloquently.

"Freeman, we grow tired of faring afoot. We asked directions of a yeoman driving a wagon down on the highroad. He told us you raised strong steeds." Fost hoped the fat, squinty-eyed peasant had been telling the truth. He knew about all there was to know about sled dogs but had little knowledge of riding dogs.

The breeder relaxed.

"This way," he said. He paused to scoop a small pouch from the nail where it hung by a red porch post, then stepped down onto the turf and led them around back of the house.

A wild clamor greeted them. Dogs of all descriptions and colors, stocky war mounts and whippet-lean racers, black and white and roan and brindle and spotted all penned in wooden kennels, flung themselves against the fence and barked madly. The breeder whistled. A towheaded urchin of indeterminate sex appeared from a shack at the end of the long aisle between the cages, wiping his hands on a dun smock.

"Master?"

The kennel master turned to them, asking "What kinda dogs you want?"

Fost pretended to study the caged beasts. His eyes left the animals and scanned the surrounding countryside. The fields, like the road, were well tended and dotted with the bulks of grazing horncows ambling over flower-decked pasture. He saw no sign of humans other than the kennel master and the urchin. That was strange; it took a goodly number of workers to keep a dog farm operational. The best maintained their own herds of cattle to feed the dogs, both to keep down prices and to control precisely the type and quality of feed the animals received. That took hands —and there were only two in view.

"It's hard times since the mountain upchucked this

spring," the kennel master drawled. "Then them lizards came through here bound down for Wirix, or so 'twas said. 'Tain't natural, those lizards. Didn't do nary a bit of lootin' and rapin'. Not a bit of it." He dug a handful of green herb from the pouch and stuffed it into the bowl of his pipe. "Then them flyin' thingies started floatin' overhead all the time. The hands got spooked. I don't mind admittin' I did, too."

He smoothed his scalplock with a gnarly hand. The urchin stood by, tugging at the hem of its smock. Her smock, Fost judged, by the small peaks in the front of the dilapidated garment.

The breeder looked around at the cages of yammering dogs. Shiny beads of moisture appeared at the outer corners of his eyes.

"You folks come by at the right time. I'm sellin' out." He made a gesture encompassing the whole establishment, dogs, dwellings, fields, cattle and urchin. "Choose what you want and name a price. I'm movin' cross the river into the Empire. Cain't take more'n some good bitches and dogs for breedin' stock. Dogs is damn trickish to move overland."

Fost stared in open amazement. The generosity of Realm dog breeders was legendary, along with that of Tolvirot bankers, Medurimin tax collectors and clerics from Kolnith. If a successful kennel master—and there was little doubt this wrinkled man was successful, judging by the size of his spread and the way it was kept—was selling out at a loss, then the threat of the *Zr'gsz* was already making itself felt.

They'd made their journey to this point as idyllic as possible, a long holiday of riding through beautiful summer lands by day and making love all night with passion and skill, as if each time was the last. Both knew that the inevitable last time might arrive soon, too soon. Though they scarcely slept, each morning they rose refreshed and filled with energy. To Fost this was little short of miraculous. In emergencies he could go from sound sleep to alertness in a single heartbeat. But without danger to goad him, he generally took long minutes to come even half awake. The fact made it curious he had chosen the life of a courier, which called for agonizingly early rising. Every morning of his life on the road, Fost complained bitterly of the necessity of arising before noon to his companions or dogs, depending on who would listen.

They picked their way down from the Central Massif and curved northeast around the Mystic Mountains. No longer did they see *Zr'gsz* skyrafts. All traffic flowed south from Thendrun. With the skyrafts went their last barrier to enjoyment.

Or almost the last. With the leisure of hours on the road and lazy hours in camp after dinner and before lovemaking, the two spirits resumed their feuding. Only threats to tie them to long ropes and drag them behind the riding dogs ever shut them up, and that only for a while.

The kennel master hadn't lied about the prices he asked for his stock. For forty klenor he provided them with two mounts of their choice and complete tack. He even skirted the subject of selling the urchin, too, but Fost evinced complete disinterest, to what seemed the girl's disappointment. By a miracle, Erimenes said not one lewd word. In fact, both genies sensed the uneasiness of the breeder and the girl and kept silent to avoid panicking them.

Fost and Moriana didn't actually benefit from the bargain. The smallest stone Sternbow had given them was worth easily ten times the price the breeder quoted. The two had between them only a few rusty sipans in the bottom of Erimenes's satchel. Finally, Moriana chose a rock at random and tossed it to the kennel master as payment. The man's amazement was so great his pipe dropped from his lips and threatened to kindle the sawdust between the rows of cages. The pair had mounted and quickly departed before he could press the urchin on them.

Moriana had picked a stocky red dog with a short, smooth fur and heavy tail for Fost. The animal wasn't quite a war mount but had the breadth of jaw to fight and looked durable enough to bear Fost's weight over a long haul. Also, it was an intelligent beast able to compensate for its rider's lack of experience. In travelling with Jennas, Fost had grown expert in riding the immense war bears of the Ust-alayakits, but riding a bear and riding a dog differed as much as flying a Sky City eagle and piloting a *Zr'gsz* skyraft.

For herself, Moriana chose a gray courser, huge of chest and narrow of skull, that could run down an antelope in a sprint. The beast was utterly neurotic, fearful of anything that lived except when it grew hungry enough to hunt, at which times it used its two-inch fangs to good effect. Moriana seemed able to gentle the creature, though it was prone to emit a shrill, unnerving keening for no apparent reason.

The mounts proved sound and the travellers made good time. Though time did not matter for them on this journey.

At least, they pretended it didn't.

Erimenes.

By unspoken agreement, Fost and Moriana had neither past nor future for the duration of their ride. But Fost privately broke the pact. There was a question that nagged him day and night and refused to go away.

The night they camped in sight of the dark line of the Great Nevrym Forest, Fost lay awake after Moriana drifted to sleep, sweetly exhausted from a bout of passionate lovemaking. For a time he watched the constellations perform their slow, circular dance overhead. Then he slipped into the forest. The scattered shunnak trees loomed above the mighty black anhak comprising most of the forest. There were few of the giants; had they grown close together they'd have prevented any light from reaching the thickly clustered trees below.

"Erimenes?" he called softly.

"Are you fishing for compliments, my boy? Your performance was adequate, I'd say. What it lacked in finesse, it certainly made up for in vigor."

Fost sighed. Moriana slept a dozen paces away and was unlikely to be awakened. What he wanted from the garrulous genie might take a long time to extract—if it could be done at all.

"Why?"

"Why what? Why was the Universe created? Why does evil exist in the world? Why did—"

"No," Fost said sharply, cutting off the spirit's diatribe before it gained too much momentum. "Why did you help us when the Hissers held us captive? Or any other time, for that matter. Of late, you've been assisting more and more and hardly ever pulling your stunt of trying to get me killed in some grisly fashion."

"It is out of the goodness of my soul. I would say heart, but alas! that noble organ has been defunct these fourteen centuries. Besides, I'm often moved to pity by the bumbling way in which you approach life. I wish to help you as a child wishes to help a sadly uncoordinated pup learn to walk without falling over."

Fost made a rude sound.

"You and Istu are equally noted for philanthropy," he said. "And I've caught you at last! You've been dead thirteen hundred and ninety-nine years, *not* fourteen hundred. Ha!"

Erimenes uttered a weary sigh.

"I have, since coming to know you, celebrated yet another anniversary of my tragic demise. Thus I came round to the fourteen hundredth year of my death. I wish I could remain thirteen hundred ninety-nine—or properly, fifteen hundred and seven—indefinitely."

Fost ground his teeth together. Trying to pin down the shade when he wanted to be contrary was like trying to grab an eel. The more so now when he couldn't yell at the spirit without waking Moriana.

"Answer the question, you old dotard," Ziore said from Moriana's pack laying nearby.

Erimenes sniffed and said haughtily, "I did."

Moving quietly and carefully, Fost picked up Erimenes's jug.

"Erimenes, I want a straight answer from you. And I want it now."

"Or what?"

"I want an answer, Erimenes." Something in his tone convinced the spirit that the time had passed for light banter.

"Very well. I'm helping you because I want you to win. That should be obvious to even you."

Fost began bouncing the jug up and down on his palm. Erimenes made choking sounds.

"Stop it! That horrid motion nauseates me."

"Tell the truth."

"I am, you fool!" Erimenes's voice lost its normal nasal overtones. Fost had never heard him speak this way before. "Damn it, can't you see why I'm helping you? Before, it was all a game to me. No matter what happened, *I* couldn't get hurt. And I was the only one who mattered." Silence. "Are you surprised?"

"Hardly." He set down the satchel and braced himself against a sturdy tree trunk.

"But that was before. Before I started to detect the black hand—or claw—of the Dark Ones in events surrounding you. By the time we left the Ramparts, I was starting to fear that what we faced imperiled not only humanity but *me*.

"And when Istu was released, there was no longer any doubt. The Dark Ones are mighty, and their malice is as infinite and ineffable as they are mysterious and unknowable. They could snuff me as you'd snuff out a candle flame. Or . . . or make me wish throughout endless ages for true death.

"No, my young friend, I cannot remain neutral in this War of Powers."

"Why don't you join the other side?"

"Really, I thought you held me in higher esteem." Fost's brows shot up. The spirit sounded genuinely hurt. "I am human, or was once. And unlike Fairspeaker and his ilk, I don't delude myself as to what the Dark Ones intend for humanity."

Fost shuddered thinking about all he'd seen, all that was promised.

"To purge the Realm as they did the Sky City."

"No." Fost stared at the satchel in surprise at the contradiction. "That is an aim, but far from paramount. They would purge humankind from the *world,* Fost. From the Universe, from every plane of being, if the theories espoused in my day of the multiplicity of planes of existence hold any truth. They intend no less than to return the Universe—Universes—to the primal Dark from which they sprang."

"I see," Fost said after a while. His voice almost squeaked through his constricted throat.

"So. Now that we've dealt with theology and cosmology, why don't you prod that lusty wench over there feigning sleep with your finger and rouse her so that you can prod her with a much more gratifying implement?"

Fost shook his head. In some ways, Erimenes hadn't changed. He had to admit being glad. To himself, at least.

Then Moriana rolled over, groping for him. He quickly slipped next to her and followed the sage's advice. After what Erimenes had said about the Dark Ones, this seemed more important than ever.

They rode boldly into the forest of Great Nevrym. The foresters were suspicious of unwanted guests, but Fost was known as a friend and there was little to gain trying to enter by stealth. Their mission was sad and aboveboard.

They were two days in when the foresters showed themselves. Riding through the forest was like moving along the nave of an enormous cathedral with the shunnak rising a hundred stories above their heads. Birds sang, squirrels chased one another along cool green avenues and at night scarlet tree toads a yard long crawled from their holes in the boles of the black anhak to trill timeless songs.

Fost had been aware of being followed, which told him no more than that the foresters didn't care if he sensed their presence. If they didn't want travellers to suspect they were near, it would take Ziore's perceptions to discover them.

They followed a broad avenue between the tall anhak. It seemed no different from any that ran through the wood, but by various subtle signs Fost knew this for the road to the Tree.

A young man rose from a bush and stepped into their path. He smiled, which relieved Fost.

"Good day," he said. "Seldom are these ways travelled by those who use feet other than their own."

"Good day, Darkwood. I apologize for the princess and myself for riding mounts in these woods. But we have a message too urgent to bear on foot."

"You, the Longstrider, say that? Oho, that's rich, indeed." He wiped his eyes from laughter. "But you must know, Longstrider who sees fit to clutter his good and proper name with the graceless noise *Fost,* that you'd be ever welcome to go upon these ways in any manner you choose."

"Thank you, Darkwood."

Moriana's gray was tossing its narrow head and whimpering. Feeling that she had to assert her part in these slow proceedings, Moriana shook back her hair and said, "You may carry along the tidings that Moriana Etuul, Queen in exile of the City in the Sky, has arrived on a visit of state to the King of Nevrym."

"Oh, indeed. Is that the way it is now?" Green eyes twinkled. He had seemed a young man at first but reading the fine wrinkles in his face covinced Moriana he was past forty. "But that's something of a problem, Your Majesty. The man you seek does not exist."

"But I . . ." She stopped in confusion, then organized her thoughts. "I don't understand."

The forest echoed with Darkwood's laughter. Fost grinned but kept an eye on her in case she decided to try to chastise this presumptuous groundling for laughing at her.

"Ah, forgive me," Darkwood said. This time he pulled a scarf from a hidden pocket to dab tears from his eyes. "But you see, Majesty, there is no King of Nevrym—unless you refer to the Tree, Paramount, Lord of All Trees. But the idea that a *man* could rule a forest, ah, you outwoods folk are droll. The man you seek is Grimpeace, ferocious to foe and fair to friend—and king *in* Nevrym, never *of* it."

Moriana smiled with visible effort.

"Please be so good as to guide us, Sir Darkwood."

"So I shall. For none is allowed to travel the ways of the wood unescorted." He smiled approvingly when she didn't try to claim they had done just that in the last few days.

They rode for several more hours. Still smarting from her humiliation over the matter of who was king of what, Moriana kept her twitchy greyhound at a long-limbed trot for the first several miles until it became apparent that the ever-smiling Darkwood kept up the rapid pace without breaking into a sweat.

"Great Ultimate, Fost, how did you ever manage to outrun a party of these folk?" she asked as she reined in the gray dog to a walk.

"I was young and in good shape," he said, slowing to match her pace. "Also I was scared cross-eyed."

By design, the road took an abrupt turn around a dense stand of anhak so that the clearing in which the Tree stood appeared suddenly to view. Moriana gasped at the sight of it. Though he'd seen it before, Fost felt his heart clutch convulsively in wonder at the sight.

This was obviously the Tree. Next to it everything else was shrubbery.

It rose over a thousand feet in the clear forest air, a giant conifer with dark green needles and a red trunk. Their master of all trees was more than the symbol and pride of the Nevrymin, it was the seat of their government as well. For hundreds of feet its bole was honeycombed with entrances, passageways, small apartments and halls as grand as the Audience Hall of the Palace of Winds. The many tiers were a history of the foresters carved in wood. The Tree still grew and every generation a new level had to be hollowed out. Stairways and catwalks spiraled around the massive trunk. When Moriana realized that the antlike figures moving along them were people, wonder flooded back anew.

"Well, my friends," said Grimpeace around a mouthful of good venison. "Where do you go now?"

Fost and Moriana traded glances. It was a good question. Oddly, they hadn't discussed it on the way from Omizantrim. They had barely thought of it.

Each sensed that the life they'd known before had perished. The world had become a strange and awful place, a battleground for forces beyond their comprehension. Even if both survived, which seemed increasingly unlikely, they little knew what kind of world they'd be living in when this new War of Powers came to a resolution.

If it ever did.

The message delivered, Fost and Moriana sat looking at one another on their side of a well-laden banquet table. It was a board fit for the Tree, forty feet long and eight across. No knife scars defaced it, as was customary at feasting tables, and spilled wine was hastily mopped up by attendants. In return, the wood, shining with a luminous luster, surpassed in beauty any piece of furniture Moriana had seen. Like the capital of the foresters, it was carved from the living wood of the Tree and kept alive by special magics known only to the Nevrymin.

"Where are we going?" Fost asked. Now that the news of the Hissers' defection was delivered, he didn't know the answer.

Moriana did.

"High Medurim," she answered.

# CHAPTER TEN

"Whoa!" cried Fost, motioning for a halt. Moriana's greyhound squealed in terror as she reined in harshly. In a single fluid movement, she dropped her bow from shoulder to hand and pulled an arrow from her quiver. By the side of the track, Darkwood stood looking on with his habitual smile. He didn't unsling his bow.

Heart racing, Moriana followed Fost's gesture. She expected enemies. What she saw made her heart leap, but not from fear.

A unicorn stag stood on a knoll to the left of the path. The trees grew sparsely there. The great beast stood between two of the black, gnarled anhaks and gazed down at the travellers, one forefoot raised.

Something in the animal's attitude told Moriana the posture was not that of a creature poised for flight. It regarded them with disdain, its eyes huge and amber, set in the capacious skull on either side of the single straight horn. Its hide was a glossy chestnut and its throat and wide chest glowed silvery. A long tail ending in a tuft of auburn was held curled over the animal's back like a manticore's sting.

"Will you shoot, Lady?" Darkwood's smile had taken on the tilt they had come to associate with some private jest. "Their flesh is a delicacy beyond compare."

Moriana looked at Fost. His mouth was compressed in a curious fashion as if he tried to suppress a grin. Erimenes swayed at his side.

"Shoot!" the genie urged, his eyes gleaming with spectral bloodlust.

"No," begged Ziore, floating beside Moriana. "He's too magnificent!"

Moriana lowered her bow, relaxed the string and slid the arrow back into its sheath.

"She's right. I could only slay such a beast if I starved. Never for sport."

As if it heard her words, the stag dipped its horn once and vanished as abruptly as it had appeared.

"You chose wisely, Highness," said Darkwood. "You'd never have hit him."

Moriana's mouth tightened. This groundling made jokes at her expense, and she didn't care for it.

"You forget I'm Skyborn," she informed him haughtily.

"Oh, I know that, Lady, and I know well you could put three arrows out of three through my chest with that monster bow of yours. But skill counts for more in hunting the Nevrym unicorn than cleverness of hand and eye. You'd've missed him, this I know." His grin widened. "Even as I'd know you'd next have seen him charging from that clump of blackleaf." He pointed at a clump of shrubbery twenty yards distant. "With his head down and blood in his eye. And I know a unicorn's fighting horn will pierce a quarter inch of the finest North Keep plate as if it were parchment."

Moriana started to protest. Thinking she'd suffered enough, Fost put in, "They're intelligent. And very cunning."

"Intelligent? Nonsense. They're mere beasts." Erimenes sniffed his contempt for such a notion.

"And are the war eagles of the Sky City mere birds?" Darkwood shook his head. "No, my friend. You've now met the third part of the triumvirate that rules Nevrym."

"The third?" asked Moriana, intrigued despite her anger.

"We're another." Darkwood doffed his triangular cap and bowed. "The last is the trees, of course."

"The *trees?*" Moriana scoffed.

"He's telling the truth. Do you think you could find your way to the Tree again unaided?"

"Of course." She glared at Fost. She was a veteran warrior. Once she'd passed over terrain she knew it by heart.

"Of course," agreed Darkwood, in an infuriating imitation of the woman's voice, "provided your intentions were peaceful toward the forest and its various inhabitants. Were they otherwise, your party might wander lost until you died of starvation." He smoothed straw-colored hair back from his forehead. "Only foresters can find their way unimpeded by the trees' magic. And where our allies of wood don't want us, we generally don't go."

"But your people are well armed and prepared for invasion." Moriana was genuinely puzzled. The many-tiered keep carved into the heart of the Tree was meant to serve as a fortress, its outer walls dotted with arrow slits and its interior honeycombed by well-stocked caches of emergency stores. Most of the humbler dwellings of the foresters were built like birds' nests high up and secure in the embrace of anhak limbs, reachable only by ladders.

"It's not unknown for Nevrymin to settle their little differences by force of arms. We are individualists at heart and not prone to taking commands of others." Reminded of this, Moriana recalled that most battles the Nevrymin fought were internecine. That was the key to the seeming puzzle of a jovial king in Nevrym named Grimpeace.

It had been Fost who explained this to her.

"He's a friendly man, but he's friendly because we come as friends. He earned his name by the way he imposed order in Nevrym when he acceded to the Tree twenty-three years ago. The Nevrymin all respect the Tree, but they're divided into factions as antagonistic and rivalry-ridden as tenement blocks in The Teeming. North Nevrymin, Central Nevrymin, Eastcreekers, Coastrunners, a score in all. Few of the factions were inclined to pay much heed to the authority of a boy who'd scarcely started to sprout his first growth of beard. They learned what the young king offered was a grim peace, indeed. Since then, banditry and sectional strife in Nevrym have been at an all-time low."

"Then, too," said Darkwood, all trace of mirth vanished from his blue eyes, "it isn't unknown for Nevrymin to guide outwoods foes along these ways in defiance of tradition and the trees."

"What kind of man would do that?" asked Ziore in wonder. Her empathy gave her an appreciation keener even than Fost's of the sacred nature of the compact between men and beasts and trees.

"You've met one, I fancy." Darkwood's voice turned winter cold. "Fairspeaker by name."

But not even the thought of Nevrymin breaking faith with their forest was enough to keep the summer in Darkwood's nature suppressed for long. He warmed and the skin around his eyes and mouth settled into well-worn smile lines.

"But the day's too lovely for talk of that, and we've leagues yet to travel before reaching the North Cape range." He set the cap on his head at a suitably jaunty angle and started off along the leaf-carpeted path.

"One question, my good man." Darkwood stopped and regarded Erimenes with his hands on hips. His grin hadn't been dented by the spirit's supercilious tone. "How do you know the flesh of the unicorn stag is succulent if your folk lack the gumption to hurt them."

The forester's cheer was the equal of even Erimenes at his most infuriating.

"My good ghost, from the height of your exalted years you must realize that any forest exists in a delicate balance," he said in the tone of one explaining a simple lesson to a dull student. "No single population can be allowed to grow unchecked. So we hunt the unicorn stag, and a most demanding sport it is." His smile showed prominent eyeteeth. "And they, of course, hunt us. We give them rare sport, too, or so I'm led to believe."

\* \* \*

Their reception at North Keep was less than cordial.

In response to five minutes' pounding on the twenty-foot-tall iron gates, first with Fost's fist and then with the pommel of his sword, a small peephole set four feet off the stone roadbed scraped open. A single bloodshot eye peered forth without any hint of friendliness.

"Go away," came the growl from within.

"We've come a long ways up the coast road," said Fost. "We're in need of food, baths, a good night's sleep. We're prepared to pay."

The latter phrase usually unlocked the domain of the dwarves. The dark maroon eye blinked once.

"We want nothing to do with your filthy money. The gate's shut for the night. Go away."

Fost's dog growled. Astride her sidestepping dog a few yards behind, Moriana tightened the grip on her reins. She didn't like the dwarf guard's tone any more than the dogs did.

"My good man, I suggest you open this gate immediately if you desire that your head should keep company with your shoulders. I am a guest of state and your rulers will be little pleased by your insolence to me."

"Who're you?" came the rude question, the eye swivelling to bear on her.

"I am Moriana Etuul, Queen in exile of the City in the Sky, and if you don't admit us at once . . ."

The eye withdrew but only to permit heavily bearded lips to appear and spit through the grill.

"*That* for you," said the eye, appearing again, "and for all decadent lordlings who oppress the people! And for their running dog lackeys, as well," he added for Fost's benefit. The peephole slammed shut.

As the clang reverberated down the valley, Fost thought Moriana's hair was about to start smouldering at the roots as Synalon's had done when she was angry.

"Why, that horrid upstart, that, that groundling! How *dare* he take that tone with me!"

"He's got three inches of iron and a foot of anhak between you and him," pointed out Fost. "That's how he dares."

"Small good that protection will do him when I loose my wrath upon him." She let reins fall and raised her hands.

"No, no, don't start flinging salamanders or deathspells or anything like that," Fost said quickly, waving his arms in hope of breaking of her concentration.

"And why not?" she demanded.

He pointed upward. Forty feet above the poorly kept road two grotesque figures squatted in alcoves set on either side of the gates. Spindly limbed with squinty eyes and oddly spurred elbows and knees, they regarded the travellers over ludicrously attenuated noses and mouths thrust out to form lipless tubes.

"And what might they be?" She eyed them with distaste.

"Old dwarven caricatures of true men," he said. "The mouths go to funnels in a room dug out of the rock. The dwarves keep a pot of lead bubbling by each in case applicants rejected for entry react the way you were about to."

Moriana dropped her hands to her sides.

"We'll have to find lodgings in the Outer Town. It's only a few miles away on the other side of the mountain."

"But it's getting dark!"

"All the more reason to start now."

When they got to the Outer Town they got some insight into the nature of the recent developments in the Realm. The moons hung high in the sky when they came around the tip of Northernmost, the mountain cradling the dwarvish citadel of North Keep. Built on a slate beach butting up against the western face of the mountain, the Outer Town was an odd conglomeration of black dwarf masonry, scattered cosmopolitan edifices of Imperial dome and column marble, prim Jorean geometry, pastel stuccoed Estil, and shantytown. The streets were paved with rubble and indifferently repaired. Though the dwarves ruled the Outer Town, it was primarily a place for the gangly Other Folk to stay while doing business. The dwarves weren't noted for their hospitality, though Fost had hoped they would invite Moriana to stay in their keep because of her royal status. For the most part, the Others entered North Keep solely to strike bargains and were ushered forth with varying degrees of politeness when the deals were done.

A smell of fish and less identifiable refuse hung in the pitted street in front of the inn Fost chose. A faded clapboard sign portrayed a flatfish grinning with drunken goggle-eyed delight.

"*The Happy Flounder*," Erimenes read as the pair dismounted and tied reins to a sagging hitchrail. "I believe they take fancifulness too far in naming these establishments."

The innkeeper was a young dwarf with a thready beard and a premature bald spot on the top of his head. He was skinny for a dwarf but had the usual protruding eyes. He examined his prospective guests with suspicion.

"What do you want?" he rapped. His prominent nose wrinkled.

"Lodgings for the night, possibly longer," Fost said hurriedly. Moriana was getting a dangerous glint in her eye. "But who knows? We may spend some time sightseeing in this quaint and hospitable town of yours."

Sarcasam was lost on the innkeeper, as it was on most dwarves.

"Vouchers?" he demanded, in a tone of bored antagonism.

Fost had no idea what the dwarf asked for and told him so.

"Well," the little man said, folding his arms across his chest and tilting his fringe beard disapprovingly upward. "I must accommodate you even if you can't pay, unless I want a drubbing from the damned militia, may their barracks roof fall on their pointed heads." He drummed blunt fingers on the counter and turned to peer through a door leading to a muddy yard in back. "I suppose there's room for you in the kennels."

"We haven't any vouchers, whatever they are," said Moriana, "but will you accept this as payment for room and meals?" She held up an emerald from the pouch Sternbow had given her.

The innkeep goggled more than usual. He snatched it away with deft fingers, held it to the dismal light of the guttering taper, scratched it along the table, and finally bit it.

"By the tunnels of Agift," he murmured. "I do believe it's real."

He pulled in a breath that swelled his barrel chest until Fost thought the jerkin would burst. He looked from the emerald to Moriana, and an avid light danced in his immense dwarf eyes. Then the glint faded and he expelled a heartfelt sigh.

"I cannot but tell you that a stone such as this would pay for my finest accommodations for a fortnight—possibly longer, depending on the water of the stone."

Moriana shrugged it off. The *Zr'gsz* had been generous paymasters. There were many more where this one came from.

"For however long, then. I doubt we'll stay more than a couple nights at most."

"I cannot change this with any currency you'd want to have." Sweat stood out on his high, broad forehead. It cost him great anguish to tell them this.

"Don't bother."

He came out from behind the counter, waddled to the door, stuck his head out into the noisome, muggy night. Nothing stirred in the streets except a fat yellow-striped tomcat roving in search of ship's rats on shore leave.

"You're strangers to North Keep," he accused.

"Not altogether," said Fost. His fingers played with his sword hilt. The publican's nervousness made him uneasy.

"But you don't know how things have stood in the dwarflands since the revolution, that much is clear."

"Revolution?"

"Of the proletariat. Since the Worker's Party seized power a year ago, the use of money and barter are outlawed. Outlanders are compelled by law to convert their negotiables into credit vouchers before dealing with dwarves."

"Who's head of state now?"

"Maanda Samilchut is the Party Chairman."

Fost frowned but said nothing.

"Normally I'd have to report your presence to the Militia headquarters on Exchange Square—er, pardon me, it's Liberation Plaza now. But, by your leave, I think I might overlook this procedure." Moriana nodded assent. The innkeeper sighed with relief and mopped his brow with a gray linen kerchief. "I take it you'd prefer accommodations aboveground, gentles?"

When the thick wood door of their second-floor room shut behind the now overly solicitous innkeeper, Fost dropped onto the low bed and broke out laughing.

"What's so funny?" asked Moriana, lowering herself more cautiously onto a bandy-legged stool.

" 'Maanda Samilchut is Party Chairman,' " he quoted. "Up till a year ago, North Keep was a republic; the President for Life was Maanda Samilchut. Before that it was a parliamentary democracy, and the Premier was Maanda Samilchut. And just before that, the dwarves had a constitutional monarchy, with, as self-crowned queen, Maanda Samilchut." He fell back across the bed and rubbed his eyes. "Need I go on? Dwarves have devilishly long lifespans."

Sitting as much at ease as he could on a chair built for someone with legs a quarter the length of his, Fost batted idly at the fly circling his head and studied the bust of Chairman Samilchut in its alcove on the wall.

"How much longer will they keep us waiting?" Moriana stopped pacing a groove in the worn stone floor long enough to ask.

"A while longer, I suspect. The folk we're dealing with are bureaucrats as well as dwarves, and both groups tend to have a cosmic sense of time."

Over by the wall the two satchels had been laid side by side so that Erimenes and Ziore could carry on their perpetual squabble in relatively soft voices. Though every now and then a voice rose in a crescendo of indignation, for the most part their quarreling blended in with the incessant murmur of North Keep.

The North Cape Mountains lacked the size of the Mystics or the Ramparts, but they were second to none in ruggedness. Taking the coast road along the western face of North Cape had spared Fost and Moriana from struggling through the sawtoothed range until the road forked inland to the southern gate of North Keep. Northernmost was the tallest mountain in the North Capes, home to that peculiar, industrious, delving, grasping race, the dwarves.

The dwarves were the miners and smiths of the Sundered Realm. Their metalwork, especially blades and armor, were renowned throughout the world. The Thailot were more skilful artificers, the Estil unsurpassed in civil engineering, but in matters involving stone or stone worked with the principle of fire to become metal, the dwarves were unexcelled.

No one knew where they came from. Some said they had lived in their mountains, which like them were short and craggy and inhospitable, when humans first arrived on the Southern Continent twenty-two thousand years before. Others claimed they predated the Hissers; still others maintained they were descended from a troupe of freaks imported to entertain a Northern Barbarian lord in the sixteenth century before the Human Era. So the stories went.

Their patron was Ungrid An, the dwarvish goddess, one of the few members of the Three and Twenty to belong to a particular race. She was a harsh, dour goddess personifying fortitude, determination and sheer hard labor. She was also goddess of political upheaval representing both repression and rebellion, which helped account for the odd political climate in North Keep.

Keep and mountain were actually inseparable. Like the Nevrymin, the dwarves made their capital inside the dominant physical feature of their domain, but unlike them they didn't work upward from ground level only. Over uncounted millennia the dwarves had burrowed deep into the roots of the mountains, some said for thousands of feet below the surface.

Fost started to rise to offer Moriana his stool. She motioned him back and went around the paper-strewn miniature desk and sat in the absent functionary's chair. Fost grinned, partly in acknowledgement of her small defiance and partly because she looked silly with her piquant face framed by her knees.

He turned to study the bust again. It had been carved recently. He could tell because Samilchut wore a severely cut tunic with a high buttoned collar. Last year at this time, her representations had been draped in a graceful toga that left one massive deltoid bare, in imitation of Jorean state garb.

Moriana started tapping her fingers on the desk. Fost allowed himself to focus on the spirits' debate.

"—obvious to anyone with the least knowledge of etiology that this couldn't possibly—"

"—piffle! That doctrine was decisively refuted by—"

He sighed and let the faraway sounds of thousands of dwarves at work in the bowels of the mountain, that strangely rhythmic pulse of North Keep, drown them out again. Their argument grew more and more abstruse with each passing day. If they followed their usual pattern, in a short while they'd degenerate to name calling and, with luck, fall into silent sulking for a blessed interval until one or the other said something and started the argument afresh.

"Ahem."

Fost jumped, blinking away the drowsiness that had been coming on him. The obvious target of the guttural throat clearing sat behind the desk holding steepled fingers to her lips.

"You certainly took your time," Moriana said to the stumpy woman in the shapeless black gown who stood glowering at her from the office doorway. "You have a favorable reply for us, I trust?"

A smile shoved up the tips of the official's thin, dark moustache. Inwardly Fost groaned. All too well he recognized the unpleasant triumph of a bureaucrat presented with the opportunity to put the dagger to a member of the public displaying inadequate respect for the nobility of the petty functionary's calling. If Moriana read the same message she showed no sign. Given her background, Fost doubted she did.

"No." She had a fine baritone, Fost noted. "Worker Samilchut has no time to spend on discarded royalty—or self-proclaimed royalty—who try to disturb the peace of North Keep with bizarre tales and schemes."

"She won't even talk with us?" Moriana stared in disbelief.

"Not at all." The official consulted the sheaf of papers in her hand. "Further, I must advise you that even if all you claim is true, you can still expect no help from the dwarves. For we sympathize with the so-called Dark Ones, as we do with all those who rise up to cast off the yoke of feudal oppression."

She snapped her fingers to summon guards to escort the

visitors out. Moriana was too stunned for words, which was probably fortunate. Fost took her by the arm, helped her from the chair and led her past the smirking official into the corridor.

Both had to bend down almost double to follow their escorts, militiamen in brown corslets topped by flat-bottomed iron hats resembling inverted pie plates. Each guard carried a lead-tipped cudgel in one hand and a lantern in the other, with short-hafted throwing hammers at their belts. Dwarves hurrying in the opposite direction either flattened against the walls or backpedalled until they came to a cross corridor they could pop into.

Fost and Moriana stood blinking in brilliant sunlight as the massive iron western gate slammed shut behind them. Fost yawned, gazing out over the Outer Town and the oily gray heaving of the North Cape harbor. With the hooked tip of the Cape itself shielding the bay to north and east, and the added protection of a long stone breakwater projecting south from the rocky, gull-decked headland, the harbor should have provided decent anchorage. It didn't. The breakwater was too short and too low, disappearing completely just before high tide each day. After a southwesterly gale, the dwarves made handy sums dragging ships off the stone docks and refurbishing staved-in hulls. Fost suspected the arrangement wasn't exactly coincidental.

At the moment, a dozen craft chanced the unseasonal southeasterly blow. Largest was a lethal and lean wardromon flying the red and black flag of the Tolviroth Maritime Guaranty company.

"If," Moriana said, speaking with the slow deliberation of anger, "if and when I am restored to my throne and powers, I will come back to this North Keep and repay the dwarves for their friendliness and hospitality. By pulling their damn mountain down around their hairy ears!"

"No, you won't," Fost said louder than he intended.

"What did you say?" she snapped.

With that look in her eyes, his only defense was the truth.

"I said you'll do no such thing. Even if you—and humankind—loses this new War of Powers, life in North Keep will go on pretty much as always. Forever, if the Vridzish have any sense. Northernmost is a fortress no amount of mining, bombarding or ramming will bring down. The dwarves can and will fight for every inch of every tunnel with the ferocity of a cornered weasel. In the days of the Barbarian Dynasty, somebody estimated that there were more miles of passageway in their Keep than there were miles of Realm roads on the entire continent. They go down for *miles*.

"And I'd think even the Hissers' pet Demon would think twice about going down too far in the shafts of Northernmost Mountain. There are things lurking in the roots of these mountains that are only a little younger than the planet. Some of the things living there the dwarves made peace with; others they keep at bay with sheer ferocity and arts not even you can guess at. If they get loose aboveground, not even the Hissers are going to want the Realm.

"Other than that, I'd imagine you can just stroll in and take over anytime you please."

"Quite impressive," complimented Erimenes. "You display hitherto unsuspected depths of erudition."

Fost had the uncomfortable feeling Moriana was trying to decide whether to cinder him or merely turn him into a newt. A gull wheeled overhead, crying down mockery on both man and dwarf. Abruptly, Moriana laughed.

"Come along," she said, grabbing Fost's arm. "Let's get back to the inn before dark. I'm tired of watching the proletarian regime in action."

The gradually opening door brought Fost awake with all senses wire-taut. A greenish dawnlight spilled across the floor from the partially shuttered window. Outside, a handcart creaked and thumped over the potholes in the street.

A hesitant footfall sounded; another. Fost lay still, forcing himself to breathe with the metronomic regularity of a sleeper, while he mentally estimated distances. In a leap he came to his feet, broadsword snatched from the scabbard hung at the bed's headpost.

"Eek!" The innkeeper cringed back against the doorpost, eyes popping, trying to pull his head into the collar of his jerkin. He looked like a frightened turtle. "P-please, gentles. I meant no harm!"

Fost became acutely aware that he stood naked in the middle of the floor menacing a three-foot dwarf with a sword nearly as long as the dwarf. Moriana stirred on the bed, wondering drowsily why her nude body was so precipitately uncovered.

"Fost, what's—oh!"

His initial fear dissolved into embarrassment. He resorted to the old masculine position: blustering rage.

"What do you mean by this, sneaking into our rooms? Come to murder us in our beds, no doubt!"

If the dwarf shook any harder, pieces of his body would come rattling to the floor.

"No, no!" he moaned.

"Aha! You voyeuristic scoundrel! Come to peep at the Princess Moriana in her nakedness, then, are you?"

"But the princess is so skinny and malproportioned, gentle sir. Why would I do that?"

Moriana cleared her throat. The conversation was clearly out of control.

"Just what is it you want, innkeeper?" she asked, sitting and making no effort to cover herself.

The dwarf glanced at Fost, who was still standing with sword menacingly pointed, then made the effort to calm himself.

"It's the militia. They're searching all over town. You must flee at once."

"But why? What do they want from us?"

"Because of the news," the dwarf choked out. *"The Sky City has stopped!"*

# CHAPTER ELEVEN

The ship sang. The lyre sang harmony.

Soprano sang the rigging, squeaking on the blocks, sighing in the warm west wind. Bass sang the hull, moaning and cracking as seams opened and closed to the play of the sea. High sang the lyre, as silver and fleeting and lonely as the cries of seabirds. And low sang the lyre in bell-shaped tones. Standing by the starboard rail with Moriana at his side, Fost thought he'd never heard a sweeter sound or one sadder.

The song dwindled and became one with the past. Fost and Moriana looked up at the ship's captain, who had folded his unlikely body between two crenellations of the stout forecastle looming over the deck. He smiled and inclined his head.

"It was Jirre herself who taught me to play," he said.

Moriana turned questioningly to Fost. He answered with a silent shrug. That the captain of the ship Wyvern was mad was indisputable. But knowing him as he did, Fost couldn't be wholly convinced he wasn't telling the truth.

Five days ago Fost's brain had reeled in incredulity at the innkeeper's tidings: the Sky City had stopped. *Impossible!* was his first reaction. The City had not simply kept immutably to following the Great Quincunx for all Fost's relatively short life, it had done so since before even humans had seized the City from its rightful owners eight thousand years ago. It had done so for two thousand years of the Hissers' tenure, since the end of the War of Powers when Felarod had confined the once free-floating City to its pattern above the center of the continent. . . .

Since the War of Powers not even the Hissers had been able to alter the City's course. Since the binding of Istu.

But Istu was no longer bound.

The word had come first to the Outer Town courtesy of a Wirixer factor who lived in a sprawling marble pile built during the occupation by the Northern Barbarians. The Wirixers had a sorcerous communications network, as did the Sky Citizens, though the Sky City had had no direct representative in North Keep for several years. The news that the City had come to a halt in the air after passing over Wirix soon spread to the Keep itself. The reaction was immediate.

The grapevine hummed with news that Chairman Samilchut was drafting an offer of alliance to be transmitted to the *Zr'gsz,* though how it was to be sent was still uncertain. The Wirixer wasn't going to do it, not while his home city was besieged by an army of the Fallen Ones. While it was quite true, as Fost said, that even with Istu on their side the Hissers would take years to reduce North Keep, Samilchut deemed it wise to try to get on the good side of a power that could stop the ten-thousand-year progress of the City in the Sky. The fact that she would be a long time losing didn't exactly encourage the dictator to seek war.

It took no great deductive powers to realize that the former ruler of the Sky City, onetime ally of the Fallen Ones, might make a nice gift for North Keep's chairman to send the People as a token of her friendship. Fost and Moriana had found themselves shivering in the wet dawn wind on the swaybacked docks of the Outer Town, wondering how they were going to reach the ships anchored out in the harbor.

Teeth chattering, Fost eyed the ships. Apparently no one left small boats moored at the dock overnight and whatever boatmen plied the harbor were still in bed on this bleak morning. He wondered if they could swim out with their dogs to one of the vessels. He and Jennas had escaped Tolviroth Acerte in similar fashion a few months ago plowing right into the bay on the backs of their bears. This time, they couldn't be sure of the reception awaiting them once they clambered over a strange ship's gunwales and asked for asylum.

His gaze kept coming back to one ship in particular. It was the largest, anchored next to the Tolvirot warcraft. Fost knew little of ships but could tell there was something peculiar about this one. Its proportions were wrong, as if its designers had set out to make it one thing and midway decided to change it into another. And it had a familiar aura to it as well, a combination of sloppiness and a ship-shapeness that reminded him of a man he knew to be dead.

"Down there," Moriana said, tugging at his sleeve. "There's a boat." Bumping its nose against the seawall like an amorous dolphin bobbed a square-prowed dinghy. They walked the hundred yards to the boat. Three men stood on the dock near it. One leaning against a pile of cordage was obviously the crewman who had rowed the boat to shore. Another, a tall storklike man in a flapping black cloak whose sleeves fluttered in the wind as he gestured gave the impression he was trying to become airborne. He had to be a local merchant.

And the third. . . .

Fost stared hard. He was well above average height for a dwarf, but there was no mistaking the shortness of limb and the sturdiness of body. His kinky hair was a golden cloud floating around his head—no pure-blooded dwarf had any but straight hair. As the disbelieving courier grew closer, the aristocratic fineness of the man's profile became apparent, another blatantly un-dwarven characteristic.

"What a strange man," Moriana whispered. "I've never seen the likes of him before."

Fost said nothing. His eyes remained on the man. He was certain there couldn't be two such men in the world—and the one Fost knew was dead.

The golden dwarf turned in irritation at the intrusion.

Immediately, his face transformed into a mask of sheer joy. Ortil Onsulomulo smiled and bobbed his outsized head. Luck had finally smiled on Fost and had continued during the past five days aboard the Wyvern.

"Yes, a goddess taught me the arts of the lyre. Do you doubt it?" He struck a chord and the listeners felt their eyes fill with tears. He strummed another chord and mirth bubbled up inside. A third and Fost and Moriana felt that some ultimate truth hovered just beyond their fingertips waiting for the tiniest exertion before they could grasp it.

"No, Captain Onsulomulo," Moriana said, shaking her head. "I don't doubt it."

"I'm sure the captain speaks metaphorically," put in Erimenes.

Onsulomulo shook his head stubbornly. His jaw set and the expression on his cheerful face hardened.

"I speak unvarnished truth, blue ghost who thinks too much about screwing." He bounced to his feet and tucked the instrument under one arm. "The Wise Ones love me. Because Fate has cursed me, the goddesses and gods pity me."

"I can almost believe it," muttered Fost. He had last seen Onsulomulo peering over the rail of the dwarf's ship Miscreate, which was being drawn up in a waterspout formed by an air elemental Synalon had called to devastate Kara-Est harbor. It was impossible that Ortil Onsulomulo lived. Yet it obviously took more than a howling elemental to stop him.

The courier still had the eerie feeling that the Three and Twenty kept their eye on him, too, just as Jennas maintained. Not only was the half-dwarf captain overjoyed to see him, he insisted on providing Fost, Moriana and the ghosts and dogs immediate transport to High Medurim—free. And more than mere transportation, Onsulomulo also offered the pair the protection of his escort, the TMG dromon Tiger.

"You, my friend," Onsulomulo had said, hugging Fost to his barrel chest, "you are the source of all my good fortune!"

It was hard to deny. Instead of smashing him and his ship to splinters, the air sprite had deposited Onsulomulo and the Miscreate in the Central Plaza of Kara-Est with loving care. It had presented the city's conqueror's with a knotty problem. No matter what their eventual plans of conquest, the City in the Sky couldn't afford to alienate either the dwarves or the Joreans. The fact that since siring his bizarre bastard Ortil's father Jama Onsulomulo had become Minister of Education for the western Jorean province of Sundown made it difficult to adopt the expedient solution of bashing in Ortil's head and claiming the elemental had killed him in combat. Ortil Onsulomulo was just not the kind of neutral one could kill with impunity, in the heat of battle or otherwise.

At the advice of Pavel Tonsho, former Chief Deputy of Kara-Est now the governor of the conquered city, the Sky Citizens had given Onsulomulo a ship, crew and a fat indemnity and sent him on his way.

The Wyvern seemed designed especially for Ortil Onsulomulo. Like him it was a freak, a crossbreed. Laid down in the Estil shipyards as a gigantic round-sterned cargo ship, its construction had been halted midway when the backing company had gone bankrupt. The receivers couldn't afford to complete a vessel of this size, but neither did they wish a half-constructed ship to go to waste. So the hull was cut down. The Wyvern was transformed into a cog. And it was *ugly*.

It had just slid—or waddled—down the ways into Kara-Est harbor when the Sky City appeared overhead. No one knew or cared if it was seaworthy; the crew sent aboard after the battle got horribly seasick on a bay as smooth as a mirror, which wasn't a good sign. But no one said the Sky City had to offer Onsulomulo guarantees. Just a ship.

He took it.

Perhaps no other mariner could have sailed the Wyvern. Probably none other skilled enough would have stayed aboard longer than three minutes. Onsulomulo fell in love with the ship at once.

He did more than sail her. He took her up the Karhon Channel to Tolviroth Acerte, a journey which made the refugee Estil seamen wonder if they wouldn't have been better off taking their chances with Prince Rann. At the City of Bankers, he took on a cargo so valuable that he hired a Shark class dromon from TMG to squire him to High Medurim, the port of delivery.

As the Wyvern's boats had warped her around the end of the breakwater, the fugitives had speculated among themselves as to the nature of the cargo. Moriana thought Wyvern carried strategic materials vital to Imperial security; Ziore, priceless art objects; Erimenes staunchly held out for aphrodisiacs. Knowing High Medurim and its Emperor Teom the Decadent, Fost tended to agree with Erimenes.

As it happened, he was as wrong as the others.

He felt the deck quiver under his feet.

"Good morrow, Magister Banshau!" called Onsulomulo, launching himself into space. Fost shut his eyes as the dwarf dropped ten feet and landed jarringly on the deck. None the worse for the experience, the captain strolled past Fost to greet the newcomer who had emerged blinking and puffing into the daylight. "I trust the morning finds you well?"

"I am *not!*" roared the corpulent man blocking the hatch. "I couldn't *possibly* be well, forced to ride in this wallowing monstrosity. How you could think for one instant that I might be, completely eludes me."

"I thought you Wirixers were used to boats and such," said Erimenes. "You live in the middle of a lake, after all."

The man glared at Erimenes with beady black eyes almost lost in a face like a full moon. He reached chubby, ring-encrusted hands to straighten the square green felt hat, then smoothed the golden silk cord fastening his purple robe about his vast equator. He shuffled bright orange toe slippers into a wider stance, as if bracing to attack the spirit, and blew out through his moustache like an angry walrus.

"Of all the nerve, you ghastly blue violation of the laws of nature!" he bellowed. "You insult my vast intelligence! Wir is a lake, and *this,* as even the ghost of a discredited philosopher ought to be able to see, is an *ocean.*"

"A discredited philosopher, am I?" bristled Erimenes. "You bilious cretin!"

"Justly are Wirixer sorcerers renowned for their wisdom," Ziore declared with fervor.

In unison, Fost and Moriana sighed. This was the cargo Onsulomulo carried to High Medurim, the cargo that rated escort by the *Tiger.* A Magister of the Academy of the Arcane Arts in Wirix was a rare commodity, but not rare enough to justify the enormous expense of TMG protection. There had to be more to Zloscher Banshau than met the eye.

A three-way screaming match ensued among the two Athalar genies and Banshau. Captain Onsulomulo stood to one side smiling slyly. The mage's elephantine rage had been deflected from him. Truly, he was beloved of the gods.

With common accord, Moriana and Fost unslung their satchel straps. They looped them over a belaying pin and went below. The music had gone out of the day.

Moriana yelped as a wave clawed at her feet before falling back to lose itself in the chaos of the sea. A few more quick heaves on the line by grinning Tolvirot sailers and she was swaying above the decks of the Tiger, dripping legs dangling from the boatswain's chain.

She was too high up for Fost to reach her. Tiger's first officer stepped up beside him, reached, plucked the tall blonde woman from the chair and handed her down as if she were a child. Tirn Devistri was the tallest human Fost had ever seen. He had the mahogany skin of a Jorean tanned the black of Nevrym anhak by the sun. It was all but unheard of to find a Jorean serving as a mercenary of any kind, not that the TMG sailors thought of themselves as mercenaries.

"Why so skittish?" asked Fost. "I thought you were used to being up in the air."

"Over land," the princess told him. "That doesn't come right up and grab you."

Ignoring a lewd comment from a female Tolvirot sailor, Fost said, "You know, you've turned the most amazing gray-green. Almost as if you had Vridzish blood."

She turned deathly pale. He let go, stepped back and watched killing rage in her eyes change into shocked hurt.

"Forgive me, I didn't know. That is, I was thoughtless . . ."

"No," she said, shaking her head sadly, "I'm the one who is sorry. I don't know why I reacted like that." She gave him a wan smile and squeezed his arm.

He watched her turn, wondering what had happened to her in Thendrun. It couldn't have been pleasant, he decided.

Captain Nariv Shend took them for a tour of her ship. She was a stocky woman of middle height and years. Incredibly broad shoulders and back showed she still took her turn pulling an oar, as did many TMG captains. There were no slave rowers on a TMG ship, only skilled and highly paid professionals.

At the moment, those professionals lounged about the narrow deck, the men barechested, the women in scant black halters. Others slept in the crowded hammocks slung between the benches below while the Tiger beat southwest under sail.

Bareheaded so that her short-cropped black hair was ruffled by the breeze, the captain herself led them on a tour of the ship.

"A Tolvirot dromon's the epitome of the naval architect's art," she informed them in a voice gone husky from bawling orders over the years. "Tiger's the latest design. She lives up to her name, too. You'll not find a tiger shark sleeker or deadlier. We're only fifteen feet shorter than that tub Wyvern—" She gestured with contempt at the larger ship, which even in the mild sea wallowed worse than the slender warcraft. "—but we're less than half as broad beamed and don't displace a fifth of what she does. And look at this." She bent over the starboard rail and pointed down at the hull. When the ship surged up as it came off the crests, they saw shiny yellow streaked with green. "Copper sheath. Cuts through water like a knife. And our spur up at the prow can punch through an enemy's hull like a spear." If Erimenes were here, Fost reflected, he'd make some comment about the captain's propensity for metaphor. Which was only one of the reasons the genie wasn't here.

She straightened and looked at them. Her eyes were pale blue and almost hidden in wrinkles etched by squinting against the harsh sunlight blazing down and glancing off the broken surface of the sea.

"That's with rowers, of course. Peaceful times, when there's any kind of wind, we sail and let the rowers off."

Fost thumped a boot heel on the stout anhak deck that covered the ship from rail to rail.

"I thought most rowed vessels were open."

"Tiger's fully armored. The deck gives us a good fighting platform in a boarding action. And you see our gunwales are pretty high, and we've these stout mantlets for added protection from archers."

She led them around her ship while they looked on and tried to ask informed questions. The Tolvirot sailors watched with amusement but no contempt.

"And up here in the forecastle, we've got the pump for our flame projector." She nodded to her first officer, who stood by the forward mast directing a sail drill in a voice like a thunderstorm. He acknowledged and went back to the drill. Like his captain and everyone else aboard, he

wore a short blue kilt with a dagger at his belt. But he
didn't wear a short-sleeved blue tunic like Shend. His ti-
tanic chest was bare. Fost eyed him, hoping that no turn
of events pitted them against one another. And in the
same thought, he hoped Moriana wasn't eyeing the enormous sailor too closely, either.

"Now the flamethrower's a tricky proposition," Shend
said as she opened a hatch in the square forecastle. "It's a
very effective weapon, but you can't get more'n one or two
good shots out of it. Can't carry fuel for more. Now
here—" A blunt hand indicated a squat, dully gleaming
brass assembly. "—here's the pump, and that's . . ."

A cry from above brought her head sharply up. Fost
saw she almost quivered like a hunting hound on the
scent. Her hand dropped to the short axe at her belt. Tolviroth Maritime Guaranty were notorious for avoiding
fights that were none of their concern, but that was only
because a finely honed instrument of destruction shouldn't
be blunted needlessly. But when the time came, the TMG
sailors took an unholy joy in battle.

A sailor, dark and sexless against a piling of clouds, sat
in a bucket at the top of the forward mast. The lookout
pointed toward the low green shoreline. They crossed
delta country where several rivers drained from Lake Lolu
into the sea. From the concealed mouth of one of those
rivers pirates often sallied forth to attack shipping.

And that was what Fost presumed the three low, black
shapes crawling like insects across the rumpled green
blanket of sea had in mind.

"An outrage!" The immense Wirixer mage quivered
with rage as he twisted a mottled silk handkerchief in his
hamhock hands. "That my personage should be subjected
to treacherous assault! Oh, woe, woe!"

"Be silent, you bulbous bag of wind," sneered Erimenes. "Be a man! You should look forward with keen
anticipation to the virile shedding of blood, as I do."

"You only do that because you've no blood to shed,"

Fost said dourly, trying to fit a conical helmet on his head so that the noseguard didn't scrape skin.

The spirit ignored him.

"Besides, these vagabonds doubtless aren't attacking us to get at you. That's merely a paranoid delusion of grandeur on your part. Likely they're just run of the mill pirates. Murderers, rapists, robbers, that sort of thing."

"Be silent, you old fool!" Ziore's voice throbbed with exasperation and worry. "They come to attack Moriana. I know they do!"

Teetering on a rail, resplendent in gilded and shaped breastplate and greaves that would have pleased the Emperor Teom, Ortil Onsulomulo laughed gaily.

"Whatever their motives, their intentions are clear." He waved a stumpy arm at the approaching ships.

"So are ours," said Moriana, holding her bow between her knees as she adjusted the buckle of her own helmet borrowed from the ship's armory.

The pirate craft had become distinct shapes with discernible details. Two were low with single banks of oars, which Onsulomulo sneeringly called pentekonters. The third was more ominous, a big bireme with staring eyes painted on the prow.

"Laid down in the Kolnith Shipyards, by her lines," the captain observed.

"You think Kolnith is backing this?" Fost asked.

"Some City State could be, but I doubt it's Kolnith. Not even the Archduke's fishheaded enough to send his lackeys a-pirating in a ship traceable to him." Onsulomulo pointed his shortsword at the pirate ships. "You'll notice their decks are fairly black with men, not to imply they are crewed by my Jorean cousins." He interrupted the lecture with a short laugh. "Each is carrying two or perhaps three times its usual crew. They've just put out from land a few hours past and don't need to worry about provisions." He sighed and shook his large, golden head. "We are sadly outnumbered, I fear."

"Woe!" lamented Magister Banshau.

Though according to the half-dwarf captain the bireme would be quicker, the smaller pentekonters coursed ahead, their rowers working frantically to drive them through the incoming rollers.

"It seems they've a basic sense of tactics," Onsulomulo said dryly.

"How do you mean?" Moriana asked.

"The two little cubs are off to worry our sheepdog while the wolf makes straight for the fold."

The cry went up, "There she goes!" from the Wyvern's rail, and Tiger slid under her bows, hitting the crests with loud bangs as she pulled for the attackers.

"They haven't a chance," said Fost.

The low, black shark-ship shot between the two oared galleys, spitting arrows in both directions. In passing, the ballista mounted amidships thumped and sent a two-yard-long iron dart smashing among the crew tightly packed between the gunwale of the pirate on her starboard. Fost heard the screams.

The bireme had already turned her bow into the west wind and made to pass to port of her fellows to intercept Wyvern. Onsulomulo shouted for his ship to come about, leading away from the distant green shore. It seemed wasted breath to Fost. They were beating into the wind as they had for ten days and could never hope to out-maneuver the big bireme.

The Tiger swung to port trying to turn about and come to grips with her attackers again. Shend had plotted well. The other pirate galley, inflamed with the lust for loot, kept coming arrow straight for Wyvern's fat flank.

Even at the distance of several hundred yards, Fost heard Shend's voice, "Star'rd oars, full back! Port oars, full for'ard!"

"A turnabout." Onsulomulo's eyes gleamed.

It was incredible. The long black hull simply swiveled in the water, as deft as a waterstrider. When her spurred prow pointed the way she had come, Shend roared, "All for'ard full!" and the ship leaped ahead as if shot from a catapult.

The men packed on the decks of the galley screamed as they saw death bearing down on them. The little galley was broadside to the swell and lost way as the rowers lost rhythm. The slave rowers were trying to tear loose from their chains and flee the path of that deadly spur.

Tiger took her broadside with a rending screech that made Fost's neck hairs rise. For a second, it looked as if the pentekonter would ride out the blow. Then the deadly iron spur tore free with a harsh squealing of sundered wood and the irresistible pressure of seventy-two strongly pulled and perfectly coordinated oars simply rolled the smaller vessel over. The watchers in the Wyvern clearly heard her keep breaking as the Tiger ran her down.

Erimenes shrieked in bloodlust ecstasy, Moriana shouted and Fost found his throat raw now. Even Banshau had quit blubbering and gazed on intently.

Tiger lunged away from the foundering body of her prey. Still apparently fresh, her rowers pulled her past the surviving pentekonter in a quick shooting pass. Again her arrows and engines worked execution on the thronging pirates while the return missile hail had no visible effect against the Tolvirot's well-shielded complement.

A hundred yards ahead of the pirate, almost in bowshot of the Wyvern, the dromon spun in another breathtaking turnabout and went head to head with the pentekonter.

"Is she going to ram?" Moriana asked.

"Do you jest, Lady? No TMG captain would ram bows-on except as an uttermost final resort. No, Highness, you'll see. Captain Shend has more daggers than one in her fine bodice."

The pirate oarsman slacked off, apparently asking the same question Moriana had. Fost heard whips cracking as the rowing master frantically sought to build up headway again. If the Tolvirot really did have a suicidal attack in mind, it wouldn't do to be caught dead in the water.

Tiger veered to port to pass wide of the pirate. He almost felt the sigh of a relief go up from the enemy ship.

"Fecklessness!" Erimenes cried disdainfully.

At the last possible instant, the Tiger swung back at her foe.

"Star'rd oars, *trail!*" Shend howled. As one, thirty-six oars snapped back alongside the ship, resting inside the line of her iron sheathing.

The pirate never had a chance. Tiger's prow ran over her oars. Damned wails and screams burst from the pentekonter as her starboard oarsmen were crushed between oars and benches. When at last the horrid grinding was over and the Tiger swung around her foe's high stern, the pirate galley lay motionless in the water.

Then with a thump and a scrape, the bireme came alongside. Fost forgot the Tiger.

Moriana had kept her eye on the approaching bireme and sent some shrewdly aimed arrows in its direction. Now she laid her bow aside and took up sword and shield. She had provided herself with a light leather jerkin for body protection and her Grasslander boots were rolled up to protect her thighs. Fost hoped it was enough. He hoped he had enough, too, with shield and helmet augmenting his tattered mail vest.

Screeching like angry ravens, the pirates swarmed up over the side. The bireme only lacked a foot of Wyvern's freeboard, so there was only Onsulomulo's crew to fend them off. Wyvern held a hundred and twenty men; the bireme easily three times that many. The fight was hopeless from the outset.

"Magic!" Erimenes cried as Moriana and Fost engaged yelling pirates in a skirl of blades. "Use your magic!"

"Can't!" she cried, taking the thrust of a boarding pike on her shield. "Too many!"

"A fireball'd cool their ardor," said the genie, mixing metaphors wildly. "Shrewdly struck, friend Fost."

"It'd set the ship ablaze, you dunce!" Fost shouted

back, as the partner of the man he'd just killed swung an axe at his head.

The battle came to him in surrealistic flashes. Bearded faces distorted with rage or pain as his blade bit home; Moriana's slim sword flickered like a tongue of flame, its tip tracing lines of blood in the air as it struck and darted away; Onsulomulo danced through the crush of sweating, bloody bodies and fought using two short swords, hamstringing, stabbing kidneys, capturing swung cutlasses between his blades and spinning them away with a scissors twist; Magister Banshau, prodded in the belly by a blond-bearded pirate, raised a shrill keening of fury, swept a large tar barrel up above his head and sent it bowling down the decks like a runaway boulder crushing half a dozen pirates to bloody gruel. They all fought well. Erimenes crowed encouragement and Ziore, wincing with pain at what she must do, clouded the minds and slowed the reactions of pirates as they closed with Moriana. But it was all in vain, as Fost knew when he thrust his sword into an angry face and counted the eighth he'd killed with no slackening in the tide of enemies. The day was lost. Sheer value wouldn't offset the crushing weight of numbers.

Then with a bang! the Tiger drove its spur through the bireme's stern and her corvus thumped against the stern to allow Tirn Devistri to lead the Tolvirot crew, rowers and all, up and over and in among the pirates.

The battle was as good as ended.

Later, Fost and Moriana lay exhausted in their stateroom. The sweat of battle had been washed from their limbs in a cold stream of water pumped by bloody, bandaged, grinning seamen. Now their limbs were clad in the sweat of lovemaking of a fervor unusual even for them. The nearness of death had made the sensations all the sharper.

Moriana lay at Fost's side running fingers through the hair on his chest. He yelped as they explored a sticking plaster the ship's surgeon had slapped over a shallow puncture where a lucky pike thrust had popped a few more rings of his hapless chain mail shirt.

"I never would have thought the Tolvirot could fight like that," she mused. "They're mercenaries, after all. They fight for money, not conviction."

"They've convictions. They're protecting freedom of trade, and that's powerful medicine to a Tolvirot. And does a highly paid artisan do lesser work merely for being higher paid?"

"I suppose not." The ship creaked and sighed about them, a note of smugness in the sounds, as if the ship, too, were happily surprised to find itself still alive and free.

"Most of all, I guess, they fight for pride. A sense of honor." He shrugged. "Most soldiers fight for that, in spite of claims for creed or country."

"You may be right." She turned to nibble on his ear.

He squirmed. He resisted, only for the sheer pleasure of prolonging the sensation. She reached down and grabbed none too gently.

"Oh, well," he said as he turned eagerly toward her. "At least we're safe. Nothing can get past the Tiger."

# CHAPTER TWELVE

The whole populace of High Medurim had turned out to greet the Wyvern, complete with a skirling and banging military band, colored streamers and a troupe of naked dancing girls and boys, without which no public occasion was complete.

"At last," Erimenes had said, puffing up like a courting frog, "we receive attention commensurate with our status."

Burly stevedores had swung Wyvern's fat stern up to the pier. The joyous tumult climaxed as the long wooden ramp was let down and the weary, shaken, but nonetheless gratified travellers set foot on the ancient stone of High Medurim. Singing traditional songs of welcome, the crowd swept forward . . .

. . . and engulfed Zolscher Banshau, hauling his vast bulk up onto its collective shoulders, bearing him forward in triumph to a state carriage waiting at the waterfront. An assembly of great and learned men, if their phenomenal beards and dizzyingly tall hats were any indication, welcomed him aboard, while gorgeous maidens wearing diaphanous robes and foil haloes placed a wreath on his head and smothered his moustache with kisses. Magister Banshau, lying at ease on a sumptuous divan, beamed from the depths of gaudy floral wreaths as if he'd been named the Twenty-fourth Wise One of Agift. Shouting with joy, the crowd pelted along the sidewalks on either side of the carriage. The band fell in behind while nude, brightly painted dancers scattered flowers and hard candies.

"Welcome to High Medurim," Ortil Onsulomulo called

down sarcastically to Fost and Moriana from the stern-castle.

Not even Erimenes had anything to say to that.

They were still standing at the foot of the ramp when a carriage appeared. A fraction the size of the one bearing away the Wirixer mage, it was impressive enough, black enamelled and polished so obsessively that a courtier could use it as a mirror. The muffled, hooded driver brought the landau to a noisy halt in front of Fost and Moriana. A curtained door swung open and a clean-shaven man wearing a gleaming black uniform stepped out.

"I am General Falaris, Imperial Intelligence Service," he announced. "You are the Princess Moriana?" Startled, Moriana nodded. He bowed perfunctorily. "Please come with me, Your Highness." He shot hurried looks in both directions. "Get in quickly before anyone sees."

Fost felt nostalgic tears sting his eyes. "Imperial Intelligence" was a contradiction in terms. Any Medurimin above the age of three knew who the shiny black landaus belonged to. They could as effectively keep secrets by hiring criers to proclaim that mysterious visitors had arrived by ship to confer with the Emperor.

The general's invitation had not included Fost. Moriana solved that problem by grabbing his arm and dragging him into the box after her. General Falaris looked doubtful at this turn of events but said nothing.

Fost went to Emperor Teom the Decadent's palace in a daze. The familiar sights and sounds of his birth city overwhelmed him. The richness, the poverty, the places of learning, the pits of dismal ignorance. He peered out from behind the golden curtains in the landau and saw urchins begging in the streets, old men, toothless and blind, directing pickpockets and cuffing the younglings incapable of stealing enough. He had been there—once.

Now he was on his way to the palace of the Emperor.

\* \* \*

"Welcome to High Medurim," Emperor Teom said languidly. Draped over the arm of his throne, his wife and sister Temalla smiled and nodded in greeting, as well.

Moriana and Ziore bowed. Fost stood upright until a none too gentle elbow in his ribs from Moriana made him bend forward at the waist. It wasn't that he meant to defy the Emperor. He was simply struck numb by meeting the man who had once possessed so much power over him as a youth.

"The blue ghost does not bow," hissed the small man at Teom's left. "He does not pay proper reverence to Your Ineffability."

Teom waved a hand. The fingers were slightly doughy and devoid of rings.

"Peace, Gyras. Were I fourteen centuries old I'd not be reverent to a mere emperor either." His voice rang in mellifluous low tones. Though he sprawled bonelessly across his gilded throne, he seemed to be a tall, well-proportioned man.

Flushing turquoise in pleasure, Erimenes performed a deep bow. His domed forehead sank alarmingly into the marble floor before he straightened.

"Your Radiance is too kind," he murmured. "Far be it from me to contradict you, however, but I must point out I am fifteen centuries old, and a shade over, rather than fourteen."

A growl emerged from Gyras's throat. Teom silenced him with a wave. The dwarven advisor drew his balding head down angrily, accentuating the hump on his back.

"I've never seen an Athalar spirit before, though I've heard of them," Teom said.

"We are alike," said Erimenes, fawning and again bowing so his head vanished through the floor clear to his brows, "for I have never before seen an emperor."

With superhuman effort, Fost bit back a reply. Fortunately, Temalla interrupted Erimenes's sally into diplomacy by fixing Fost with big dark eyes made bigger by a liberal application of kohl and saying, "Oh, but you must have had a *long, hard* journey." Her husky voice accentuated the adjectives with undue emphasis. The Empress's voice had a curious quality about it that sent shivers up Fost's spine.

"Yes," Teom said. A light came into his brown eyes. Reading his mood, his sister leaned forward and slipped a hand into a fold of his robe. She was of medium height, plump and with tightly curled brown hair hanging to her shoulders. Though she had not withstood the onslaught of middle years as well as her husband-brother, she was far from unattractive. The breasts hanging above the high waist of her blue gown were ample without being ostentatious, and the gown's gauzy fabric was drawn taut by her position poised on the throne arm, revealing a pleasing curve of hip and thigh. Her left hand toyed with the ringlets framing Teom's face, while her shoulder rose and fell in a gentle motion.

Fost held his breath when he realized what she did to her brother. Teom's eyes were shut and he sighed in pleasure. Fost felt Temalla's eyes burning into his. Moriana tensed at his side.

"You are welcome to High Medurim," the Emperor repeated breathlessly, "though I'm afraid it was a bit unorthodox."

It had been that, Fost thought, looking everywhere but at Teom's lap, his sister's smiling face, Gyras's hot glare and the narrowing of Moriana's eyes. He wound up gazing down at his feet. The sight of his boots among the mad geometric patterns of the carpet intensified his unease.

Teom stiffened, then sighed. Temalla's smile broadened. Unspeaking, she promised Fost unspeakable delights. Sweat poured down the insides of Fost's tunic. He was very glad its hem came down below crotch level. Teom's eyes opened.

"I apologize for the furtive way you were brought to the Palace," he said, as if nothing had happened. "Given the sensitive nature of your mission—Magister Banshau gave us a somewhat garbled account by means of that mystical communication Wirixer mages use—we thought it best your arrival be kept secret for the moment."

"We are most grateful that Your Effulgence chose to receive us as promptly as you did," said Moriana. "Now, if we could get down to the matters I've come to discuss."

"No, dear Princess!" Teom cried, holding up his hand. "We have ordered an extraordinary session of the Assembly for day after tomorrow to hear your proposals. Time enough then for me to hear what you've come to say."

"So much for secrecy," muttered Fost. Gyras looked as if he'd just found a family of dung lizards nesting in his beard.

"Time enough to send these beggars packing, Your Magnificence," Gyras said in a voice like two stones grinding together.

"Gyras," chided Temalla, "where's your hospitality?" She jumped to her feet and stretched with a litheness belying her years. "Personally, I'm looking forward to entertaining our visitors." She looked directly at Fost. Will you excuse me? I'm late for my riding lesson." She glided out, licking her fingers.

"Good Gyras," said Teom, rising, "we thank you for your attendance on our person." At this formal dismissal, Gyras folded his hands across the front of his frayed gray robe, looked plague and poison at Fost and Moriana, then followed the Empress out. "Now, my friends," Teom said. The words trembled with barely suppressed excitement. "I should like to show you my great Project. It was to complete this Project that I imported Magister Banshau to High Medurim. And once you behold with your own eyes what the Magister's science has made possible, I believe you shall understand the extravagant reception we gave him!"

\* \* \*

"And here on the right," the Emperor waved his hand so that the fingertips protruded ever so briefly outside the shade cast by the parasol, "we have spider monkeys from the Northern Continent. Careful, there, good Erimenes! If you regard them too obviously they tend to become excited. And they fling handfuls of dung with fearful accuracy." He chuckled indulgently at the quaint proclivities of his pets.

Erimenes recoiled.

"Why do you care if they pelt you with offal?" demanded Ziore. "They couldn't possibly hit you."

"It is beneath the dignity of an Athalar scholar to be bombarded with excrement by members of inferior species. Besides, what if one of the little monsters drops a ringer in my jar?" He shuddered and turned his aquiline profile away from the monkeys' wizened, curious black faces.

"On the left are more exotic specimens. Lizard monkeys from the Isles of the Sun." Fost peered at them with interest. Though shaped like the mammalian monkeys across the gravel walkway, the lizard monkeys were obviously reptilian. Their skins were scaly green, their eyes glittering black beads, and tiny hands and feet three-clawed. Their bellies were yellow, as were the ruffs of skin around the necks of the males. They had prehensile tails, several hanging upside down regarding the humans with sprightly curiosity.

Moriana shuddered and turned away. No doubt they reminded her of the *Zr'gsz*. Fost thought they were cute, but as he reflected on it, they began to make him uneasy. In the Library of High Medurim he had once read that many savants, including Wirixer genetic magicians, believed humanity had evolved from monkeys not dissimilar to those penned on the right side of the walkway.

Might not the *Zr'gsz* . . . ?

He hurried to catch up with Moriana and Teom. The Emperor was as proud as a small boy showing off his famous menagerie. It was indeed impressive. Pens on either side contained small bits of alien environment for the comfort of the imprisoned fauna. He sauntered past tall tanks of some durable crystal filled with water, through which clouds of fishes small and not so small swirled and flashed brilliantly in the evening sunlight.

"Where are the naked dancing girls?" demanded Erimenes in a petulant whisper. "The orgies in the street, the extravagant displays of wealth? I am sorely disappointed in this High Medurim of yours, Fost."

Fost winced. It wasn't his fault. Still, he had been raised on tales of the opulence of life in the Imperial court. It had been something of a shock when they were ushered into Teom's presence in the private audience chamber and found it so austere. Likewise, Fost wondered at finding Teom attended only by his sister-wife and the dwarf advisor. Where were the coveys of courtiers said to follow him everywhere, panting with eagerness to obey his every whim?

He admitted his puzzlement to Erimenes.

"But you did see nude dancing girls, Erimenes," he pointed out. "This morning on the pier. They came out to greet Magister Banshau along with the cherubs and savants and that tinny marching band, remember?"

"But they were too far away to *see* anything."

As they came back within earshot, Teom was pointing with pride at a shaggy mountain with a tail at both ends and two huge yellow tusks curving from the vicinity of the thicker tail.

"A Jorean mammoth, from Amsi Province in the south. They tame the beasts as dray-animals, I'm told, as we do hornbulls." He indicated a block of ice melting in the corner behind the listless, hairy giant. "It's fortunate we have an adequate ice house in the Palace. Otherwise, the poor beast would swelter to death in this frightful heat."

He turned to nod at Fost, his smile mocking.

"Perhaps I had motives beyond secrecy in receiving you

so surreptitiously and informally, friend Longstrider. Perhaps I felt a yearning to meet with people who had been to strange places and done wonderful things, and talk with them as *people*—not as mannikins decked with plumes and ribbons and walled off from all true contact by layer after layer of protocol. And without a flock of gaudy, useless songbirds fluttering about cooing in awe at my every utterance. Their songs are pretty, I confess, but they are also empty." He reached out and touched Fost fleetingly on the shoulder with his long, soft, pallid fingers. "Perhaps one day I should like to sit down and hear you tell me about life in my city's streets." His tone was serious and his eyes were touched with bleakness. Fost almost missed his next words. "That might be the most alien environment of all, to me."

Then he laughed and turned away, his robe swirling about his legs.

"And perhaps a man as well-travelled as you should consider how keen must be the hearing of an Emperor to survive Palace intrigues long enough to keep the throne."

Fost hardly thought of himself as a citizen of Medurim any more. But still . . . the Emperor had touched him and named him friend. In a way, that was as strange and wonderful as anything befalling him.

They came to the end of the rows of enclosure,

"Here's a sentimental favorite of mine," Teom said. It was a seashore enclosure, a rocky beach and a pool dark with seaweed. Resting with half its bulk in the water was a mottled brown sea toad as big as Magister Banshau and covered with warts. "It's three hundred years old," Teom said. "It sings with a beautiful, high soprano when the moons are full. But mostly I keep it because it reminds me of my dear, departed mother, the Dowager Empress." He snuffled and wiped his eye. Fost stared. The thing *did* look like the late Dowager.

"What do you think of my menagerie?" Teom asked. He made a slight hand gesture and a balding servant appeared from nowhere bearing iced goblets and a flask of wine. Erimenes nodded. This was more like it, although the servitor didn't fit his conception of what a servitor should be. Too old, too male.

Fost sipped the cool wine. It was sweetened to the verge of cloying, but refreshing nonetheless.

"It's beautiful, Your Supremacy," Moriana said. "But am I correct in assuming it's not the Project you spoke of?"

"Indeed you are, Princess." Teom had taken no wine himself. "When you've refreshed yourselves, I will show you the great work whose culmination Magister Banshau has brought about." He closed the parasol and handed it to the servant.

Moriana set her empty goblet back on the tray held by the immobile servant, saying, "I'm ready."

Teom led them through a door in the northwest corner of the Palace. Inside was cool and dim. They passed down a narrow corridor toward a shine of lamplight and a low murmur of conversation.

A stentorian whoop of joy echoed around a large chamber as they entered. Magister Banshau stood before them, his garish garments mercifully hidden under a white smock, holding his hands above his head and performing a dancing bear two-step of glee. He saw them and uttered another joyous bellow.

"Your Imperiousness! I have succeeded! I, the Magister Zolscher Banshau, now assume my undoubted rightful place among the greatest of Wirixer mages!" And he seized Teom by the arm and waltzed him around the room.

A few old men in robes who sat crosslegged in a semi-circle on the floor looked up reprovingly at the commotion, then went back to reading in droning monotones. Fost spared them barely a glance; even the bizarre specta-cle of the Emperor of High Medurim practically swept off his feet by a balloon-shaped wizard couldn't compete for his attention with the beast occupying the center of the room.

It was huge, the size of the Jorean mammoth and more, sporting a featureless hump, corpse-white and touched with blue-gray near its base. It lay in a pool of horribly bubbling brown, viscous liquids. The wrinkled, robed men were arranged around the pit, and they appeared to be reading to it.

"It looks," Erimenes said, tapping his nose judiciously, "like an enormous mushroom cap."

"You're right, my excellent Athalar friend!" Banshau released the Emperor and started to grab the genie. He only succeeded in dispersing Erimenes's thin substance. As Erimenes coalesced in a blue whirlwind, the mage grabbed Fost and kissed him wetly on both cheeks. His moustache was redolent of wine and salt fish. "It is a fungus. But a fungus such as the world has never seen!"

How a new breed of fungus merited such excitement escaped Fost.

"Where is—where is it?" Teom almost danced with excitement.

"There." Banshau pointed to a door opposite the one through which they'd entered. In a single bound Teom was pulling it open and tumbling inside like a child opening his Equinox presents. Fost followed, careful not to jostle the imperial personage while craning his neck from side to side to see.

The cubicle was bare of furnishings. A small, round man sat crosslegged on the stone floor. His skin was very pale. At the sound of the door, he raised his head. His cheeks swelled in an infectious smile. Colorless eyes surrounded by laugh-lines glowed.

"Your Radiance," he said, bowing.

"O Oracle!" cried Teom. He fell to his knees. "This is the greatest moment of my life! My name shall live forever for this!"

"And mine," added Banshau.

"Oracle?" Erimenes's brow creased. "I remember the Magister saying something about an Oracle aboard the ship. Who is this Oracle, anyway?"

"I am, honored sir," said the pale, round man. A pudgy hand pointed past the kneeling Emperor and Fost to the swollen fungus mound. "And that is the Oracle, as well." His merry laughter pealed like a bell.

"Many years ago," the Emperor said around a mouthful of food, "a certain Wirixer mage was on an expedition to the Isles of the Sun. He gathered specimens himself, since several of his assistants had been killed and eaten as a result of some slight unpleasantness with the Golden Barbarians." He paused to wet his throat from a goblet of iced water. "He was wading in a tidepool, whistling to himself. He lost his footing and stopped whistling while he caught his balance—only to hear the last few bars of his tune whistled back at him from nearby.

"On investigating, he found the sound had come from a fist-sized growth at the edge of the pool. A small amphibious predator lived nearby; the fungus imitated the cries of various seabirds and lured them into the creature's reach. In turn, its droppings and the remnants of its meals nourished the fungus. Remarkable symbiotic development." Temalla made a face at the mention of droppings. She picked a leg of roast fowl from the silver platter and began to tear at it with small, neat teeth, gazing at Fost as if she'd decided to have him for the next course.

"The mage brought the fungus and its partner home. He waited until it produced spores, then went to work. The work was long and exacting, but over generations the Wirixers altered the nature of the fungus. It was found to have a rudimentary consciousness. By selective breeding and the most cogent and subtle genetic enchantments they expanded it until it equalled a man's. And then exceeded it.

"Their aim was to produce a variety of the mimic fungus that could store information, sort it within its own, well, *mind,* and not only produce facts but actually make deductions of its own."

"But why bother, Your Sublimity?" asked Erimenes. "You've the Library. It's the greatest in the world. Or was, when I lived."

"It's the greatest still, though recently it has fallen into neglect. At times, it seems I am the only Medurimin with any interest in abstract knowledge." He took a bite of the seaweed pod marinated in brandy. "Be that as it may, the Library possesses over ten million volumes. It contains within its walls virtually the sum total of human knowledge, of history, of nature, of the workings of politics and the Universe. And ninety-nine parts of a hundred is as good as lost. No human intellect can absorb a fraction of it."

He leaned forward. His dark eyes glowed with passion.

"But Oracle's intellect can. For the first time in human history, man can actually make use of the immeasurable trove of facts."

Fost felt his own pulse race. He remembered his frustrations as a boy under the tutelage of the pedant Ceratith, when he had completed learning how to read and in part appreciated the sheer size of the Library. He had been frustrated to tears when the truth first struck him. To his small-boy mind it had been like being confronted with all the sweets in the world and knowing if he lived to be a thousand he could sample only a paltry few.

"How does Magister Banshau come into this?" asked Moriana. "I gather he wasn't involved in development of the Oracle himself." She leaned to the side to let a serving maid refill her goblet. Dusky breasts threatened to pop from the maid's tight, skimpy bodice. At long last beauteous serving girls had made an appearance, to Erimenes's vocal delight.

"You gather correctly, Princess. What Banshau did,

and what has earned him all the bounty I can bestow, is discover a new kind of nutrient. It enhances the Oracle's mental energy level so that it is capable of telepathy and projections and similar feats. Mental feats such as flourished in lost Athalau."

The jolly, white-skinned little man who had been in the room adjoining the fungus solemnly entered and sat quietly beside Moriana. Teom smiled broadly and gestured to the man, saying, "Tell them about this wonderous accomplishment, Oracle."

The man nodded, then spoke.

"This is similar to the mental magic that flourished in Athalau, what is now termed intrinsic magic as opposed to extrinsic, which involves manipulation of elementals and demons and other forces external to the magician."

Fost looked at Moriana. She returned a small smile. Then she stiffened a little. Teom laughed.

"Ah, you perceive my little jest."

"I don't," said Fost. "What's wrong?"

"Nothing is wrong, Fost," said the Teom. "This being you see beside the princess is nothing more than a mental projection created by the fungus."

"A Wirixer spell," the little man said. "I can teach it to you, Highness, since your mind is both powerful and agile." He laughed at Moriana's thunderstruck expression. "The Wirixers have been at the game of magic almost as long as your folk, Princess. Do not begrudge them their little abilities."

While this interchange took place, Erimenes was growing livid, turning gray-blue with the veins standing out at his temples. If he'd been corporeal, Fost would have feared him to be on the brink of apoplexy. Erimenes was far from resigned to the existence of a second Athalar spirit. Oracle's projection struck him as a cheap imitation of himself. It was too much to bear. He was on the point of fulminating when Oracle turned to him, eyes widening.

"Oh! It comes to me now. Your pardon, sir, I have only recently attained consciousness. But you are the spirit of Erimenes? The mighty Athalar philosopher known as 'the Ethical'?"

Guardedly, Erimenes admitted he was.

"This is marvelous! You are a great man, sir. Your life and works are a part of history. Ah, to think I meet in person a man of such legendary erudition and wisdom." He clapped his hands together—through one another. Oracle blinked rapidly and said, "Please forgive me. I haven't learned all the possibilities of projection yet."

"Pardon me, Your Magnificence," Fost cut in. "It's astonishing that Oracle can project his image like that. But I don't see the importance."

Teom waved his fingers airily.

"The projection is a mere trick, a side effect, if you will. You saw the old men sitting around the nutrient pool reading?" Fost nodded. "Well, now Oracle can absorb knowledge directly from men's brains. Not only can it pick up the accumulated knowledge of a learned man's whole life, but it can read new material as fast as a man's eyes can scan a page. Can you imagine the lifetimes that will save teaching it?"

Having stripped the drumstick to bare bone, Temalla flung it over her shoulder and slumped back in her chair.

"You've grown so tedious, Teom," she complained. "All you can talk about is that horrid giant toadstool."

Teom's fist slammed down onto the table, setting goblets dancing. His own crystal goblet jumped off the table to shatter on the floor.

"It is *not* a giant toadstool. Oracle is the greatest achievement in High Medurim in a thousand years. It is my Oracle who will bring about a renaissance of knowledge and wisdom and make Medurim mighty again."

Sneering, she yawned ostentatiously and raised her arms above her head, squeezing her shoulderblades together so that her heavy breasts jutted straight at Fost. Areolas like targets showed clearly through the gown's flimsy fabric.

"You spend all your time with that unnatural thing!" Inch-long lashes batted at Fost; he almost felt the wind. "I'm sure Sir Fost would never neglect me so."

He felt as if someone had poured molten wax into his stomach. Damn the woman! Why didn't she leave him alone?

And why did she have this effect on him?

"Unnatural?" Teom's voice rose to a shrill scream of outrage. "Unnatural, you witch? How can you say that about my creation?"

"Because it is. And it's not your creation."

"I sponsored it. Without my patronage it would never have been completed!"

"But what's it good for?" the Empress shouted. "Will it fill the Imperial coffers? Can you eat it, drink it, make love to it?" Her lip curled and her voice lowered. "But knowing you, dear brother, you probably could. And enjoy it!"

"It would make a livelier bedmate than you."

In the thick silence, Fost and Moriana rose and murmured excuses which went unheard amid the gathering storm. Scooping up the genies' satchels, they pushed through a group of serving maids that had crowded around to watch. As they began walking rapidly toward their suite, they heard the explosion of a shrewdly hurled crystal decanter against a wall.

No sooner had they entered their chambers and chased out the dewy-eyed blond youth and girl they found already in their bed, than Moriana went to Fost and ripped his shirt open from collar to navel.

Swaying, he put a hand on the wall to steady himself. They were both more drunk than sober.

"What'd you do that for?"

Her hands slid cool and smooth along his ribs. She

undulated against him, her breath warm and sweet in his ear.

"The way that slut Temalla's been making eyes at you," she purred, "I thought it best to give you something else to think about tonight."

Moriana kept him occupied until dawn, when they both slipped into an exhausted sleep.

The next morning, they took advantage of their leisure to tour the fabled Imperial Palace. They wandered to and fro along the marble corridors, gazing at paintings hung on the walls and statues standing in silent alcoves. The place had been decorated in early plunder. Whatever hadn't been nailed down or too heavy to move, the Imperial Army had taken from its country of origin. There was no scheme to the collected art. Much of it was dross, much incomparably fine. What impressed Fost was that the collection spanned two continents and almost a hundred centuries.

The sun was high when they drifted into the western courtyard. It was a garden replete with tinkling fountains and divided into nooks and crannies by an ornamental hedge. Fost suggested it had been designed as a trysting ground. That gave Erimenes much satisfaction imagining past activities.

He waved a vaporous arm at a marble statue in a niche as they passed along the grassy path.

"That's what I call art," he announced. "Consider the interplay of line and form, consider the dynamics of the poses, the subtle imbalance inherent in the juxtaposition of human form and delphine. And such mastery of expression. Behold the girl's face. Was ever a transport of ecstasy made more concrete? And see how the dolphin smiles as it . . ."

"Dolphins always look like that," said Ziore. "Can you find no pleasure in art that isn't lascivious?"

A puzzled frown creased his face.

"Why, no. Why should I?" Then he brightened and said, "During my own lifetime it was definitely established that male dolphins were altogether willing to mate with human females. Keeping in mind that this is High Medurim, Moriana, you really ought to consider . . ."

Fost would have liked to hear Moriana's retort. He never had the chance. Just at that moment they rounded a corner to see Gyras sitting on a bench, huddled head to head with another. As arresting as the dwarf's appearance was, it was the other who brought a gasp from Moriana's lips and made her hand drop to where her sword normally hung.

Gyras spoke to a *Zr'gsz*.

The Hisser saw them before Gyras. He came to his feet in a fluid motion, a dazzling white smile splitting his dark green face.

"What have we here?" His voice was a well-modulated baritone, quite human in pronunciation and inflection. "You must be the Princess Moriana, and you, sir, you'd be Fost Longstrider." He clasped clawed hands at his breasts and bowed. "I am honored to meet you."

He was as tall as Fost, clad in a single garment of shimmering gray cloth that reached down to his sandalled feet. His shoulders were broad, his waist lean. Gyras hurriedly pushed himself off the bench, landing with a thud.

"May I present Zak'zar, Speaker of the People." Shrewd eyes studied Moriana. "I take it you've not met?"

Moriana's lips moved but no words emerged.

"No, we haven't," Fost supplied. The words ripped at his throat.

"But he's an enemy!" Erimenes shrieked. "How can you welcome this viper into your nest?"

Zak'zar bowed again.

"And you would be Erimenes the Ethical. It is a pleasure to meet you, too, sir."

"I assure you, fellow, the pleasure is entirely yours! Lord Gyras, what does this mean?"

Gyras feigned astonishment.

"Surely, you do not think we would convene a debate and hear only one side, especially one as important as this?" Malevolent glee shone in his huge eyes. He raised one eyebrow before saying, "The revered Speaker arrived the day before you did, my friends. I'm surprised your good friend His Radiance the Emperor neglected to inform you."

# CHAPTER THIRTEEN

The languid young officer leaning back in the uncomfortable chair on Fost's left stifled a yawn with the back of his hand. The President of the Assembly was hammering for order to quell a minor riot taking place on the floor.

Ensign Palein Cheidro said to Fost, "The Guilds oppose going to war with the Hissers. It'd disturb their precious status quo." He examined the lace at the cuffs of his blue velvet doublet.

The President recognized a nervous cricket of a man from Jav Nihen. Fost didn't even bother listening to a speech he'd heard a dozen times before, reworded but essentially the same in content.

"Why do the Guilds oppose war? They were quick enough to back the Northern Adventure when I was a boy."

"That was a war conducted safely on foreign soil," explained the ensign. He smiled a lazy half-lidded smile. "Until a suicide commando raid landed and burnt a dozen warehouses, that is. *Then* the Guilds cried to bring home the troops. If you offered them a really safe war against some foe too primitive to strike back at Medurim, they'd jump at it right enough. Think of the fat government contracts."

"But that large gentleman denounced expansionists," Ziore said. "Do you say the Guilds really want a foreign war in spite of that?"

"My dear lady, do you mean to say you actually believe what politicians say in speechs? Oh, my."

In Fost's youth, the Imperial Life Guards had been a fighting organization of renown. Ensign Cheidro made him wonder if the Life Guards had been devalued along with the money. Painfully thin, cat-elegant, dressed always in outfits that cost a common trooper a year's pay, Ensign Cheidro didn't fit Fost's image of a member of an elite unit.

Whether by coincidence or otherwise, no more invitations to dine in the Emperor's apartments were forthcoming after Fost's chance meeting of the *Zr'gsz*. On the morning after, the ensign had appeared stating he was to be their guide. That he was also their keeper was left unsaid.

The debate over Moriana's petition to the Empire to declare war on the Fallen Ones had now dragged into its second day. During the long-winded disputes, Fost had come to a grudging liking for the officer, highborn fop or not. Cheidro had wit and used it utterly without regard for place or prestige of each speaker.

"Why do they go on so?" Fost heard Moriana complain. "I thought they were discussing whether or not to hear that damned lizard."

As if on cue, a small man with impressively broad shoulders bounded to his feet and shouted, "We won't listen to the snake! We border folk have had enough words. It's time our swords spoke for us!" The men around him rushed to their feet, waving their fists in the air and shouting.

"Assemblymen from the Marches," Cheidro said in bored tones. "Excitable fellows."

"Order!" cried the President, using his gavel freely.

"Up yours, Squilla!" the small Marcher shouted back.

The turmoil grew until a figure rose in the center and climbed from the floor toward the spectator's gallery. Silence fell as the commanding figure leaned forward, hands on the railing.

"Foedan speaks rarely, and never without effect," said Cheidro. "This could bode ill if he favors hearing Zak'zar."

"Assemblymen," began Foedan in a voice like a bass drum striking up a slow march. "The question is not

whether the Speaker or the princess is right or wrong, it
is whether we should hear what Lord Zak'zar has to say in
answer to Moriana's request that we make war upon his
people. There can be but one answer. In fairness, we must
hear him before making so grave a decision."

Squilla pounded down the tumult greeting the words
and called for a voice vote. No roll call was needed. Over-
whelmingly, the Assembly voted to permit Zak'zar,
Speaker of the People, to plead his case.

Moriana sat staring at Foedan as the vote was called,
twisting the hem of her tunic as if it were the Kolnith
Assemblyman's neck.

Zak'zar walked out on the floor of the Assembly Hall in
silence. The usually rowdy delegates seemed hypnotized
by the Hisser. He held all their attention in one clawed
hand—and he knew how to wield it.

"I will be brief," he said. He let the small ripples of
comment die before continuing. "You are asked to go to
war with my People. What have we done to you? We
menace no Imperial holding. No resident of any City State
has suffered at our hand. What wrong have we done that
you would raise hand against us?"

"The Princess Moriana Etuul's written petition claims it
is your duty as humans to resist *Zr'gsz* aggression. What
aggression? And if it be the duty of your people to fight
mine to the death, why did she come of her own accord to
Thendrun seeking our aid in reclaiming her throne?"

A babble of voices washed about the podium. He raised
his hand, stilling them.

"The Princess Moriana tells you we treacherously
seized the City in the Sky from her, our ally. Examine
the record. Who first built that fabled City—and who
seized it by treachery from its rightful owners? We assisted
her in unseating Synalon—but for our own ends. Is this
wrong? Who among you would not resort to subterfuge to
avenge the murder of your kinfolk and reclaim from
thieves the house you built? We only took back what was
ours.

"I come before you in the name of my People, bearing the willow-wand of peace. For your own sakes as well as ours, I ask you not to grasp instead the firebrand of war!"

He bent forward, voice dropping to a sonorous whisper that penetrated to the farthest reaches of the room.

"Weigh well your decision, men of the Empire. Much hangs in the balance." He straightened and strode from the podium amid a barrage of cries.

Moriana vaulted over the rail and scattered Assembly-men in all directions as she moved forward. Head back, eyes ablaze, she walked down the aisle to the podium Zak'zar had just vacated. Squilla faced her, gavel raised as if to repel her attack on orderly procedure. Their eyes met; he fled before her.

She needed no gavel to bring the hall to silence, any more than the *Zr'gsz* had. With hair streaming about her head like liquid fire, she launched into an impassioned speech.

The door to the Assembly Hall crashed open. Moriana paused, one fist raised in emphasis of a point. An old man stalked into the room. He walked ramrod straight in spite of the burden of years. Gray hair hung lank about his haggard face. The lips Moriana remembered so well were now twisted from emotions too great to be expressed. He was clad in scarlet and his eyes shone with fanatical light.

"Sir Tharvus!" she exclaimed.

The only survivor of the three Notable Knights who had ridden beneath her banner at Chanobit Creek stopped and flung out his arm to point at her.

"Do not heed this witch!" he shouted. "Her wiles lured my brothers and thousands of our countrymen to their deaths.

"On peril of your souls, don't listen to her!"


"So what happens now?" Fost asked.

A smile pushed up the ends of Cheidro's moustache.

"Why, what always happens when there's an impasse in a matter close to His Effulgence's heart."

"What's that?"

"He throws a party."

"This is more like it!" crowed Erimenes. Fost stirred from his fog.

"What is?"

A tall, lithe girl, nude except for diagonal stripes of blue and gold, walked by on the arm of an officer in a purple plumed helmet.

"This is!" A sweep of Erimenes's vaporous arm indicated everything.

At long last the travellers were face to face with the seamy, steamy decadence of High Medurim. The Golden Dome was every bit the voluptuary's vision of heaven popular repute made it out to be. Niches lined the wall, dark and inviting. Already Fost dimly made out writhing tangles of pale limbs in alcoves across the circular chamber. In the center, a round pit was filled with lustrous furs in careless profusion. Tables bowed under the weight of delicacies. Serving maids circulated everywhere to keep the wine and high spirits flowing. Many wore no more than kohl and inviting smiles.

In the middle of the pit reared a dais. On it lay a throne and on the throne sat the Emperor. He wore a ludicrous tentlike garment patterned in white and black diamonds.

Here and there Fost saw forms or faces he recognized. Magister Banshau sat with his chubby legs dangling over the edge of the pit, his garb standing out even in this profusion of color. He held a wine jug in one hand and the shapely thigh of a young noblewoman in the other. He looked mightily pleased with the world. Over by the far wall stood the dignified Foedan of Kolnith. His doublet was askew, his hair rumpled and he gazed on the crowd with bleary-eyed gravity while a short, plump redhead poured brandy into a snifter the size of his head.

At the center of an eddy of gay costumes rode Zak'zar, laughing like any rakehell at something the two young women he had his arms about said, a striking, chilling figure in a robe of woven midnight.

"Great Ultimate!" Erimenes shouted in Fost's ear. "Look at *that*, will you?"

Moving through the crush with lithe grace was a strange and beautiful figure. Her body was that of a voluptuous woman but it was clad in soft, short, creamy fur. A long, sensitive tail swung behind her. Her face combined the best characteristics of human and feline. Her ears were pointed and set high on her head, poking out from the midst of a lustrous cascade of blue-black hair. And at her back was folded a pair of wings.

"I'll be damned," said Fost with feeling.

"So you like Ch'rri?" A slender blonde woman in a short tunic, her hair cut boyishly short, dropped onto the bench at Fost's side. "She's quite a sight, isn't she? If you have a taste for the exotic."

"Uh, Ch-chu-chri?" Fost couldn't manage the throaty purr.

"Ch'rri," the blonde woman repeated, laughing at Fost's doleful look. "She's the only one of her kind, poor thing. Another Wirixer experiment. Or work of art, perhaps. One of their genetic wizards wanted to see what a winged cat woman looked like, and she was the result." She frowned. "She's a terribly lonely thing. But she does know some interesting ways to make up for it."

"What are you waiting for?" demanded Erimenes. "Introduce yourself! You're the hero of the hour, Fost. You'll sweep her off her feet!"

"I think that sums it up well, spirit," boomed a voice. Fost turned to look at the group approaching. "Wild tales of your exploits are flying all over the city. We'd be honored to hear the truth from your own lips."

The speaker was a rangy man in a flame-colored robe. His head was shaved and a gold earring swung from one earlobe. A tawny-haired woman, taller than Fost and with a patch over one eye, walked to one side. On the other was a shy, towheaded youth.

"I'm Sirsirai. This is Osni, and Jerru." He nodded to each of his companions in turn.

Something in the way they moved clicked in Fost's brain.

"You're fighting masters," he said, almost accusingly.

The one-eyed woman bobbed her head in agreement.

"Erimenes cleared his throat, then said, "What you've heard about Fost is true. All of it—and none of his marvelous adventures would have happened without me . . ."

Across the room, Moriana smiled and nodded mechanically and fended off still another smiling face. She was a celebrity. That she had balked at wearing frilly, fleecy finery in favor of her russet and beige tunic and trousers seemed to draw rather than repel the revellers.

"Why don't you relax?" said Ziore. "Enjoy yourself."

"You're as bad as Erimenes," she accused, then softened her tone. "I'm sorry. That was unfair. But I've no appetite for this sort of thing."

"That might be a pity," Ziore said, her voice holding a tone of longing.

On his dais, Teom sat fondling his chin and regarding various gorgeously painted and costumed courtiers, male and female, who had arranged themselves in front of his throne to vie for his attention. Deciding, he flicked his little finger. A slender woman in a feathered skullcap and sky blue tights widened her eyes in happy anticipation and scampered to the dais in response to his summons. His knees spread. She knelt between them, took hold of the tentlike robe and hiked it up about his Imperial waist. Beneath it Teom wore trunks and a codpiece of epic proportions that laced up the front. Licking her lips, the woman undid the laces . . .

And fell back as something sprang out at her.

All sound ceased as every head turned to see a giant wooden phallus crowned with a painted jester's head bobbing at the end of the spring which had launched it from Teom's crotch.

It was the signal for the orgy to begin in earnest. Flinging his pink-trimmed orange blouse off, Magister Banshau teetered with his splayed toes gripping the edge of the pit.

Then with a happy mating-walrus bellow, he launched himself into the sea of naked bodies below. A crowd stood watching as Zak'zar took advantage of a physiological peculiarity of his race to pleasure simultaneously two naked and ecstasy-flushed young women who lay back to back on a buffet table.

Tapers were touched to cones of incense. Thick musky smoke rolled into the air, scents of sandalwood and amasinj mingled with the tangy sweet aroma of a Golden Barbarian narcotic herb. Ch'rri the cat woman grabbed a passing serving boy, shoved him down on a stool and climbed astride him, folding her wings protectively about them so that no one quite saw what happened. Ortil Onsulomulo, his golden body naked except for a woman's green scarf wrapped around his neck, danced in a jig while a clutch of noblewomen of middle years giggled and grabbed at a certain portion of his anatomy. Erimenes pointed out to Osni that Onsulomulo either disproved a certain racial canard pertaining to dwarves or proved the one about Joreans.

"And so there I was," explained Fost, warming to his audience, "in the dark, and that little bastard Rann came at me with his scimitar." He broke off when he saw the expressions of his listeners. "What's wrong?"

"You crossed blades with Rann?" asked Jerru.

"Twice. Once in the foothills of the Ramparts and again in Athalau."

Osni's one eye went round as she asked, "and you lived?"

"As far as I know." Fost started feeling defensive.

"It seems the rumors don't do you justice, friend," declared Sirsirai.

"What do you mean?"

"Prince Rann Etuul," said Osni, "is without question one of the top blademasters alive today. To think you faced him twice, and lived . . ."

The room started to spin around Fost. He spilled his goblet of wine, then realized he had been steadily draining it, only to have it automatically refilled. He had no idea how much he'd drunk.

"Excuse me," he said thickly. "I've got to get some fresh air."

He put Erimenes's satchel on the bench before stumbling away.

"Never mind him," said Erimenes. "He tends to be long-winded, like any hero." The genie smiled slyly. "Why don't you take off your clothes and forget all this idle chatter?"

Fost made his way out into the gardens. He breathed deeply and tried to quell the revolt in his stomach.

A finger was laid across his lips. He started, turned, saw it was Empress Temalla. She was nude. She took his hand and led him off through the shrubbery maze.

He followed numbly, fascinated by the way her buttocks moved when she walked. She pulled him into a secluded cubicle and pushed him down into the cool grass. The broad leaves of the shrubbery rustled inches away. Her body shone softly silver in the moonlight as she swung herself astride him and shuffled forward on her knees. The smells of crushed grass and her musk were heady in his nostrils. He took a deep breath and a double handful of her behind and lost himself in the pleasures she offered so freely.

Moriana sat on the floor with her knees drawn up and her back to a wall. Not even Ziore could pierce the armor of her loneliness. She felt drained, defeated. Sir Tharvus's appearance in the Assembly Hall the day before had destroyed her hopes of fielding an Imperial army against the Hissers. The Empire would react only when the lizard men came swarming across the River Marchant. Then it would be too late.

She sensed someone over her and looked up into the liquid brown eyes of Emperor Teom. He extended a hand to her. After a slight hesitation, she took it and let him lift her to her feet and lead her out of the Golden Dome. They passed within arm's reach of Ensign Cheidro, engaged passionately with an auburn-haired youth. He never looked up.

As the evening wore on and various participants wore themselves out, some mischance brought Erimenes and Ziore face to face with their jars laying side by side on a table.

"What are you staring at, you vapid bitch?" Erimenes asked with that special tact he reserved for his fellow Athalar.

"The man who blighted my life! Whose obscene philosophy deluded me into denying myself all worldly pleasure in favor of a life of serene meditation." Her face twisted in anguish. "Meditation! I'd trade a lifetime of it for one hour of passion!"

"What do you know of passion? Ice water would run in your veins, had you veins!"

"Bastard!"

"Bitch!"

"Asshole!"

Heads began to turn. Grinning a cat's grin, Ch'rri appeared carrying a bronze waterpipe in a ringed stand. Her tail was held upright, its tip twitching mischievously. She set down her burden next to the two jugs.

"What game do you play now, darling Ch'rri?" a male voice asked.

She held up a vial filled with yellow crystals. Delighted gasps rose from the onlookers.

"*Tusoweo*," a man breathed. "Enough to make a statue of Felarod jump off its pedestal and start buggering tom-cats!"

The short-haired blonde who had sat by Fost earlier ran up with a clear glass bottle containing aromatic oils. Ch'rri pulled the cork, emptied the bottle and smiled wickedly.

Ch'rri shook a pinch of the yellow crystalline tusoweo

into the waterpipe's bowl. Holding a smouldering incense cone to it, she puffed it alight. A thick yellow cloud welled up. Her slit pupils dilated.

"—your mother!" Erimenes was saying with malicious precision. "*And* your father. Wha—?" Ch'rri picked up his jug and popped home the basalt plug. He disappeared with a dismal squawk of rage. She pulled out the plug again and poured the spirit into the oil bottle.

"Now, you just wait a minute," he protested as he spilled like smoke into the new bottle. "Just because this is an orgy doesn't mean you can take indecent liberties with my person! What are you doing? Great Ultimate, you can't pour that hag in here with me!"

Having plugged and reopened Ziore's jar, the blonde was doing just that. Hissing and spitting like cats, the two genies whirled in a dizzying vortex inside the glass jar, each trying to keep his or her substance discrete from the other's.

Ch'rri drew in a deep lungful of the yellow aphrodisiac smoke. Leaning forward, she puffed it into the bottle and hurriedly corked it.

Coughing sounds emerged. For a moment, the spirits were obscured by the thick vapor. Then it was absorbed, and the pink shade and the blue glowed with a new intensity.

"I say, woman, don't jostle me like that," said Erimenes. "I . . . my word, I felt it. I *felt* it!"

"And do you feel this?" Ziore asked in an unspeakably lewd slur.

His response was a wordless wail of ineffable lust.

The bottled genies began to spin again. This time they quickly blended into a purple vortex.

"Ohh!" cried one and "Ahh!" moaned the other.

The mutant cat woman's experiment, combining the most powerful aphrodisiac known to sorcery with two highly telepathic spirits, produced spectacular results. A lust so pure and fierce it was almost tangible pulsed from the jar and expanded like the wavefront of an exploding star. Every being it touched went into immediate sexual frenzy. The occupants of the dome yowled as one and went for each other. Out in the streets of High Medurim, pandemonium reigned. Dogs madly humped cats, cats screwed rats. Married couples who hadn't touched each other in years broke bedsteads all over the city. Lonely night watchmen pounding their beats were seized with un-accountable yearnings to pound something else.

Time passed, to the accompaniment of groans and moans and glad cries.

In darkness, a traitor's hand opened a hidden door. Masked and muffled figures slipped into the Palace. Steel glinted.

The door of Emperor Teom's bedchamber burst open. Three men lunged into the room. Stark naked, sitting astride the Emperor and gasping in the throes of passion, Moriana still reacted to the danger. She threw herself clear of Teom, rolling toward the sword-carrying trio, seizing the furs on the bed as she hit the floor. Continuing her roll, she came to her feet and threw the fur pelt into the assassins' faces. It caught two of them by surprise, and they flailed at it as if it were a living attacker. The third sidestepped and lunged at her.

She grabbed at a tall wrought-iron lampstand and swung. Bones crunched. The man dropped. Oil spilled over him, then the ghastly odor of burning flesh filled the air.

A second assassin struggled free of the fur and ran at her, sword high. She tossed the lampstand in his face, then wrested the sword from his hand. She disembowelled him with his own weapon. The third would-be murderer still struggled on his knees. A single blow split his skull.

Through the handful of seconds of the savage, silent battle, Teom had sat huddled on his bed, watching, quivering, his face waxy. He silently rose and beat out the flames devouring the first assassin while Moriana shouted for help.

Fost lay face to face with Temalla while she sleepily twined fingers in his hair. Through a mellow fog of intoxication, satiation and exhaustion, Fost heard a flurry of cries coming from the north wing of the Palace.

"Istu take it, where're the others?" he heard someone nearby whisper. A soft drumming of feet came and a masked swordsman ran by their little alcove in the shrubs.

Without thinking, Frost launched himself in a flying tackle. Over they went, the assassin's hooded head crashing into a bush. Desperately, Fost tried to pin the man's sword hand while driving a fist repeatedly into his assailant's body. The man grunted and kicked. His knee caught Fost in the groin. It was a light blow but still set off bright explosions of pain.

It also sobered him. He groped at the man's belt, found the dagger, used it. The assassin squealed through his mask, then lay still.

The dead man's sword in his hand, Fost ran to the Golden Dome knowing he couldn't find his way out of this labyrinth in any other direction. He burst through an open archway and sagged against the door frame as a wave of lust hit him like a blow. His flaccid organ stirred and thrust out straight ahead of him like the bow of a ship.

Ch'rri was on hands and knees in front of him, wings poised above her back, purring like a bass fiddle as a man in black took her from behind. The man's head was covered by a hood. Though the initial irresistible psychic impulse the spirits had sent out had long passed, the sexual energy still crackled in the air.

Fost wrenched himself away, unlike the assassins in the Dome who had been intent on murdering the celebrants. As Fost ran for the north wing, a suspicion formed in his mind. He had seen the two jugs laying side by side and apparently empty on the table and beside them a squat glass bottle in which a purple whirlwind spun and motes of light danced intolerably bright.

He reached the north wing. Off to his left he heard

shouts and the clash of arms and then the unmistakable booming of Magister Banshau's wrath.

"Oracle!' he cried to himself, then set off at a run.

The corridor widened into an antechamber just before the door that led into the laboratory. A hasty barricade of furniture blocked the hallway, a group of hooded killers and *Zr'gsz* defending it against a squad of Household Guard. The door into the laboratory had been broken down but the Wirixer mage, totally naked and clumsily wielding a paddle used to stir Oracle's nutrient slop, prevented their entry. A low caste Hisser, back broken by a blow from the paddle, lay kicking at his feet like a dog run down by a carriage.

Even as Fost watched, a Vridzish spearman sank his weapon deep into Banshau's vast belly. The killers swarmed into the laboratory.

A lithe, naked figure vaulted the barricade, steel flashing in both hands. A Hisser swung on Ensign Cheidro with a mace. With a speed scarcely less than a *Zr'gsz*'s, Cheidro whipped his blades into a defensive cross, caught the mace and sent it spinning away with a deft twist. His rapier licked out and killed the Vridzish. Fost hurtled the barricade, joined the effeminate Life Guard, helping him clear the enemies remaining in the antechamber.

"You're well named, Longstrider," Cheidro said in an unruffled nasal drawl. "That was quite a leap."

Fost smiled. Some of the Household Guards, encumbered by heavy armor, had finally struggled over the barrier. They charged into the laboratory.

The unarmed and untrained sages tending Oracle had died under the *Zr'gsz* onslaught, but none before impeding the headlong rush for a few brief instants. Their deaths allowed Fost, Cheidro and the Household Guards to burst among the intruders like a bomb.

Fost sighted Zak'zar and made for him. A black steel sword in hand, the Speaker of the People had engaged one of the Household Guard when three more rushed him, shortswords poised for the kill. He pursed his lips and blew. Black vapor issued forth. The inky cloud swept over the three. They screamed as the flesh festered and fell from their faces in black gangrenous lumps. They collapsed as their bodies rotted inside their armor. The Guardsman Zak'zar duelled gaped in horror. The Speaker hacked him down.

"Beware the cloud!" cried Fost to the men behind him. Zak'zar turned to Oracle. With a feeling of fatalism, Fost hurled himself at the handsome Vridzish.

Spitting a curse in his own tongue, Zak'zar swung back to meet the attack.

"So you've chosen this way to die, Longstrider?" He grinned.

Zak'zar dodged with impressive speed as Cheidro hacked at him.

"Perhaps you'll do the dying, friend," said the young ensign.

By unspoken consent, Fost and Cheidro separated to attack the Vridzish from two sides. Zak'zar took a cautious step backward. The spur on his left foot found only empty air.

"You gentleman have the tactical advantage. Make of it what you may!"

Fost and Cheidro attacked. In a prolonged contest, a human had the advantage over a *Zr'gsz;* the lizard men were quicker but lacked staying power. Zak'zar was obviously exceptional in more than his command of manspeech. Fost felt his reactions slowing, though the fury of the Vridzish's defense did not flag. A sudden slash opened a long gash down the left side of his chest, and Fost knew that the fatigue lag in his reflexes and Cheidro's would hand the *Zr'gsz* both their lives. The Hisser's grin showed he knew, too.

The door to the north side of the room caved inward, riding a yellow fireball. Masked men ran to bar the way, only to fall like grain before a scythe as Foedan of Kolnith hewed his way through using a huge sword.

Zak'zar's blade slowed to visibility as he glanced toward the flash and thunderclap. Cheidro's rapier pinioned his right shoulder. Tearing the blade free in a welter of blood and a horrid sound of snapping sinew, the *Zr'gsz* wheeled and sheared through the young ensign's face.

Reversing the longsword in his claws, he raised his arms into the unprotected swell of Oracle's flank. The hilt of the sword abruptly turned incandescent. Fost heard the sizzle and smelled the stench of frying flesh. With an explosive hiss, Zak'zar dropped the weapon and jumped back. He blew his black breath. Moriana dismissed it with a wave of her hand.

She made a quick sweep of her fingers and a semicircle of blue flame crackled and roared to the height of a tall man's head. The *Zr'gsz* was trapped.

"Have you anything to say before you fry, serpent man?" she called.

His hair smouldering from the nearness of flames, his right shoulder a torn and gaping ruin, Zak'zar showed sharp teeth in a smile.

"This round goes to you, Lady. But we shall meet again quite soon, and I believe I can promise a different outcome!"

"Meet again?" Her fine features showed disbelief. "Not unless they've integrated Hell!"

"I'm not due there for quite a while, yet. It may be that you will precede me, unless your pitiful friends manage to defeat the army of the People that even now prepares to cross the River Marchant!"

The listeners gasped. Fost's face stung with the infernal heat of the flame. He marvelled that Zak'zar endured them so calmly.

"An army! Where would you get the men?" Moriana asked.

"Haven't you divined that? It is an army of the Children of Expectation. Since our exile from the City in the Sky, entire generations have grown to adulthood and then entered hibernation in vast crypts beneath Thendrun, waiting

for the day we'd meet you in battle. I number myself
among them, Your Highness. I have waited six thousand
years for the day of final victory."

"You won't live to see it!" screamed Moriana. She flung
forth her hands. The flames devoured the wall.

Before the hungry blue tongues reached Zak'kar, the
Speaker disappeared. There was a sharp crack! as air
rushed to the space he had vacated. Then the only sounds
were the disappointed clucking of the flames, and the
moans of wounded men.

# CHAPTER FOURTEEN

"It seems we've been through this before," Ziore remarked, looking down at the armies spread out at the foot of the bluff. Moriana had to agree. In many ways, the impending battle shaped up like the conflict at Chanobit Creek.

Vigorous interrogation of the assassins captured in the Palace revealed a plot laid by Zak'zar in collusion with the Guilds of High Medurim—and Gyras, late advisor to Emperor Teom. The hunchback had been intercepted riding along the coast road that led to North Keep. After undergoing suitably painful torments, the dwarf was impaled as an object lesson for others.

Had Teom been with a Medurimin woman trained from birth in helplessness instead of Moriana, or had the dozen assailants infiltrating the Golden Dome not succumbed to the libidinous emanations from Erimenes's and Ziore's coupling, High Medurim would now be dominated by the Fallen Ones. Ten days after that night of lust and slaughter, Fost still had nightmares. One image in particular haunted him. Exhausted and bloodied, he had been helped back into the Golden Dome. He saw Ch'rri the winged cat woman kneeling above the body of her erstwhile lover licking the blood from her whiskers and paws. In good feline fashion, she had taken her pleasure from the lust-crazed assassin, then ripped him to pieces.

Badly shaken, Teom had named Fost a Marshal of the Emperor and given orders to march for the River Marchant. In two days, the Imperial Army issued forth from the high walls of Medurim, winding in a mile-long serpentine of trudging foot soldiers, baggage wagons and proud war dogs stepping out beneath armored riders. Temalla was left behind to cope with the administrative tangle ensuing from the attempted coup. Not the least of her problems was cleaning up after rioting had broken out the night of the attack when the Watch had attempted to arrest over seven thousand Medurimin for fornicating in the streets in violation of the traffic code.

As rapid as Imperial response had been, it had not come quickly enough to prevent the Vridzish from pouring across the Marchant and laying waste to half the Black March. Like locusts the *Zr'gsz* devoured everything edible in their path, including human inhabitants who didn't flee in time. Unlike locusts, what they couldn't consume they put to the torch.

A hundred spires of smoke reared up into the blue sky beyond the black ant-mass of the *Zr'gsz* armies. For the hundredth time since the sun came up, Fast tried to estimate how many there were. For the hundredth time, he gave up when the numbers became too hopelessly huge.

"Why did Zak'zar tell us about the Children of Expectation?" Fost asked, pulling up a clump of black-tipped grass and thumping the sod around its base listlessly against his thigh.

"To seize psychological advantage," said the short, round, bald man in the white robe. Oracle tuned himself to Moriana's mind and succeeded in projecting his image several hundred miles from High Medurim as a result. "We already know the Hissers had greater numbers than expected. By letting us know where they came from, Zak'zar also gave us reason to fear there'd be so many we couldn't possibly win."

Fost plucked out a blade of grass and chewed on it.

"Yes, if they've been stashing away the rising generation for thousands of years . . ." He let the sentence trail off. It was too depressing to finish.

"Well, Fost my boy," Erimenes said avuncularly, "see how you've come up in the world under my tutelage?

You're now a bonafide hero, and Marshal of the Empire as well, with a fine suit of armor and a strapping black and white war dog."

"Marshal of the Empire, indeed." He spat out the grass. "Being Marshal doesn't mean those highborn fools listen to me, much less take my orders."

"But Foedan of Kolnith and the Border Guards heed your counsel," Ziore said. She favored Erimenes with a wink of surprising lewdness.

"That's all well and good," replied Fost. "The high and mighty chivalry of High Medurim and the knights of the other City States all think Foedan's a traitor to his class. And the Border Guards and militias of the various marches—never mind their experience—are considered nothing more than low born dabblers in the fine art of war."

He pointed with an armored arm.

"Behold the main strength of the Medurimin army. Fifteen thousand spearmen, every one of whom is a conscript wanting nothing more than to be somewhere else. Then there are eight thousand regulars of the Imperial Army, who look sharp in drill and who have never seen blood shed outside a barroom brawl. Then the infantry. On both wings are men who will win the day for humanity, if you care to listen to their boasts. Six thousand knights from Medurim and the City States, all of whom can be relied on to do the worst thing possible in any given circumstance. Sandwiched between are the only troops likely to do a damned bit of good, longbowmen from Samazant and Thrishnor, and there're only a scant four thousand of them."

"But what of the Borderers and the militiamen you think so highly of?" asked Ziore.

In disgust, Fost waved at men drawn up well to the rear of the front ranks.

"Back there where they can't get in the way of the precious cavalry."

Oracle rubbed his plump chin with fingertips. It was a mannerism he'd picked up from Fost, which unnerved the courier every time he saw it.

"Is not the reserve a good place for them?" the projection asked. Fost swallowed hard. The sunlight contrived to shine through Oracle's body.

"It may turn out that way," Fost answered, "if the battle isn't lost before they can come to grips with the Hissers."

Moriana walked over and laid tender hands on his shoulders. He couldn't actually feel her hands, since his body was encased in a lobster carapace of metal, but he still appreciated the gesture. He reached up and clasped her hand to his.

"At least you're near me, love," she said quietly.

Fost's joy at hearing those words was short-lived. The two genies had heard the words, too, and triggered off a now-common response.

"Yes, my own true love," Erimenes said in a disgustingly honeyed voice. "And I shall be here, not far from your side!"

Ziore batted nonexistent lashes and said, "Never leave me again! Oh, swear you won't, my blue darling."

"Never, so long as we both shall live, sweetums."

"Sweetums?" Fost and Moriana cried in unison. They shared a groan. It had been like this ever since the night in the Golden Dome. Neither ghost was a stranger to lust, but with the discovery that they could at long last *do* something about that particular passion, they had fallen in love—sticky, sweet, gooey love—and had become hopelessly mired in emotion. They lapsed now entirely into unintelligible baby talk.

"Do you know," Fost declared, "I liked you both better when you fought all the time?"

"How could you take that seriously, Fost?" Erimenes shook his head in pity for his friend's ignorance. "That was but gentle teasing. From the first sweet moment we met, we both knew that it was love."

"Isn't he poetic?" Ziore sighed to no one in particular.

"No." Fost rose and pulled on his gauntlets.

Moriana pointed to a dark form high above.

"Ch'rri's signalling," she said. "The *Zr'gsz* skyrafts have taken to the air."

Fost shuddered, remembering Ch'rri and her lover, her dead, dismembered lover.

"At least the damned City's not with them. Nor the Demon." Where City and Demon were, they didn't know. Moriana was blocked from directly scrying her lost Sky City, but her perceptions did tell her that it and its resident demon floated somewhere to the southeast. It was little enough that they wouldn't have to match strength with Istu.

Yet.

"I'd best mount up," Fost said, eyeing his war dog. He was not happy about riding into battle on the back of a dog. He managed to stay aboard one—and that was about all. But the fact remained no one in the Imperial Army took orders from any unmounted commander. Even the border men were peculiar that way.

After banging his head against the wall of noble obduracy and class pride, Fost had resigned himself from any direct role in the conduct of the battle. He knew he lacked the experience to be a field officer commanding vast armies of men, yet his choice still nagged him because few of the Imperial nobles and swaggering regular army officers had more experience than he. Fost had settled for command over Moriana's own guard, a unit of volunteers. To Moriana's surprise, the men from the Marches had joined her personal unit in large numbers, some of the veterans from the fiasco at Chanobit Creek. And even a hundred lancers from Harmis, domain of her lost lover and champion Darl Rhadaman, had joined the unit.

Moriana's unit had a vital role to play. They were to ensure that Moriana could work her magics in safety during battle. They were to keep out of the thick of fighting off on the left flank. That was fine with Fost. He had little taste for battle. Personal combat, yes, man to man, face to face. He savored that, sometimes. But not the wholesale butchery promised this day. That sickened and scared him.

A line of skyrafts appeared above the *Zr'gsz* army and floated silently forward. Fost swung into his saddle and waited.

Responding listlessly to the insistent notes of their officers' whistles and the lead-tipped cudgels of their sergeants, the conscript spearmen shuffled forward. The *Zr'gsz* moved toward them in a wedge, black massed ranks of low caste spearmen and slingers in the center. Higher caste Hissers rode giant lurching lizards on the trailing flanks. The wind shifted and brought a rank reptilian smell wafting across the Imperial lines. Dogs began an excited barking.

The first wave of skyrafts swooped toward the Medurimin ranks. Arrows sleeted down. Screams of agony and shocked surprise rose, spectrally thin at this distance. Moriana bit her lip. Her biggest concern was choosing the precise moment to use her magic. She had only so much strength and she had to marshal it against the moment of crisis, of greatest tactical need. She looked left and right along the bluffs, checking the preparations she'd made. All seemed in order, but the time for magic wasn't yet.

"It's hard to let those men die," said Ziore quietly.

"My only consolation is knowing they trade their lives so future generations of humanity will be free of the Hissers. And Istu."

Trying to psych his mount into believing he was both calm and in command, Fost looked to Oracle and asked, "How're you doing?"

"Well, I think. Magister Banshau himself is overseeing the balance of nutrients in my pool." There was a spot of light against the darkness—or Dark, as Fost thought with a thrill of horror. Despite the Hisser spear in his belly,

Banshau lived and would recover. There are worse armors than several inches of flab.

The skyrafts rained down a continuous storm of arrows on the Imperial foot soldiers. Already, the ill-dressed lines began to waver, though the Medurimin had not yet come to grips with the foe.

"Poor bastards," Fost said with feeling.

Moriana's fingers itched with the need to hurl spells, to smash the Hissers who fought from the smug safety of their skystone rafts. But she knew she had to conserve her strength.

The borderland archers had opened on the flitting rafts. The *Zr'gsz* craft were slower and less maneuverable than Sky City eagles. Many shafts found their marks. Small, twisting shapes began to fall among the ranks of spearmen.

Deep thrums punctuated by tocking sounds announced that the Imperial catapults had joined battle. A big skyraft suddenly slewed in air, spilling dozens of occupants to their deaths. The shot had probably been loosed by one of the crews of refugee Estill artillerists Fost had bribed away from Ortil Onsulomulo. They were superlative with their missile engines, though the Imperial crews were far from poor.

The lines of foot soldiers met. A clash of arms and clamor of voices went up. Fost thought it impressive, but Moriana found it almost anticlimactic. It was wholly unlike the rending clash with which her knights and Grassland allies had met at Chanobit.

Almost at once, the Imperial infantry began to be pushed back. Moriana's muscles started winding themselves into knots.

"Commit your cavalry, damn you!" she shouted at the enemy commander.

But the *Zr'gsz* general, whoever he was—Zak'zar?—was much too canny. He knew that to approach the Imperial cavalry too closely with his own mounted troops would trigger a charge. Haughtily disdainful of their border reserves, the knights would never think of charging in support of their own infantry. So the Vridzish held his mounted men back as long as possible, his infantry chopping up the footsoldiers unmolested by the knights.

"I see it," Oracle murmured. "If the *Zr'gsz* cavalry were not closing on the flanks, the knights would charge the foot soldiers. The lizard riders are bait of a sort, aren't they?"

"Of a negative sort, yes," Fost said sourly. "Shrewd of you to see it." His mouth twisted. "Shrewd of that damned serpent to think of it."

It began as a tiny ripple along the line of conscript spearmen. Men in the front rank turned in fear from the flashing stone-edged weapons of the Hissers. Poorly armored, they still had the advantage over the *Zr'gsz*, who wore none at all. But it would take men much better motivated to face the inhuman speed and ferocity of the *Zr'gsz*. The first rank turned and shoved back in panic on the men behind, who resisted and then sought flight themselves. In moments, the whole formation was beginning to erode like a dirt clod dropped into a fast-running stream.

A squadron of Imperial cavalry surged forward on the far right flank. Fost saw a black chalice on a white pennon at the fore and smiled grimly. Foedan led his Kolnith knights into *Zr'gsz* lines, knowing his fellows would have to cover him against a countercharge of Hisser cavalry. No sooner had the Kolnithin driven deep into the body of the Vridzish foot soldiers than the Imperial knights and the *Zr'gsz* lizard riders charged one another.

Moriana had seen the giant lizards the Hissers rode before, sprawling green monsters with a crest of long yellow spines running down their backs. Not even she had seen them in full charge. Awesome as the full charge of the Northern heavy cavalry was, the lizards' charge was even more awesome. The whip-tailed monsters raised their bloated bodies off the ground and sprinted with legs at full extension. Six thousand dog riders met fewer than half as many *Zr'gsz,* but the Hissers' lizard mounts gave them the edge in height and speed. At first contact, the Imperial squadrons on the right flank reeled and fell in confusion, while on the left the Hissers were brought to a halt. As the resounding surf-boom of the collision died, the battle degenerated into swirling melee, *Zr'gsz* and humans hacking one another with axe, mace and sword. Triangular lizard heads darted to snap knights from their mounts and crush them in sawtoothed jaws; dogs grabbed wattled throats of the dragons and clung, tearing out huge gobbets of flesh.

"Strike!" Moriana commanded, raising her arm. For hundreds of yards along the bluffs, pageboys struck padded hammers against brass gongs. The Imperial treasurer winced at the expense of gongs and ridiculed them as an extravagance. But Moriana had got her way; the gongs were her most lethal weapon.

The reverberation of hundreds of gongs filled the air, dampening even the mad tumult of battle. Moriana closed her eyes and concentrated all her energy, her being, her very soul, on modulating the booming waves of sound.

With Ziore to help draw the memory from the depths of her mind, and Oracle to analyze the memories, Moriana had been able to determine the exact pitch which the undying toad creature Ullapag had used to induce torpor and death in *Zr'gsz* venturing too close to the skystone mines of Omizantrim. Now she altered the voice of the gongs until they cried out in the inaudible voice of the Ullapag.

Skyrafts began skidding crazily all over the sky, scattering their passengers like a farmer scatters handfuls of seeds. The relentless advance of the Vridzish foot soldiers in the center and the lizard riders on the right stopped as if it had run into a wall. The riding dragons uttered hissing squeals of fear and fled, their senseless riders dropping from the saddles.

The rout of the Imperial center was stemmed. Even the ranks of the regulars were being disrupted by the panicking conscripts.

With the upper hand already, the left wing cavalry squadrons ran the stunned lizard riders off the field. Fost was shouting and pounding on his saddle.

"You've done it, Moriana! You've won the battle for us!"

Oracle noticed the black cloud forming above the battlefield.

"I beg your pardon, Your Highness," he said to Moriana. Her eyes opened and glared at him. She needed every ounce of concentration.

He pointed to the cloud. Her eyes went wide.

"Get down!" she screamed.

Fost flung himself face down on the sod. His dog bolted and smashed into a silver dome that hadn't been there seconds before. As he lay blinking, he realized the jagged purple lines of afterimage were caused by lightning. The pewter dome above flickered and went out of existence. He looked at Moriana. Her face was drawn and pale.

"I don't know if I can do that again," she said, her voice weak.

He scanned the line of gongs—or where the line had been. Charred corpses remained behind where humans had once stood. He swallowed hard. Had it not been for Oracle's alertness and the quickness of Moriana's reactions, they would have shared the fate of those feckless pageboys.

"Why is the cloud going away?" demanded Erimenes. "It could blast our whole army to rubble."

"The *Zr'gsz* sorcerer—or sorcerers—must spend their life energies to cast spells, just as I must. They couldn't maintain the lightning cloud." She smoothed hair back from her forehead. "Its work was done, anyway," she added bitterly.

The left wing's pursuit of enemy cavalry ended abruptly in disaster when the deadly vibrations ceased. The Hissers turned back on their pursuers while a living sea of footmen swamped the knights from the side. The dogs began to mill in confusion. Having lost momentum, the heavy riders were doomed. They could work destruction on their foes, but it was only a question of time before the last was dragged from his saddle and slain.

The center gave way to total flight. The Imperial ranks behind began to fall apart as the supposedly invincible regulars joined in the disorderly retreat. Behind them, the men of the border states waited, grim and firm.

When Moriana's force dome winked out, Fost's war dog had run down the face of the bluff where it was intercepted by the picket of Black March bowmen guarding the foot of the hill.

"I'll be back," Fost promised, and began picking his way down.

Summoning her resources, Moriana began to fling forth spell after spell. None worked as well as the vibrations; that had been their best chance and she knew it. The *Zr'gsz* magic met her every spell and cancelled it. She felt the deadly frustration her sister must have felt during the battle for the Sky City, when the Heart of the People harmlessly absorbed her most potent magics. But one thing encouraged her. The *Zr'gsz* magic was all defensive. No lethal conjurations were loosed against the Imperial armies.

On the other hand, the *Zr'gsz* were winning without them.

"Here, Marshal," a grinning boy said, handing Fost the reins of this dog. Fost nodded, trying to look gruff and martial.

"Thanks, son." He hoisted himself into the saddle. The skitterish beast danced and growled.

The *Zr'gsz* foot soldiers advanced again, harrying the

routed Imperial forces. The Marchers waited tensely, weapons ready, but the Hissers didn't come their way. The green tide swept past their knoll in pursuit of fleeing foes. Fost looked that way and tried not to wince. It seemed the end of the battle wasn't far off.

His dog turned and caught sight of the enemy. Fost's dog was a fine charger, a mount fit and trained to be ridden by a knight. And like the Imperial knights, it was bred to be headstrong, ferociously brave, and as dumb as a stump.

The dog charged.

On the hill Moriana sank down sobbing as her legs gave way.

"It's no use," she moaned. "I can't go on!"

"Don't give up," Ziore gently urged.

"Don't you understand? Every spell I try they counter before it's completed. It's over. I'm sorry I brought you into this."

Hesitantly, Oracle touched her shoulder. She didn't feel it. He couldn't project a tactile illusion this far. He cleared his throat.

"If I might suggest something . . ."

"I'm telling you, I don't have any power left!" she shrieked.

"Highness," Oracle said softly, "that might be so, but you might be able to make them *think* you still have power. Or rather that another does."

Moriana looked up at Oracle, the idea germinating in her brain. She slowly smiled and rose. The damned Hissers would never forget this day after she—and another—finished with them.

Fost tried valiantly to stop the animal but his lack of skill in riding betrayed him. His arms flailed wildly and it appeared that he urged on his troops. None heard his cries: "No, you forsaken son of a bitch! No! Stop! Halt! Oh, shiiit!"

Shieldless, unhelmeted, Fost rode through the surging masses of *Zr'gsz.* He struck out in truly heroic fashion, left and right in great looping arcs, so fast his blade blurred like a hummingbird's wings. His usual berserker madness failed to take him. What gave Fost such superhuman strength was stark terror.

He swept among the reptile men. His blade lopped limbs, crushed skulls, stove in chests, and Fost did not tire. He didn't dare.

The low caste *Zr'gsz* were much less intelligent than the darker skinned nobility. They could cope well enough with normal battle situations: Find enemy, kill enemy. Nothing in their limited experience prepared them for anything like this.

The Hissers' front ranks ran up against the lines of Borderland spearmen—and recoiled. The Border Guards and militiamen from the Marches had already stood firm in the face of their own fleeing comrades. Now they met the full force of the *Zr'gsz* charge and did not yield. But off to their right the surviving wing of cavalry was being pushed back slowly. It wouldn't be long before the lizard riders overwhelmed the knights. Then they would fall on the border men like an ocean wave falling on a sand castle.

A tall noble in whipping black robe and shiny green armor turned the wedge-shaped head of his riding dragon toward Fost and kicked it into a run. Still hewing frantically, Fost saw the lance drop to the horizontal. He had no shield and in the crush of reptilian bodies surrounding his dog he couldn't dodge.

He was a dead man.

He stopped the wild flailing of his arms. Immediately, fatigue turned them leaden. He gripped his sword two-handed, trying to make himself believe he had a chance to knock the lancehead aside before it skewered him. He saw the *Zr'gsz* grin above the rim of the shield, saw the triangular lancehead streaking toward his chest. . . .

With a scream of demonic fury, the nobleman was plucked from his saddle by sudden claws seizing his head from above. His plumed helm fell away. Black blood fountained from his punctured eyes. With a drumming of wings, Ch'rri bore the Vridzish up and away. Fost swatted the riderless dragon across its scaly snout with the flat of his blade. It turned tail and ran.

From five hundred feet in the air, the body of the *Zr'gsz* warrior plummeted down to smash into the ground not ten feet from Fost. The Vridzish bounced once, limbs waving like a rag doll's. Then it lay still.

The low caste Hissers scattered in all directions. Fost raised his eyes to the terrible apparition hovering above his head. He saluted Ch'rri with his bloody sword. It seemed an appropriate tribute.

But Ch'rri paid him no heed. Her blue slit-pupilled eyes stared toward the north where men of the Empire made their final stand. Fost followed the gaze. He couldn't believe the sight.

*Jirre had come.*

Tall as the sky she strode across the hills. Her hair blazed golden and her eyes were emeralds. Her flowing robes shone green and gold. In one hand she held a lyre, in the other a sword. Beholding her, men forgot their mortal peril to drop to their knees and worship.

*Jirre had come.*

Jirre, named by some priests the foremost of the Three and Twenty Wise Ones of Agift. Jirre, of all the gods one of the bitterest foes of the Dark Ones.

Vridzish hissed in dread, "The devil-goddess! She comes again!" The lower caste foot soldiers knew Jirre and hated her, as they hated all gods of Light.

Half mad with fear, the nobles and officers tried to bring their troops into a semblance of order. Clouds of arrows were loosed at the apparition. She did not deign to notice. Skyrafts drove at her, *through* her. All to no effect.

Jirre struck her lyre. A pure, sweet tone throbbed in the air. The *Zr'gsz* skyrafts crumbled to dust beneath their crew's clawed feet. She swung her sword, and the Hissers fell. They fell without mark of violence on their bodies, but fall they did up to the very feet of the hard-pressed border men.

On the hilltop, Moriana raised herself on tiptoe and held her arms high above her head. Ecstatic, she felt the power pulsing through her. She blessed Oracle for his inspiration, for the idea of the illusion of one whom the Fallen Ones dreaded above all others.

"It's working!" she cried as the *Zr'gsz* armies disintegrated below her.

Fost flung his sword down so hard it buried itself to the hilt in the soft, blood-drenched turf. He jumped off the dog's back, letting it run off to drag down any fleeing Hisser it could catch.

He stood shaking on the now stilled battlefield. The *Zr'gsz* that still lived were in full flight back toward the River Marchant. Many wouldn't stop running until both their hearts burst from exertion. The armies of the North stared into the sky at their deliverer. Teom came to the door of his great pavilion and dropped to knees before the Goddess.

"Well done, Moriana! Will *done,* girl!" Erimenes cried.

"You've beaten them," sang Ziore.

And the apparition turned to face Moriana. The princess turned white.

"*Daughter,*" boomed Jirre. "*We love you well but never again can any of the Wise aid you in this manner. Only because you opened a pathway was I able to come. I cannot come again. But know that we will do what we can, that Night shall not claim this world again.*

"*Farewell, most-favored daughter. Know that I love you above all.*"

And Jirre was gone.

"That's what I call verisimilitude," said Erimenes with a knowing wink. Moriana couldn't control the shaking of her hands or the cold knot in her stomach as she continued to stare into the space recently occupied by Jirre.

# EPILOGUE

The hills and meadows of the Black March shivered with joyous celebration. The night air rang with boasts and jubilation. Many brave men had fallen but others still lived. Foedan of Kolnith was there, his huge domed head swathed in bandages. And Sir Tharvus, one of the pitiful handful surviving the catastrophic pursuit of the routed *Zr'gsz* by the cavalry on the left, sat as far from Moriana as possible, giving her poisoned glances over the rim of his goblet.

But seated at the great table of honor inside Teom's pavilion, Fost and Moriana picked at the sumptuous banquet spread before them with neither joy nor appetite.

Emperor Teom had knighted Fost where he stood in the middle of the battlefield, and the battle-weary survivors had hoisted him on their shoulders, bearing him directly to the pavilion.

Moriana arrived in much the same way. Their eyes met. An infinity of meaning flowed between them.

"Now tell me, Your Highness," said the knight sitting at Moriana's right, "how did you get the Lady Jirre to answer your call?"

She slammed her fist down on the table. Heads turned toward her.

"I did *not!* It was an illusion," she said.

Disbelieving, the heads turned away and returned to light conversation or serious consumption of food and wine. Fost laid his hand on Moriana's leg and gave it a reassuring squeeze. She nodded acknowledgement without looking at him.

"Erimenes," he heard Ziore whisper. "You were magnificent!"

"Of course."

Fost shut his eyes and shook his head.

At the head of the table, Teom pounded for silence with the golden pommel of a sword never drawn in anger.

"Silence! Let us have silence! I propose a toast!"

The noise died. He rose, resplendent in a gilded breastplate sculpted in the likeness of a muscular torso, with a robe of yellow lacebird silk thrown over his shoulders, the jewelled rings on his fingers shining with inner lights of their own. He raised his goblet.

"To the Princess Moriana," he cried. "Mightiest sorceress of the Realm, favored by the Lady Jirre, and . . . and . . ." His Adam's apple rode slowly up and down. Even the rouge and paint on his face failed to give him color. Tense silence gripped the revellers as all eyes followed his to the uppermost part of the pavilion.

"Greetings," said Zak'zar, Speaker of the People. "I foretold we would meet again, dear cousin Moriana. And so it has come to pass. A corner of his mouth twisted. "Not precisely as I predicted, I grant you, but this is after all no victory you've won. A petty respite, at best."

He floated at the top of the tentpole, his body radiating a cold black light. Sputtering on a mouthful of wine, the captain of the Guard bellowed for archers.

"It will do no good. I am not here. Only my likeness. A trick your Oracle knows well." He inclined his head toward the pale, round man beside Fost.

Fost found his voice and said, "You're bluffing, Zak'zar. We whipped you from the March like dogs."

Zak'zar's laughed chilled him to the bone.

"See then, friends, what *we* were doing while you were whipping dogs."

He stretched forth his hand. A globe of intense blackness formed. A point of light danced in the middle, expanded to become a picture. The City in the Sky floated over the slate roofs and boxy pastel structures of Kara-Est.

Fost wondered why he was showing them the conquest of the seaport by the floating City; this was old news. Then he realized no eagles winged over the City and saw the strange blackness that filled the Well of Winds in the center of the City.

A black vortex extended downward from the Skywell. Where it touched, stones, people, entire buildings were uprooted and drawn upward into the blackness where they ... disappeared.

"Istu!" The name ran through the tent.

"Istu," Zak'zar agreed. "Do you see what the great victory you won today signifies, Pale Ones? Do you, my cousin?"

Moriana wouldn't look at him. Her eyes were fixed on her plate, her face hidden by her golden hair.

"Why do you name her 'cousin,' you wretched creature?" Ziore shrieked at him.

Counterfeit surprise crossed Zak'zar's face.

"Why shouldn't I call her that, good Ziore? Surely, you cannot object if I call my blood kin by their right name?"

"You lie!" Fost screamed as he came to his feet.

"Ah, poor Fost," Zak'zar said, a sad chuckle escaping his throat. "Do you truly think you can change the truth by denying it?" He raised his head to address them all. "Know you the truth: nine thousand years ago an Athalar-trained adept came to Thendrun to receive the secret of true magic, not the petty mental tricks which the Athalar knew how to play."

Erimenes sputtered in outrage.

"Azrak-Tchan, Second Instrumentality of the People, gave her the secret of true magic, which is the providence of the Dark. He also gave her a child." Heads swung toward Moriana.

"This Moriana, surnamed Etuul, received great powers. But it was her daughter Kyrun, half human and half *Zr'gsz*, who possessed them in full measure. She aided Riomar shai-Gallri, accursed traitress, in casting my folk from the Sky City. So the blood of the People entered the Etuul line. And it has been passed down from that day to this. And renewed, perhaps, by the late Instrumentality Khirshagk, blessed be his name."

"He's dead?" demanded Moriana, looking up sharply.

"He is. He delivered Istu from bondage and fulfilled the role for which every Instrumentality had trained."

"You're lying, you filthy scum, *lying!*" Fost screamed, shaking his fists at the Hisser.

"Am I?" Zak'zar asked softly. "Moriana does not deny it.

"I hope you will find some measure of happiness, all of you, in the time you have left before we come for you with He Who Will Not be Denied. Farewell to you all. And to you, cousin." He folded taloned hands across his breast and faded.

Moriana sat in a silence and isolation unlike any she had ever known.